THE WORK OF A NARROW MIND

THE WORK OF A NARROW MIND

FAITH MARTIN

ROBERT HALE · LONDON

© Faith Martin 2015
First published in Great Britain 2015

ISBN 978-0-7198-1607-9

Robert Hale Limited
Clerkenwell House
Clerkenwell Green
London EC1R 0HT

www.halebooks.com

The right of Faith Martin to be identified as author
of this work has been asserted by her in accordance with
the Copyright, Designs and Patents Act 1988

2 4 6 8 10 9 7 5 3 1

Typeset in Palatino
Printed in Great Britain by Berforts Information Press Ltd

CHAPTER ONE

Ex-DI HILLARY GREENE pulled her old Volkswagen Golf, Puff the Tragic Wagon, into the car park of the Thames Valley Police HQ in Kidlington, and turned off the ignition. Puff coughed once before falling silent, and Hillary sighed in sympathy. The old car's MOT was due soon, and she had no idea if the old boy was going to pass.

She climbed out into the early morning air, smoothing down her navy-blue skirt as she did so, then pulling her warm winter coat a little tighter around her as the brisk wind whistled past her ears. It was the first week of November, and soon the fireworks of Bonfire Night would be terrifying every neighbourhood dog and cat in Creation. And, as she walked towards the entrance to the large, not particularly pretty building, she supposed, glumly, that both uniform, and the ambulance service, would have their usual hard work cut out for them, one arresting drunken revellers, and the other treating their burns.

After a lifetime of such experience, the stupidity of the human species invariably failed to amaze her.

She pushed through the doors, but instead of heading to her office, made straight for the desk sergeant instead.

She'd worked as a DI in this building for more years than she cared to remember before taking early retirement two years ago. Unable to withstand the tedium, however, she'd soon returned, accepting a civilian post working cold cases for the Crime Review Team, which hung its collective hat in the basement, down amid the old paper files, antiquated heating system and spiders.

When she'd first started there, the small investigative team that she worked for had been headed by Superintendent Steven Crayle. But Steven was now heading on and up to better things, and today, the new man in charge had arrived to learn the ropes. And this was why she was headed for the desk sergeant.

She hadn't been a raw, wet-behind-the-ears green recruit for more than a week before she'd learned the very valuable lesson that if you wanted to know anything – and that meant *anything* – the person to ask was the desk sergeant.

As she approached the reception counter that was his fiefdom, the particular specimen on day duty looked up and was patently ready for her. A big, beefy man, with thinning hair and a wide grin, his big brown eyes crinkled at the corners as he beamed a welcoming smile at her.

'All ready to meet the new boss then, Hill?' he pre-empted her cheerfully.

She undid her coat, giving the sergeant a quick peek at her smart navy-blue skirt suit and warm, paler-blue poloneck sweater combo, and her low-heeled, comfortable and sensible black leather boots. She wore no jewellery (in her younger years as a humble WPC she'd quickly seen that ear-rings could be ripped out of your ears in a fight, and a necklace used as a choker – literally). Her make-up was discreet but effective, and her usual bell-shaped cut of chestnut brown hair hung just to the top of her shoulders.

'I expect I'll pass muster,' she said laconically.

In response, the sergeant gave an appreciative wolf-whistle.

'Does your wife know you're safe to be let out?' Hillary grumbled with a smile. She'd reached her half-century just last year, but had finally managed to lose the stone or so in weight that she'd always been meaning to shed, so she knew that she looked good.

Or so a certain, very good-looking superintendent was always telling her.

'So, come on then,' she said, rolling her sherry-brown eyes in a telling gesture. 'what do you know about our Rollo?'

Commander Marcus Donleavy had appointed Superintendent Roland "Rollo" Sale, from today her new boss, as head of the investigative branch of the CRT. And although Hillary had put out her own feelers about him, she knew that the desk sergeant would have by far the best gen.

'What exactly do you need to know?' he teased with mock innocence, widening his eyes elaborately and leaning a meaty elbow on the counter, before propping a whisker-darkened chin into his cupped hand and fluttering his non-existent eyelashes in her direction. 'He's a perfect pillar of the community and what not, surely? Being a super and all, and passing the commander's scrupulous interviewing techniques and vetting.'

Hillary sighed heavily. Just why did every desk sergeant and his grandmother enjoy taking the piss whenever possible? On the other hand, she might just as well ask why cats miaowed.

'Come on, come on, give,' Hillary grumbled, waving a hand briskly in the air in the universal gesture to hurry up. 'I need to know just how far and how fast I need to cover my arse.'

The desk sergeant grinned. One thing you could say about Hillary Greene – she was an old trooper who knew just how the game was played.

'Well, there's not much juicy stuff, so you can relax,' he said, settling down for a good chat. 'He's out of Aylesbury, originally. Not a university graduate, so no fast track for him, which I say has to be a blessing. He's had a few good collars, but nothing spectacular. He's not' – he mimed rolling up a trouser leg – 'one of that lot, so there's nothing iffy there either.'

Hillary blinked, wondering vaguely if Masons really did

roll up their trouser legs, then wondered why everyone she knew (but mostly the men, it had to be said) seemed to be so paranoid about who might, and might not, belong to their ranks. For herself, she'd never cared a jot, and had made it quite clear. Which just might explain, she mused, why nobody had ever bothered to approach her to sound her out about joining.

A flea in the ear did tend to offend.

'He came up in a steady rise through the ranks, like I said,' the desk sergeant rambled on. 'Been married to the same missus for yonks, like thirty years or something like that, three kids, all boys, all grown up. None of them joined up with us though,' he added significantly, and tapped the side of his nose.

Hillary nodded. Now *that* was genuinely interesting. A lot of coppers joined the force because their fathers, uncles or brothers had already done so. It became, in effect, the family business. So the fact that her new super had three sons, but none in the police service, gave her pause for thought. Had he actively encouraged them not to join? If so, what did that tell her about his attitude? Or, conversely, had he always hoped or assumed that at least one of his sons would follow his career path, and was, therefore, now a disappointed man?

'We'll have to see if he's sensitive about that,' she muttered thoughtfully.

'Yeah, we've already got feelers out about it,' the desk sergeant informed her complacently.

'So, what else?'

'He's in his mid-fifties, so not too long off retirement himself I reckon. Three or four years tops. He hasn't had any trouble with the Complaints, no disciplinary issues, and doesn't seem to like the media much. So you won't catch him trying to hog the camera or press for telly interviews.'

'He's not all bad then,' Hillary said happily.

'No. So the fact that he's not out to up his profile with a view to promotion tells you something else, don't it?' the canny

8

sergeant offered innocently.

Hillary nodded. It certainly did. 'He's not about to step on anybody's toes.'

'And that can only mean one thing, right?' the desk sergeant nodded his head sagely.

Hillary smiled slightly. 'The brass regard him as a safe pair of hands,' she said succinctly.

The sergeant nodded in agreement. 'Right. Well,' he said with a small sigh, 'it makes sense, when you think about it. Your Steven set it all up and got the ball rolling. And since you've been getting good results that way, now that the commander has booted him upstairs, all they wanted was someone with experience to keep everything nicely on track and ticking over; someone without too much ego, or without anything to prove, as they would only go and muck it about just so that they could make their own mark.'

The desk sergeant grinned wolfishly. 'And there'd be plenty of them to chose from. So a safe and steady super coasting to retirement is just what the doctor ordered. 'Sides' – he cocked a knowing eye at her – 'we all know that Commander Donleavy sees you as the real star of the show anyway. So who does it matter who's technically in charge anyway?'

Hillary shot him a sour look. 'Don't know why you lot keep coming up with that old chestnut,' she said flatly. 'The commander and I are hardly like that.' And she held up a hand, her two fingers crossed firmly together, indicating closeness.

The desk sergeant grinned, but held up his hands in a gesture of surrender. 'OK, OK, have it your way. But we all know better. Oh yeah, one other thing about Sale,' he added seriously.

Hillary, who'd been about to move off and head for the stairs, turned back.

The desk sergeant crooked a finger to beckon her further in and leaned over the counter, casting a pantomime-obvious look around to make sure that they weren't being overheard. 'One thing I did hear about him, that you might like to keep in mind,' he said darkly, lowering his voice as he did so.

Hillary, willing to play along, leaned across the desk and cocked her head to one side. 'What?' she whispered back.

'Word has it – there's no dirt on the old man when it comes to a bit of how's your father!'

Hillary reared back, putting a lock of mock-horror on her face. 'Crikey!'

The desk sergeant's lips twitched. 'I know. Scandalous, ain't it? A man who doesn't cheat on his missus? I mean, what can you do with a super who doesn't like to chase the WPCs around the desk?'

Hillary shook her head woefully.

'My old man said you should never trust a boss who didn't have wandering hand trouble,' he said gravely. 'Know why?'

Hillary blinked, thought about it for a moment, then nodded. 'Yeah. It probably means the bugger is up to something else, and who knows what unsavoury substance you might accidentally tread in before you know just where it's safe to put your feet.'

The desk sergeant roared with laughter, making a couple of passing PCs grin across at them. 'Got it in one.'

'Great,' Hillary said, twisting her lips wryly. 'Well, when I find out just what it is that we need to watch out for, I'll be sure to let you know. You can spread the word to the others.'

'Righty-o, Hill. Oh, by the way, exactly when is your fella due to head over to St Aldates?' he asked, super casually.

Hillary shot him a nice-try look. 'If you're talking about Superintendent Crayle,' she said blandly, 'his new posting begins officially in two weeks' time.'

'Better watch himself in the big city then,' the desk sergeant grinned. 'A good looking boy like that.'

Hillary laughed. The 'big city' of Oxford lay all of three miles up the road. 'I'm sure he's old enough and mean enough to watch his back,' she said drily.

'Word is that you do that for him, Hill.'

Hillary said something very pithy and extremely Anglo Saxon in origin to this blatant bit of cheek, and left the desk sergeant smirking knowingly and in a very good mood.

Still smiling herself, she headed downstairs into the depths of the building, her mind still very much on Superintendent Steven Crayle. Her thoughts, however, weren't so much particularly amused, as rather more pensive.

Steven Crayle was six years her junior – hardly a 'boy' in anybody's language. He was good looking, sexy, smart and ambitious. And when she'd first joined his team nearly two years ago, he hadn't been particularly welcoming, seeing her as Donleavy's choice, an ex-DI with something of a mixed reputation, being foisted on to him by the top brass.

And just a week or so ago he'd asked her to marry him.

Now that he'd accepted a promotion, and moving on from the CRT meant that he'd no longer be her boss, he was expecting her answer any time soon.

And she still had no idea, yet, what that answer was going to be.

With a sigh, she walked down the labyrinthine corridors to her own tiny office, that had once, literally, been a stationery cupboard, and unlocked the door. There was just room inside for a tiny desk, one chair, a filing cabinet and her computer. She hung up her coat on the hook on the back of the door, slung her bag under the desk and booted up the computer.

She dealt quickly with her e-mails, and tackled some of the seemingly endless supply of paperwork in her IN tray, then walked back through to the larger communal office, where her team worked.

Her eyes went first to Jimmy Jessop, her 62-year-old right-hand man.

Jimmy had been a sergeant for most of his forty-year career on the force, and had retired after putting in his time. He'd confidently expected to take up an allotment, enjoy the holidays he'd never got around to taking, and generally get to do all of the things that his beloved and long-suffering wife had always wanted them to do but hadn't been able to, because of his job. But, barely six months after retiring, he'd suddenly lost his wife.

And the waiting list for an allotment was nearly three years long.

So now, here he was, back at HQ, and working as a civilian consultant on the CRT and thinking himself very lucky indeed. Hillary Greene was, in many ways, the best boss he'd ever worked for. Although she'd been married to the late, unlamented, and extremely bent copper, Ronnie Greene, everyone knew that she herself was as straight as they came. What's more, she'd had a conviction rate second to none during her days as a DI, even earning a medal for valour after getting shot saving her former boss and best friend, Phillip 'Mellow' Mallow. Since joining the CRT she had yet to fail to solve every cold murder case given to her by the super. Speaking of which, Jimmy expected them to be getting another case soon. Maybe even today, given that the new boss was being shown the ropes. It made sense to show him how the process worked from scratch.

The thought of a new case made him very happy, like an old hunting dog spotting the white tail of a rabbit disappearing across the field. Not that he didn't already have a fair bit on his plate as it was, though.

'Guv.' He nodded a greeting at her and gave a brief smile.

She nodded back, and her eyes moved on to the two newest recruits.

The majority of the team was comprised of computer and forensic boffins, who solved the bulk of cold cases by comparing old, stored, DNA samples and matching them to new crimes, as well as using all the other, latest scientific methods available. Databases were also used to cross-reference past crimes and pick up the traces of repeat offenders still at work.

But some of the more one-off, mostly murder, cases needed a more active, old-fashioned approach to detection, and that was where she came in. Because of budget cuts, however, the small investigative team within the CRT was always going to be a low priority. Consequently, it was now manned only by herself and Jimmy, as two civilian ex-police personnel, and by two youngsters who were, ostensibly anyway, thinking about joining the police force in the near future. Because they weren't actually in uniform however, and hadn't yet been through police training college, they were also civilians, worked part-time, and thus could be used as relatively cheap labour.

It was part of Hillary's remit to train up these assorted 'wannabes', sorting out the wheat from the chaff, and eventually passing the best of them on up the line, where it was hoped they'd become official, not to mention semi-seasoned police officers.

Sam Pickles, who was now in his last year at university, had been one such success story, and Hillary missed seeing his cheerful, freckled face about the place. But she was confident that, after finishing his degree, he was going to join up, and would probably, one day, make chief constable.

Now that he was gone, however, she had two more green kids to deal with. Well, Wendy Turnbull at least fitted that category, as far as Hillary was concerned. At twenty-four she almost certainly wouldn't regard herself as a kid, but her Goth appearance didn't do her many favours in wanting to be seen as an adult. Today, she was wearing black leather leggings, with a black and red lacy top and what looked like a knitted black shawl, tied over her skinny shoulders. Her short spiky hair was dyed at the tips in a vibrant lime green colour, and full black mascara, eyeliner, and eyeshadow, plus pale face powder, made her look like an escapee from an Addams Family film set.

She was busy tapping away at her computer and was so engrossed in what she was doing, that she hadn't even realized

Hillary was there. She was a cheerful kid, which was always a bonus, a bit gung-ho and still naïve in many ways, Hillary mused, but she was at least eager to learn. Whether she'd actually make a good police officer was still up for debate, in her opinion.

With a wry smile, Hillary turned to the last member of her team and by far the most problematic: Jake Barnes.

Jake, at thirty-three, was poles apart from Wendy in almost every way. At six feet tall, with short brown hair, and grey-green eyes, he was a fit and good-looking man, who was dressed today in an expensive navy blue suit. It looked like it had cost a thousand pounds, and probably had, for Jake had made his fortune young and early, during the dot.com boom, and had retired at the ridiculous age of twenty-five, a very wellheeled young man indeed. Divorced, childless, he'd joined the CRT supposedly because he wanted to 'give something back to the community'. And with his computer skills, unquestionable business prowess and forward thinking, media-smart savvy personality, it was hardly surprising that the brass had snapped him up like greedy vultures when he'd volunteered for the programme.

But although, along with Wendy, he'd worked with Hillary and helped solve their last murder case, she knew that there was far more to Jake Barnes than he was letting on.

'Guv,' Jake said now, giving her his usual slightly shy, quiet-but-confident smile.

Hillary quirked her lips at him and moved her glance back to Jimmy, who nodded slightly. He obviously had something to report to her, and she nodded back that she understood as much.

She'd asked him to keep an eye on the new boy, or the Boy Wonder as Wendy had cheekily dubbed him, and wondered exactly what it was that Jimmy had now got on him.

Well, time would tell. First things first.

'I'm just off to see the new boss. Is he in?' she asked the old sergeant.

'Guv, I think he's in with Steven. I heard voices in his office when I passed,' Jimmy said.

'Have you seen him?' It was Wendy who spoke, looking up eagerly from her lap top. 'What's he like?'

'Haven't clapped eyes on him,' Jimmy said laconically.

'Damn. I hope he's nice,' Wendy said fretfully. 'It's horrible if you're lumbered with a boss you can't get on with. Not that I'm saying that I can't get on with people, mind,' she added anxiously.

'Well, I'll report back and let you know,' Hillary promised with a wry smile. And so saying, she turned and walked smartly towards Steven's office.

Steven Crayle had got in to the office early that morning, and wasn't surprised to find Roland Sale arriving not long after him.

He'd approved of Donleavy's choice to take over his old role at CRT, on paper at least, liking what he'd read of Sale's past record, and now that he'd spent nearly an hour talking to the man in person, he saw no reason to change his mind.

Sale still lived in Aylesbury, where his wife was too settled to want to move. But the commute wasn't that bad, and the superintendent certainly spoke fondly of his wife, Joyce, and was clearly prepared to do things her way. Divorced himself, Steven readily admired any married couple who managed to stick it out these days, let alone when one of them had a job like theirs.

At 58, Sale was around five feet ten inches tall, with brown-turning-to-grey hair, hazel eyes and a slim build that was just beginning to show signs of developing a bit of a gut. He was dressed in an old, but respectable grey suit, and he looked comfortable sitting in Steven's office. Which was just as well, since it was soon to be his own. A second desk had been brought in temporarily, so the two men could work in tandem as Steven showed him the ropes.

'So that's all the admin sorted,' Steven said now, shutting a folder and handing it over to him. 'It's all on the computer, of course, and the secretaries will help you out if you get bogged down. The committee meetings can be a bit of a pain, but actually there's less paperwork than you might think.'

Roland Sale nodded. 'That's fine. Everything's clear so far. And I understand how tight the budget is for this place. I thought we were squeezed, but what you managed to accomplish down here on so little is an eye opener. So tell me about the team – how does it work, having mainly civilians reporting to you? I have to say, out of all the things that I've heard so far, that's what's worrying me the most,' he admitted openly.

'Yes, it's not totally like running an active investigation unit,' Steven agreed. 'On the other hand, in many ways it is. First off, your primary investigator is ex-DI Hillary Greene. You've seen her solve rate. It speaks for itself.'

'Yes. Very impressive. She's a bit of a legend in these parts, or so I hear,' Sale said cautiously.

Steven smiled a shade grimly. No doubt, before accepting the post, Sale had done his homework. And he wasn't surprised that he must have had mixed reactions when looking over Hillary's personnel file. 'We'll come back to her later,' he said cautiously. 'Let's start with Jimmy. Ex-sergeant, good, steady man.'

They spent some time discussing Jimmy's history. 'And there's no doubt that both of them see Jimmy as Hillary's wing man,' Steven concluded. 'They're tight, and work well together. And between them, they train up and work the wannabes, as Hillary calls them.'

'Yes. I'm not sure I like the thought of untrained youngsters working cases,' Sale said flatly.

'Me neither,' Steven agreed just as flatly. 'But with all the budget cuts, it was either them or no one. Actually though, apart from a few hiccups, it's been OK. Sam Pickles is going to make a first-class officer in a few years' time, and of the two we've now got, both look promising, in different ways.'

'Hmm. I can see why Commander Donleavy appointed Jake Barnes. Is he really worth that many millions?'

Steven grimaced slightly. 'Yes,' he said shortly. 'The top brass liked his profile, obviously. He's media-smart, and just the sort of role model they were looking for. His joining the CRT in such a junior role was something of a coup for the PR team.' He picked up Wendy Turnbull's file, anxious to get off the subject of Jake Barnes.

Not long after Barnes had joined up, Hillary Greene had found him snooping on her computer. She hadn't been surprised. From the first moment she'd met him, she'd sensed the man had some kind of hidden agenda. And, what's more, she'd persuaded Steven to keep quiet about it, until they could figure out just what it might be.

That hadn't sat particularly well with him, but he had learned to trust Hillary's judgement and instinct. And she was right when she said that they needed to gather more proof and evidence before going to the top brass with it. Nobody was going to thank them for tarnishing the gilt on the brass's new golden boy, after all, and , as Hillary had also pointed out, if Barnes *was* up to something illegal, as opposed to just being an inveterate snoop, then it was their job to catch him in the act.

Crime prevention being, sort of, the point.

So they'd had one of the technical boffins set up a tracker on her computer, so that they could keep tabs on whatever it was that Barnes was looking for on her computer system. So far, though, he hadn't accessed it again. Hillary had also asked Jimmy Jessop to keep a tight watch on him, and he was regularly reporting back to Hillary.

So, given the fact that Steven didn't feel particularly comfortable playing things so close to his chest, it was hardly surprising that he felt guilty about keeping Roland Sale in the dark. After all, in two weeks' time, Jake Barnes would be Sale's problem. Not Steven's. Or even Hillary's - not officially. And if it all blew up in their faces, it would be Sale who'd take the majority of the flack - the brass being notoriously clever at passing the buck.

At some point he'd have to have a word with Hillary about bringing Sale fully into the loop even though he already knew that she wouldn't like it. With a sigh, Steven Crayle contemplated the stormy weather that they had ahead of them. He was already feeling distinctly jittery as it was, waiting for her to give him some sort of clue as to how she felt about them getting married.

Forcing his mind back to the task at hand, he picked up another folder. 'Now, Wendy Turnbull is a very different kettle of fish. But she has something about her,' he said with a smile, tossing across the file. Sale caught it neatly.

Ten minutes later, they'd finished discussing the two newbies, and the talk returned inevitably to Hillary Greene.

'So, what's she like?' Roland Sale asked, accepting the mug of coffee Steven handed over to him.

Sale had already noticed that the younger man had made it from his private stash of Columbia beans that he kept locked in his top drawer, and the high-quality brew seemed typical of the man himself.

In his mid-forties, Acting Chief Superintendent Steven Crayle was dressed in an impeccable dark-blue suit, with a maroon and pale-blue tie. He was tall and lean, and looked like the sort who kept himself scrupulously fit by playing energetic squash or something equally athletic. He had crisply styled dark hair and dark eyes, and was well barbered, and smelt of something expensive and tasteful. Perhaps because he was not a good-look-ing man himself, Roland Sale knew that women would instantly be attracted to Crayle. He was what his Joyce would have called a fox.

But for all that, Sale wasn't fooled by the well-manicured elegance of the man. He'd read enough about him to know that his latest promotion was only the latest in a long line and, from their conversation so far, he could tell Crayle had a mind as smart as the rest of him. He was also tough and incisive, which came as no real surprise to him, given the CRT's great record so far. Although, if there was any truth to the rumours, that wasn't all down to Steven Crayle. Hillary Greene had to take some of the credit.

'I mean, the woman as opposed to the legend,' he said now quietly. 'If she's the best weapon in the arsenal, I need to know what I'm dealing with here. So please, be honest.'

Steven smiled, wondering just how much Sale had found out or guessed.

'When Commander Donleavy first told me he'd appointed her, I wasn't best pleased,' he admitted, deciding to be up front and honest about it. Well, reasonably so. 'Not that I was worried about her ex, Ronnie Greene, you understand,' he put in quickly. 'An internal inquiry team had already cleared her and found her totally innocent of having anything to do with that animal parts smuggling ring he had set up. Neither did she see a penny of that bloody fortune he made. Besides, that was all ancient history by then. He'd been killed in that car crash years before she came to us. Besides, her work ethic was well known, and her solve rate has always been through the roof.'

Sale nodded.

'But after taking that bullet for Mellow Mallow, and then sticking by her sergeant through all that later trouble, she was something of a superstar as far as the rank and file were concerned. And all that baggage wasn't something that I par-ticularly wanted to deal with,' Steven swept on, taking a sip from his own mug of coffee.

Again Sale nodded. 'Her sergeant, Janine Tyler, was married to Superintendent Mallow, wasn't she?'

'That's right,' Steven agreed. 'And when her husband was shot and killed, she then killed the man responsible. Acting in self-defence of course,' Steven added, with absolutely no inflec-tion in his voice whatsoever.

'Right.' Sale let that sit for a moment. 'But she contacted Hillary right after the incident, and DI Greene went out to the scene, even though she was no longer Janine Mallow's superior officer. And Hillary's boss made certain accusations that she'd covered up something about it.'

'Yes. But that was never proved,' Steven said flatly and a shade coldly, and then felt the need to warn him. 'Her old boss later got transferred. To Hull.'

Sale winced and rubbed a finger thoughtfully across his chin. 'To Hull, huh?'

'To Hull,' Steven confirmed blandly.

Sale sipped his coffee and let the silence settle a bit. He was no fool and knew just what he was being told. 'I did hear back from my contacts, that Commander Donleavy really rates her as a detective. He didn't like it when she retired, I gather?'

'No, he didn't,' Steven said. And then had to smile at the understatement.

'And when she came back he made sure that she got the top spot here,' Sale pressed, just to be sure that he'd got the political lay of the land right.

'Yes. Of course, her record alone made that inevitable, so nobody cried foul. But when the commander told me to give her only the cold murder cases,' Steven admitted, with a small grin, 'I have to admit, I wasn't happy to have my hands tied. So I found the coldest, deadest cases and handed them over, knowing damned well that she'd have to end up with egg on her face.'

'Didn't she complain?' Sale asked curiously, and looked surprised when a wide smile crossed the younger man's handsome face.

'You've got a lot to learn about Hillary,' Steven said softly. 'First, don't assume – like I did – that she'll fail to close even the deadest of dead-end cases. She's that good.' He ticked off another finger. 'Secondly, always bear in mind that she sees any set-back as a challenge. And third – she'd rather have all her teeth pulled, and without the benefit of Novocain, before she'd be caught dead complaining or whinging about *anything*.'

Sale smiled. 'Got it.'

'Now I tend to hand her the cases that really stick in my craw, knowing that there's a damned good chance that some murderous bastard who thought he'd got away with it, is finally going to get what's coming to him. For instance' – he shuffled through the files and produced one from the stack – 'a young mother of three, killed in her own kitchen.'

Sale winced. 'I hate those kinds of cases.'

'Exactly: we all do. This is another case in point.' He tapped a finger on another buff-coloured folder. 'A young man, a student at one of the Oxford colleges still in his teens, who should have had his whole life ahead of him. And then there's the last one she closed, a thirty-something chap, by all accounts a thoroughly decent sort, who left behind parents devastated by his loss. She solved them all. Of course, you don't have to do the same thing: you can hand her cases on whatever basis you see fit.'

Roland Sale nodded thoughtfully. 'I rather like the way you go about it.'

Steven smiled acknowledgement. 'Speaking of which, my last case of choice for her is this.' So saying, he picked up a folder and opened it.

As he did so, he heard a sharp rap at the door, and called out, 'Come in.'

Roland Sale looked up as a woman entered the room. She had a very attractive, maybe rather old-fashioned hour-glass figure, and was dressed in a no-nonsense blue suit. She had that shade of reddish-brown hair that Sale had always liked, and a pair of beautiful but laser-like pale-brown eyes that instantly zeroed in on Steven.

Sale didn't need to hear Steven Crayle say her name in order to guess her identity.

'Ah Hillary, that's good timing. I was just about to discuss your new cold case.'

Hillary Greene looked at her lover, then turned to the stranger in the room, who was already getting to his feet and was holding out his hand.

'DI Greene. Roland Sale.'

Hillary shook his hand with a brief smile. 'I don't really have a rank any more sir,' Hillary pointed out mildly. But nobody in that room was in any doubt just how redundant those words really were.

CHAPTER TWO

'I was just telling Superintendent Sale, here, the criterion I use when I hand out your cases,' Steven said, with a slightly wry smile in the older man's direction. He'd already noticed that Hillary's eyes had gone straight to the open file on the desk between them, and that she'd tensed slightly with anticipation. A quick glance at Roland Sale told him that he'd noticed her instant preoccupation too.

'Knowing your appetite for cold murder cases, I thought that the best way for Superintendent Sale here to learn how things work, is to start you on a new case, and let him see the process through. It goes without saying, that from now on, you'll be reporting back to both of us.'

'Understood, sir,' Hillary agreed easily.

They'd already discussed every aspect of Steven's move and every possible repercussion for them. Although Hillary wasn't feeling exactly happy to see him go, they'd both, albeit tacitly, acknowledged that, given the state of their private life, it was probably best that he was moving on. After he'd met with Donleavy's choice of replacement, he had been able to report back favourably , which had been a relief for them both. The last thing they needed was for Hillary to be stuck with a boss for whom she couldn't work.

Right on cue, Roland Sale now spoke up with a smile. 'I have to say, I'm as intrigued as you are to see what the case is and how you'll go about working it.' Privately, he was under no illusions that he still had a lot to learn.

'Then let me summarize it for the both of you,' Steven said, retrieving the file, but barely needing to refer to it, since he'd been studying it for the last two days.

'Sylvia Perkins,' he began, 'was seventy-five years old when she was found battered to death in her home on the 22 February, 2010. Fingerprints at the scene and in the house were all traced back to either the victim herself, or close friends and family. There was no DNA evidence of a stranger found, so the attacker didn't leave any trace of himself – or herself – behind. There were no witnesses to the crime either, which was, as you can see, brutal.'

Both Sale and Hillary drew in a low, level breath, and Steven, catching Sale's eye, nodded. 'Yes, I know. Violent, needless death is always nasty, but we all really feel it when it's some poor old soul who stood no chance of fighting back. The old deserve to die peacefully in their beds, with their family by, not at the hand of some vicious thug.'

'Sir,' Hillary used the single syllable to both acknowledge the truth of his point and to urge him to carry on.

'Not that Sylvia, by all accounts, was particularly frail,' said Steven, taking the hint. 'She was still, according to her friends and family, fit and active. She still drove, for instance, only a small run-about, but it helped maintain her independence. She only used to go to the local shops, and never drove more than ten miles away from home it seems, but even so, she was no housebound, doddery old lady.'

'But, from the glimpse I saw of the scene-of-crime photos just now,' Rollo Sale said flatly, 'she wasn't strong enough to fight off her attacker.'

'No,' Steven agreed, dividing up the graphic and gruesome photographs of the victim *in situ*, and giving half of them to

Hillary, and the other half to Sale. Both of them flipped through them with set, grim-lipped concentration.

'Murder weapon?' Hillary asked simply.

'Not found at the scene, but it was widely assumed and believed to have been a brass poker. As you can see from this...' He showed them a picture of a fireplace, where a largely ornamental fireside set had also been photographed. It showed a small, never-used little brass coal shovel, a hard-bristled brush in the same pristine state, and a pair of brass coal tongeus. All three hung from a roundbased stand with hooks. 'The poker that would have completed the set is missing. According to her neighbours and family, it was generally agreed that the set was normally complete, although no one could swear to it a hundred per cent. Like a lot of old folk, she had a large collection of knick-knacks, ornaments, photo-frames and stuff, so nobody would have had any reason to particularly notice if the set was complete or not.'

'But the autopsy confirmed that a small ornamental brass poker would have fitted the bill?' Sale asked.

'Yes. The battering to her head was consistent with a heavy, rounded, thin metal implement. So it was probably the missing poker, but even though there was a fingertip search made in the garden and surrounding area, it was never found, and it was assumed that her killer took it away.'

'And did Mrs Perkins's house have a working fireplace sir?' Hillary asked, always careful to use Steven's title around anyone else.

'No, her house was mainly oil central heating. She lived in a little hamlet called Caulcott, about five miles from the market town of Bicester,' he added for Sale's benefit. 'Sylvia married her husband, a farm labourer called Joseph Perkins, not long after the war. They lived there all their married lives – nearly fifty years of it – and together they raised three daughters. Joseph worked on the local farm, but died out in the fields of a heart attack in ...' – he turned a page and consulted the information there – 'June 1998. As I was saying, the house is now oil-heated – or was at the time of her death – but there would originally have been an old fireplace and working chimney of course. Like a lot of people, Sylvia kept an arrangement of dried flowers there'– he pointed out some more scene-of-crime photos 'and decorated it with the brass fire screen and the fireplace set.'

'Sounds like the killer didn't necessarily come prepared then,' Hillary said, speaking her thoughts out loud, again for the benefit of her new boss. 'Selecting a murder weapon from the immediate vicinity usually indicates an unpremeditated crime, – unless, of course, it was meant to look that way, and the killer is trying to be clever.'

'On the other hand, do the elderly usually make someone so angry with them, that after a furious argument, someone picks up a poker and brains them with it?' Sale asked. He didn't sound, Hillary noted, adversarial, but rather genuinely interested. She knew from what Steven had learned about him that he hadn't handled that many murder inquiries in his career, and none as the senior investigating officer.

'It's not usual, certainly,' Hillary conceded. 'But just because you're senior in years, doesn't necessarily mean that all the old motives don't still hold true.'

'Money, sex, revenge, power,' Steven quoted drily.

'So who did get her money, sir?' Hillary asked, going straight for the most likely on the list.

Steven smiled. 'Ah yes, that would be her eldest grandson, and the original SIO's best bet. Robert 'Robbie' Grant.' Steven shuffled some more papers, and sighed. 'Sylvia's eldest daughter, Mary Rose, had two children, Robert and Julie. Julie apparently is doing well, married, kids, and works in a Boots store in Oxford. But Robbie has a sheet as long as your arm. And started early.' Steven held out a piece of paper, then hesitated visibly about which of the two people seated opposite him he should give it to. 'Sorry, I haven't had a chance to make duplicates.'

'Please, give it to Mrs Greene,' Roland Sale said at once. 'She's the SIO.'

'Call me Hillary,' Hillary said at once. Whilst she'd never had any trouble in being called DI Greene, being called *Mrs* Greene always made her feel like screaming.

Still, perhaps someday she could be called Mrs Crayle instead, a voice popped up mischievously in the back of her head. With an annoyed mental flick she kicked the thought aside and reached for the paper Steven was handing her, giving it a quick once over.

'Started young, with shoplifting,' she read out loud. 'A bit of aggravated assault, time in Juvie, before heading up the scale a bit.' She checked the dates. 'At the time of his grandmother's death, it was still petty stuff. Now he's serving time for robbery. Held up a shop with a mate with a shotgun. Charming. And you say he was Sylvia's main legatee? What are we talking about exactly? Did she own the house?'

'No, the Perkinses were strictly working class, and always rented. But he had all her life savings, the contents of the house, and her car. All told, about twenty-five grand, I suppose. That's a lot of money for a kid like Grant.'

'And I dare say he went through it like water?' Sale put in grimly. He was thinking that the nest egg had probably represented years of hard work and scrimping and saving on the part of the hard-working grandparents. But it wouldn't take a scrote like Robbie Grant much time to blow the lot.

'Within six months,' Steven confirmed. 'He wrecked the car during a race with some of his mates, and bust his leg pretty bad. The rest went on booze and probably his drug of choice.'

'And the original SIO liked him for it?' Hillary repeated. 'Just who was that, sir?'

'DI Linda Jarvis. Know her?'

'Heard of her,' Hillary said, thinking back. 'Tall woman, dark hair, I think I've seen her around the station house. Heard she was good. I'd like to catch up with her and compare notes.' She turned to Sale and smiled. 'When you investigate cold cases, the original senior investigating officers can sometimes take it personally. You know, it can often feel as if you're second guessing them, or that opening their case sends the message that you don't think they were up to the job, or that you think you're better than they are, that kind of thing. Needless to say, that's hardly ever the case. I'm sure Linda Jarvis did a first class job. And I always like to get the original SIO on board if I can.'

'Afraid you can't this time, Hillary,' Steven said quietly. 'DI Jarvis died last year. Car crash the other side of High Wycombe. One of those multi-car smashes in fog. Some stupid idiot was going too fast behind her and....' He shrugged graphically.

'Shit,' Hillary said simply.

'Yes. Will that be a problem?' Sale asked, again with what sounded like genuine curiosity.

'Not necessarily, sir,' Hillary said. She liked it that Sale was prepared to ask questions when he didn't know something, instead of making out like he knew it all. She was beginning to agree with Steven's favourable impression of the man. 'Although it's easier to have the original SIO to refer to, it's not as if opening a cold case is merely a process of repeating what they've already done. What would be the point of that? The forensics people are the ones to go to if it comes to going over old evidence with new, improved techniques. What we do here, is reinvestigate the old-fashioned way, using a different pair of eyes. I try and winkle out any lead, no matter how small or insignificant, that the original team might have missed, or dismissed as being too tenuous. As you know, in any fresh murder inquiry, the first forty-eight hours are crucial.'

She turned a little in her chair, glad to see that Sale was listening attentively. 'As you yourself know, in the rush and need to get results fast, you always have to prioritize what's important and what's less so. Also, as time goes by, an investigation that's stalled or not going anywhere, starts to bleed personnel, and then being allocated enough time becomes a problem, as the department gets other cases piled on top of their workload. There's always only just so much that you can realistically do. That's where investigating a cold case is very different and comes into its own. For a start, both my team and myself will be dedicated to the Perkins' case exclusively. What's more, there's no rush, and no pressure; we can take our time and check things out in a way that DI Jarvis and her team never had the luxury of doing. There's bound to be T's she didn't cross, and I's she didn't dot. And you never know when one little detail might prove crucial.'

Sale nodded. 'Yes. I can see the advantages of that. But surely, after the passage of time, aren't things always that much harder? In this case, 2010 isn't that long ago, but I know you've closed cases where twenty years or so have passed.'

'Yes, but sometimes, having that distance can be a good thing as well,' Hillary pointed out. 'Witnesses who were too scared to speak at the time, can feel more sanguine about opening up now. After all, "years ago" can seem like another planet away. Also things can become clearer with the passage of time that weren't so obvious then. For instance if someone kills a victim for money, they lie low before taking advantage of it. Then, years later, when we reopen the case, and find they're living the life of Riley without any adequate explanation for it, they suddenly stand out like a sore thumb. It's rarely as simple as that, obviously, but there are signs to look out for. So, like most cases, it's a matter of swings and roundabouts.'

Sale nodded, then glanced across at Steven. 'Sorry to interrupt. You were saying Robbie Grant was the number one suspect? I take it that DI Jarvis wasn't able to bring it home to him though?'

'No. He had the motive all right, but Jarvis couldn't put him at the scene of the crime. His alibi was so-so, but there were no witnesses who saw him at his grandmother's house that day, and no forensic evidence placing him there,' Steven carried on. 'Not that he visited the old lady all that much. But it seems that he was the apple of her eye nonetheless. Who can say why?'

'She had all daughters, sir,' Hillary pointed out philosophically. 'And Robbie was her first male grandchild. It's perhaps not surprising that she'd have a soft spot for the boy.'

'And besides, she was of the generation that would have thought the oldest male relative should get everything anyway, I suspect,' Sale added pragmatically.

Hillary nodded and caught Steven's eye and smiled slightly. Yes, the new super might not be all that experienced in their particular field, but he was on the ball all right.

'So, was he the only suspect?' Hillary asked, pushing on.

'No, there were others. Linda Jarvis found someone with a motive other than money,' Steven admitted, with a small grin. 'Care to guess which on the list it was?'

'Sex,' Hillary said promptly.

Sale blinked.

'Right,' Steven said. 'Or rather jealousy, which stems from the same thing. Like a lot of senior citizens, Sylvia was a member of a social club for the elderly. Small rural communities especially rely on them to organize day trips and outings, provide a Christmas dinner, entertainment nights, bingo, fetes, what-have-you, anything to stave off the dreaded disease of loneliness.' He waved a hand in the air. 'Four of the local villages clubbed together to form the Forget-me-not Club. According to witnesses, Sylvia and a woman called Ruby Broadstairs were both interested in the same man: one Maurice Ritter.'

'A bit of a silver fox, huh?' Hillary asked with a grin.

'Apparently. A widower, seventy-six, with all his own teeth, one presumes. He was much sought after on dance nights it seems,' Steven said. Like all coppers, he knew that sometimes you needed levity to brighten a grim and ghastly situation.

'His cha-cha-cha was legendary?' Sale put in with a smile of his own.

'More like his tango, if it got Sylvia and Ruby all steamed up,' Hillary riposted.

'Whatever,' Steven said, with a grin. 'Again, according to what Jarvis's team found out, Ruby and Sylvia genuinely generated a good bit of ill-will and ill-feeling between them over this Maurice character.'

'Not coming to blows, surely?' Sale said, sounding aghast.

'Nothing that physical, I think,' Steven agreed.

'But again it came to nothing?' Hillary pressed. 'Did Ruby have her own transport for instance?' she added.

'Yes, and no,' Steven said, answering her questions in order. 'She lived in one of the neighbouring villages and relied on her son to run her around. Nobody saw Ruby or her son's car around Caulcott at the time of Sylvia's death. Don't forget we're talking about a small rural hamlet here, so an unknown car would stick out, even in this day and age.'

'On the other hand,' said Hillary, determinedly playing devil's advocate, 'if it's that small a community, most potential witnesses were probably out working on the farm, or had commuted to London, or wherever. Most rural places around here nowadays are a mixture of the relatively wealthy white-collar workers who motor up to London or Birmingham, but like to actually live in a country retreat. And people who still actually work the land and rely on tied cottages. So what are the chances that anybody would be in their homes, and nosy enough to see which car passes by, or who's visiting who?'

'True,' Steven said. 'But luckily for DI Jarvis, there were several people of Sylvia's age living nearby who were a good source of reliable information. Unfortunately most of it was negative.'

Hillary, sighed. 'So, nobody could put the scarlet woman at the scene?'

Steven's lips twitched. 'No.'

'Anyone else in the frame?' Sale asked.

Steven lifted his hand in the air and rocked it gently from side to side. 'Iffy. It seems that Sylvia Perkins didn't get on with one of the local farmers and landowner, Randy Gibson. And since he's always going to be around, with or without a tractor and/or a sheepdog trotting at his heels, nobody would have particularly noticed his comings and goings anyway.'

'This is the same farmer that her husband worked for?' Hillary asked, sitting up a bit straighter.

'Yes, it is. And therein, as they say, lies the rub. According to family and friends, Sylvia always blamed Mr Gibson for her husband's death.'

'But you said it was a heart attack, right?' Sale asked, a little confused.

'Anything dodgy about it, sir?' Hillary put in.

'No, not as such. Doctors were happy, and there were witnesses. But Joseph Perkins was nearly seventy at the time of his death. He was one of those who never retires, apparently. But it seems Sylvia had wanted him to do so for some time. She complained bitterly to her daughters that Gibson was pressurizing him to keep on working long hours, and again, according to Sylvia, the pay wasn't what it should be.'

Hillary leaned forward slowly. 'What did the farmer have to say about it?'

'Oh, he maintained that he had just been doing Joe a favour. Keeping him on, even though physically he was long past his best. Said he did it because Joe was always nagged at home and needed the excuse to get out of the house. Says he didn't give him any of the more strenuous jobs to do any more.'

'And did he admit to paying him low wages?' Hillary asked.

'Yes, eventually. But he claimed that was because Joe wasn't worth full wages anymore anyway. He maintained that Joe had no problem with it.'

'Hmm,' Hillary said, then did a bit of mental arithmetic. 'But her husband had been dead twelve years or more by the time she was killed.'

'Right.'

'So it all seems a bit tenuous. Why did it take so long for things to come to a head between them? If, in fact, it did?'

' DI Jarvis thought that too, but she mentioned it in her report because everyone kept telling her that the victim had a "running feud" with Gibson. Always bad-mouthing him, and going out of her way to attend council meetings to vote against him when he asked for some small bit of planning permission, that sort of thing. She even wrote to a Ramblers Association, urging them to use some defunct footpath across Gibson's land just to inconvenience him.'

'Ah,' Hillary said. 'So the thinking is, she might have come up with some other piece of harassment that finally hit home. Makes sense. After years of putting up with her, he might have confronted her and then just lost his rag.'

'It fits in with the unpremeditated argument,' Sale agreed. 'He calls on her, trying to either make peace or talk her out of whatever it is she's up to. They argue, it gets heated, he loses his temper, looks around for something and ... whack.'

They were all silent for a moment, thinking about the awfulness of it.

'Just how many blows were there to her head?' Hillary asked quietly.

Steven leafed through to the autopsy report and scanned it. 'There were no other bruises to the body, apparently, but the pathologist reckons there were eight blows to the head, two of which he reckons were delivered to the back of the head when the victim was standing. Three more when she was in a kneeling or in some sort of semiprone position, and the rest when she was probably collapsed on the floor.'

'So, not quite frenzied,' Sale said, 'but hardly a single blow either. Nobody could claim that it was "an accident" or' – he made more speech marks in the air – 'that "I only hit her a couple of times before I knew what I was doing". Which tells us what, exactly?'

'Well, whoever did it, be it Gibson or someone else that she'd made angry, they certainly meant to make sure that she was dead,' Hillary took up the argument. 'Nothing else really fits, like you said. If it was someone who went literally berserk, they'd have rained down fifty, sixty, maybe even a hundred different blows on her, and they would have attacked her body as well, not just the head area. We've all heard of cases where someone seriously off their head simply can't stop striking the victim.'

Sale winced, and Steven paled slightly.

'But in this case, it seems as if whoever killed Sylvia hit her enough to make sure that they'd done the job, but not enough to suggest they were out of control whilst doing it. Unless there was some other reason why they confined it to just the eight blows. It might be that whoever did it, simply didn't have the stomach for more,' she said flatly.

'So no question of it being borderline accidental,' Steven said. 'I agree. That's why I want you to work on it, Hillary. Whoever killed Sylvia Perkins has had nearly five years to think that they've got away with it. I don't like that. And I know DI Jarvis didn't like it either. She fought hard to keep the case open longer, but was overruled by her DCI. As usual, I'll have the rest of the case files sent up to you, and I'll copy this summary for both of you. Any questions?'

'No, sir,' Hillary said, and rose to her feet. She turned to Sale, 'It's good to meet you, sir. I think we'll work well together.'

'Likewise.' Sale shook the hand she held out, smiling widely. 'And I don't see why not.'

Both men watched her leave, then Sale slowly leaned back in his chair. 'So that was Hillary Greene. My senior investigating officer. Impressive.'

Steven nodded. Then caught Sale's eye, and hid a sigh. He wasn't looking forward to this next bit, because, like most men, he never liked having to explain himself or his actions. And, also like most men, he never felt comfortable discussing personal matters. But it had to be done.

'I'm not sure if you're aware of it, but if not, perhaps you should be. Hillary is also my partner. I mean, we're an item,' he added, somewhat awkwardly, since even he didn't know, really, how he could best describe what he and Hillary had together.

Roland Sale slowly nodded. 'Yes. I had heard some station-house gossip to that effect,' he said carefully. Then smiled. 'Congratulations. She is, as I said, very impressive.'

Steven smiled slightly. 'I think so. But I don't want you to get the wrong idea about how it works around here. I've never given her any special treatment, and you don't have to either. We are both, and always have been, professionals, first and foremost.'

'I never thought otherwise,' Sale said, meeting his gaze levelly. Although he had, of course, wondered. But now that he'd had a chance to see for himself just how things were, he felt himself relaxing marginally. Besides, once Steven Crayle was gone, the CRT, and how Sale chose to run it, would be no concern of his.

'So now you just leave her to get on with it?' Sale asked, sensing the younger man's unease, and getting back to business.

'Basically, yes. She'll report back and I'll supervise, and have my say of course. But with an officer of her calibre, my input is rarely needed. But since I, and soon *you*, will be the only one to have the actual authority to instigate power of arrest, whenever she needs to charge someone, it'll be up to us to make the actual collar. She is, remember, a civilian now, even though to all intents and purposes, you think of her as your DI. Then, of course, we have to baby sit the case through the courts, but you know how *that* goes.' His lips twisted, and Sale grimaced.

'Oh yes. Pray for a good prosecutor.'

Steven grunted an assent. 'And in the meantime, we get on with supervising our other on-going cases. Most of these are serial rapists, burglars, arsonists and what have you. And we get on to the majority of them via the computer boffins who've set up data bases and computer programmes designed to pick out recurring patterns and cross-reference, wherever possible, DNA matches and MOs.'

Steven got up and pushed away from his desk, Sale following suit. 'And that all takes place in the biggest room we have in this warren. So it's time to introduce you to the forensics people and assorted computer experts. Rumour has it that some of them have lost the use of their eyes and developed bat-like radar, since they hardly ever venture out into the daylight, but don't let that scare you.'

Sale laughed. 'I'll try not to.'

As Detective Superintendent Sale got to grips with how the bulk of work in the CRT was done, Hillary Greene returned to the small communal office, and set about organizing the troops.

'Right you lot, we've got another murder case. Wendy, can you get on to records and make sure they send all the hard-copy boxes and folders up here.' She handed her the paperwork with the case-file number on it. 'And then I'm afraid you and Jake are going to have the usual major sorting-out job on your hands.'

'Great!' Wendy said, and then frowned. 'Not the major sorting-out job, I mean, that's always a pain. But another murder case! Yay!' She thrust one fist into the air.

Hillary smiled. 'Glad to hear you're so enthusiastic. Let's hope you can say the same come five o'clock this afternoon. I want you and Jake to sort out the timeline, witness statements and forensics, all in order. The original SIO is out of the picture, I'm afraid, so all we've got to go on is her records. Jake, you're the computer whiz and organizational genius – by tomorrow morning, we need to have the bulk of what we need at our fingertips.'

'Guv.'

Hillary turned to Jimmy and hid a wink. 'Jimmy, my office. And bring some coffee, will you?'

'Guv.'

Hillary returned to her cubby hole and cleared a corner of her desk, and was perched with her bottom firmly on it, leaving the sole chair free for Jimmy when he came in, holding two mugs.

She took hers and nudged the chair with one foot. Jimmy sat down gratefully.

'So, what's the Boy Wonder been up to then?' she asked softly.

Jimmy blew across the top of his mug and took a tentative sip. It was still too hot.

He settled back into his chair and looked at his guv'nor thoughtfully. He'd been keeping an eye on Jake Barnes for some time now, and had begun to think that maybe Hillary had got it wrong about the lad after all. He certainly hadn't come back to HQ after hours in order to hack Hillary's computer again, that was for sure. And apart from a few visits to some nightclubs, and to see an older woman that Jimmy had later discovered was his mum, he hadn't been doing anything to cause them alarm.

Until yesterday. And now Jimmy had to hand it to his boss. The lad was definitely keeping secrets.

'He went to visit Crimmins & Lloyd. Know 'em?' he asked succinctly.

Hillary frowned. The name rang a bell … 'Not solicitors?'

'That PI outfit, guv. You know, last year, the ones who got the gen on that tabloid journalist who was later done for phone hacking.'

Hillary sighed heavily. 'Right. A two-man outfit, one ex-army, intelligence probably, and the other one who used to work for a big London firm that specialized in industrial espionage. Plenty of financial backing from some source or other not obviously apparent, so they're not short of a bob or two, and a reputation for getting results on even the toughest of jobs. And discretion guaranteed.'

'That's them,' Jimmy said laconically. Like most coppers, he had little use for private eyes. Unlike the species usually found in pulp American fiction, the real-life johnnies were usually nothing more than a pain in the police service's collective arse. But this pair, even he had to grudgingly admit, had clout. And expertise.

Hillary sighed. 'This pair know what they're doing at any rate,' she echoed his thoughts unerringly, 'and as such, they wouldn't have come cheap.'

'But our lad can afford them, can't he?' Jimmy pointed out.

'I don't suppose you were able to find out what he wanted them for?' Hillary said, without much hope.

'Didn't even try to find out, guv, not without reporting back to you first,' Jimmy admitted with a shrug. 'First off, I reckon there's no way that I could have scoped them out without getting caught. They've got cctv at their offices that would give our people wet dreams.'

Hillary nodded. 'No, you're right, of course. And if we tried to approach one of their receptionists or secretaries with a view of having a quiet chat, they'd be bound to report back to their bosses. Outfits like Crimmins & Lloyd can afford to pay their people top money. And with that comes loyalty. And the last thing we need is for Jake to realize we're on to him.'

'So, the question is,' Jimmy said, taking a gulp of his coffee, 'what does our lad want finding out so badly, that he'd hire the A-team to find it for him?'

Hillary sighed and shrugged. But she had the feeling that they'd soon be finding out. 'Well, continue to keep an eye on him. But don't lose sleep over it,' she added, somewhat guiltily, 'you're already going above and beyond, as it is, Jimmy.'

Jimmy grinned at her over the steaming mug. 'Truth is, guv, nowadays I don't need as much shut-eye as I used to, so I don't mind sitting obbo. Besides, it's more entertaining than anything that's on the goggle box nowadays.'

'You should be at least getting overtime,' Hillary said. But they both knew that was just pie in the sky. If they were to find out what Jake Barnes was up to, they'd have to do it off their own bat. And out of their own pocket.

'No worries guv,' Jimmy assured her. Like Hillary, he was too intrigued by what the Boy Wonder was up to, to care about a little thing like getting paid.

CHAPTER THREE

THE NEXT MORNING, Jake Barnes was in early, blissfully unaware that his savvy boss suspected anything. He'd spent a long and productive day yesterday, beavering away along with Wendy copying and up-dating the Sylvia Perkins case, and he was anxious now to get a few hours' reading in. He wanted to get a good handle on the evidence before Hillary Greene started testing his mettle.

Although he didn't regard Wendy as serious competition, he was determined to keep his job and make progress in it. It was vital that he made himself indispensable, and impressed Hillary Greene. What's more, if he wanted to challenge Jimmy Jessop for the position of her right-hand man – and he did – he knew he had to earn his spurs, and fast.

So when Hillary walked past the open office door at 8.30, she saw his dark head bent industriously over the files and, with a slight, enigmatic smile, walked on to her office. There she spent an hour catching up on general admin, and making sure that she had everything she needed for the day at her fingertips before heading to the communal office.

Like the rest of her team, she'd spent the previous day acquainting herself with DI Jarvis's investigation of the murder, and now it was time to give the paperwork a rest and get active in the field, always the best part of the job. But should she reward Jake for his obvious hard work, or give free rein to Wendy's enthusiasm?

She paused in the doorway, but it was Jimmy who looked up at her first. Despite his protestations of yesterday that he didn't mind the extra work that keeping an eye on the Boy Wonder entailed, he had to smother a yawn. So that was one less decision she had to make – it was a cold and raw day, and the old sergeant deserved an easy ride.

She smiled at him briefly. 'OK, Jimmy, I want you to spend today in the office with the experts. See if they can find any similar MOs that fit the Perkins case. It's possible that she might be one in a series. Perhaps even the first.'

Jimmy nodded. 'Guv.'

'But we'd have heard, surely, if any other old ladies had been killed, wouldn't we?' Wendy asked, with a small frown. 'I mean, I know it's a bad old world and all that, but if many other old ladies had been bashed to death, they'd have made some sort of headlines, wouldn't they? And if they didn't, they bloody well should have,' she added hotly.

Hillary nodded. 'Yes, they would,' she said, amused and a little touched by the youngster's passion, and went on to explain patiently what Jimmy had instantly surmised. 'But that wasn't exactly what I was asking Jimmy to find out. Of course we'd know if we had a serial killer on our hands – alarm bells would have rung well before now if there'd been a spate of killings similar to that of Sylvia Jenkins. But one of the most obvious lines of inquiry that we have to follow is that of a robbery gone wrong. Now we know from the files that nothing was missing from Sylvia's house as far as her family and friends were able to tell,' she swept on, before Wendy, who'd just opened her mouth to say it, could point that out, 'and we know at the time that DI Jarvis's team couldn't find any evidence of any individual or gang targeting the elderly in remote rural spots, but it's just possible that Sylvia was the first. So just say for argument's sake, that she was, and whoever broke into her home had the fright of his or her life, and for a while was scared into lying low. That would have meant that they'd have stayed off Jarvis's radar maybe for the whole term of her investigation. But since a good few years have now passed, if some light-fingered sod had merely intended to rob her but ended up killing her instead, it's highly likely that he, she or they would have felt safe enough by now to pick up where they left off. And that would leave a trail for us to follow.'

'So you want me to look out for any elderly people, male or female, living alone, and in small country villages, who were robbed or burgled of their valuables,' Jimmy took up today's lesson. 'And if any of them were assaulted. If so, make special note of it if they were hit around or about the head.'

'Right,' Hillary said. 'It's a chore and a long shot, but we'd look like incompetent idiots if we didn't follow it up. And then, when you've done that, you can ask them for a list of known thieves who like to mug the elderly out on the street, and who were active around the time of Sylvia's death. And why do I want him to do that?' she tossed out into the room in general, but it was Jake Barnes who leapt on it.

'Escalation,' he said flatly. 'Muggers are usually junkies desperate to get cash for a fix. Consequently, they're not very well organized. But some aren't addled by drink or drugs, and are more calculating, and could have upgraded to following possible victims in the hope that a home invasion would net them more profit. Jewellery, small, easily portable valuables and so on.'

Hillary nodded. 'Yes. And if Jimmy and the boffins can find some likely candidates who were actively mugging old ladies at the time of Sylvia's murder, we need to know about it. Jimmy, there are bound to be quite a few names on a list like that, so you can follow them up. Getting alibis for them after five years won't be easy, but give it a try. You never know, one of them might make your copper's nose itch.' It was the type of thing that needed an experienced copper, and could be done at Jimmy's own pace, and at his own convenience.

Jimmy nodded. 'Guv.'

Although Hillary was privately pretty sure that the Perkins case was going to turn out to be a far more personal and a strictly one-off affair, she couldn't afford not to cover all her bases.

'Wendy, I want you to drive out to the village and do a canvas for me. Find out who's still alive and living in the area, and set up interview times for them.'

'Right, guv. Do you want me to take photos of the house and surrounding area as well? I've got a great digital camera on my phone.'

'Sure, why not? ' Hillary said, although what possible use they could be she wouldn't like to say. But there was just something of the eager young puppy about the Goth that would have made her feel guilty if she'd slapped her down.

'Jake, you're with me. We're going to start by interviewing her family, and we might as well start with the eldest daughter.'

'Guv,' Jake said with alacrity.

Wendy, who would have liked that job far better, taunted good-naturedly under her breath as he passed her. 'Swot! Teacher's pet,' and something far less complimentary. Jake, who had good hearing, as did Hillary, grinned at her in passing, and flipped her a friendly finger.

Wendy stuck her tongue out.

Hillary hid a sigh. It was going to be one of those days.

In Jake Barnes's lush and lovely E-type Jaguar, Hillary leaned back in the cream leather passenger seat and let the scenery fly by as they headed towards Minster Lovell, the village where Sylvia's oldest daughter now lived with her second husband.

Her mind, however, was not so much on the upcoming

interview as it was on Steven Crayle. Just a month ago, she'd been sure that he was about to break up with her. She'd sensed that small but inescapable shift in his behaviour that told her something had changed in their relationship. It was true enough, but she'd been wrong about the cause of it. Far from trying to gently disentangle himself from her and her life, he'd asked her if he could become a much bigger part of it instead.

Which had totally thrown her.

Hillary shifted uncomfortably in her seat, but she was not one to shirk painful thoughts. When she'd thought he was going to end their affair, she'd found it surprisingly hurtful. She'd thought herself old enough and mean enough not to get snared up in anything too emotionally dangerous. And yet, she'd found the idea of not seeing him again, of not having him sleep over on her narrowboat, of not spending weekends with him, walking, or simply chatting and relaxing together, almost paralysing.

So when he'd asked her to marry him, she'd been unprepared for it. Instead, in her mind, she'd already been rehearsing the words that would save her pride and face, and allow him to wiggle free. She'd had her big, "It's OK, I'm a big girl now, I can handle it, so so long and don't let the door hit you on the bum on the way out" speech all set and ready to go.

So she'd been left, almost literally speechless, when he'd asked her if she'd ever given any serious thought to them getting married.

After a while she'd managed to croak out something – something no doubt inane and inadequate. She seemed to have some vague idea that she'd said that she hadn't really given it much thought, and that it was a serious step, and something that shouldn't be rushed into and needed careful consideration. And all the while, he'd continued to smile at her, that small, slightly sad smile, that made her feel like squirming inside.

Because she knew what he'd been thinking, of course. What

he *must* have been thinking, and probably still was. That, after the débâcle of her first marriage, she was so wary of ever trusting another man again, that he'd been a fool to even ask her.

Ronnie Greene. She'd been so young when she'd met, fallen for, and married Ronnie Greene. She'd been a newly promoted DS, and he'd been a DI in a different division. Good looking, popular, with a reputation for being a shade brutal, a shade canny, he'd turned out instead to be utterly bent, and a serial womanizer as well.

He'd made her life miserable for nearly seven years. She'd been in the process of divorcing him when he'd been killed in a road-traffic accident, and had saved her the bother. Of course, by then, he'd been under investigation by an internal review board for serious corruption. For years he'd been amassing a small fortune from bribes and kick-backs, and who knew what else. He'd also organized a lucrative animal-parts smuggling operation using contacts he'd made over the years in the criminal underworld .

And she'd known nothing of it. Suspected nothing. The humiliation of that alone was enough to make her squirm, even now. How could she have been so bloody stupid? So wilfully blind?

She'd been investigated too, and cleared. And, oddly enough, her own reputation hadn't really suffered that much as a result. Her record in many ways spoke for itself and she'd had good guv'nors, who had stood by her.

But although that was all many years in the past now, it still cast a long shadow, and she'd vowed – never again. Which was, perhaps, understandable. Marriage, she'd learned the hard way, was a minefield: men were untrustworthy. It simply wasn't worth the hassle. That had always been her mantra. There had been a few (very few) scattered love affairs over the years – she was not a nun, after all – but she'd never seriously fallen for another man. She'd made damned sure she didn't.

Until now, it seemed.

But did it really make sense to stick so religiously to her single way of life? The little voice of hope persisted in niggling away at her. Steven Crayle was so many miles away from Ronnie Greene they weren't even in the same solar system. And the woman she'd been then, naïve, trusting, gullible and blinded by love's young dream, bore no relation to the woman she was now. So why assume that taking another chance would automatically end in disaster?

And yet … and yet…. The thought of actually remarrying gave her a severe case of the heebie-jeebies. Just why did Steven want to tie the knot anyway, she wondered crossly? Why couldn't they just carry on as they were? Nowadays, nearly everybody simply remained partners. It was so much easier, and legally, far less messy. There were many advantages to just—

'Can you just check the sat nav, guv?' Jake Barnes's voice suddenly and abruptly pulled her out of her funk. 'I think the house must be up here on the right somewhere but I don't know the village.'

Hillary blinked and glanced around at the pleasant, tree-lined street that Jake had turned into. Not far from the market town of Witney, Minster Lovell overlooked a pretty valley. At this time of year though, the leaves were fast losing their leaves and becoming skeletal, and the grey, overcast sky felt oppressive and ominous.

The houses here were detached, stone-built, sturdy-looking specimens. Mary Rose Perkins, daughter of a humble farm-labourer and his equally working-class wife, must have done well for herself.

'Her second husband is part-owner of an accountancy business in Witney, guv,' Jake Barnes said. He'd seen her looking around and mentally pricing up the real estate, and had read her mind. 'Her first husband worked in a butcher shop, and they lived in a council estate in Bicester, where they bought up their two kids. They divorced not long after her mother died. Mary Rose then took a job as a secretary at the accountancy firm in Witney, and obviously caught the eye of Ewan Gentley, the senior partner. They've been married barely a year.'

'Thanks for the background info,' Hillary said. 'Nice to see you've done your homework.'

Jake smiled a gentle smile of satisfaction as he turned off the ignition, and the Jaguar's self-satisfied purring ceased.

Hillary climbed out and glanced around, a wind presaging rain blowing her hair across her face. Some late-flowering Michaelmas daisies and the last of the chrysanthemums and a few straggling dahlias filled the borders in the garden of number eight, where they walked up a gravel-packed path towards the front door. After they had rung the doorbell, it was promptly opened, as if the occupant of the house had been looking out for their arrival.

The woman who looked out at them was perhaps in her late fifties, but obviously knew how to make the best of herself. Her fair hair, which should, if left to nature, have turned to silver by now, was instead a gentle platinum blonde, and had been cut in a gentle swoop to sit just below her ears. Her make-up was light but well applied, and suited her. Wide hazel eyes looked at them warily. She was dressed in well-tailored pale beige slacks that had been teamed with a russet-coloured soft polo-neck jumper that cleverly hid any sagging lines at her neck which might have given away her true age. A simple gold chain hung against the cashmere at her throat.

Her cheekbones were taut, and she had the look of someone who'd recently had her face lifted, and Botox had definitely recently been flirted with.

'Hello. You're the people from the police?' Sylvia Gentley, formerly Grant, asked them, her voice a shade tight and strained. 'A woman rang yesterday and said that you'd be dropping by. This is about my mother, yes?'

'Yes. That would have been my assistant, Wendy Turnbull.' Hillary held out her own ID, and Jake did the same. Briefly, she explained who she was, and what it was they were doing on her doorstep.

Mary Rose nodded, and stood to one side to usher them in, but Hillary wasn't sure just how much of her speech the other woman had taken in. 'So you're taking another look at my mother's death, yes?' she said, as she showed them through a spacious, wooden-floored hall to a living area carpeted in moss green. A cream-coloured leather sofa was flanked by two matching armchairs, nestled around a low wooden coffee table, facing a working fireplace. A fire crackled cheerfully in the hearth, instantly improving chilled spirits.

'Please, sit down,' Mary Rose asked diffidently. 'Would you like some tea or coffee?'

'No, we're fine just now, thank you, Mrs Gentley,' Hillary said. 'I'm sorry if talking about this upsets you. But murder cases are never closed, you know, and periodically we do take another look at them in the hope of finding something new.' She briefly went on to cover her own background and expertise, all the while watching the murder victim's eldest daughter thoughtfully.

She looked ill-at-ease and unhappy, and Hillary thought she knew why. No doubt DI Jarvis hadn't made any secrets of her belief that Mary Rose's son was one of her prime suspects. And having that child now in gaol, whilst trying to live the middle-class respectable dream, was always going to be a difficult one to juggle.

Hillary was not surprised that the husband was nowhere in evidence, although at this time of the day, he'd have been at the office anyway. She had little doubt that the husband would not be hearing about the police visit any time in the near future. She wondered, vaguely, if he even knew that his late mother-in-law had met her end violently. Or that one of his stepchildren currently resided at Her Majesty's pleasure.

'At this point, I really just want to get an overall view of the case,' Hilary began carefully. 'Your mother and father had a happy marriage?' she asked, deciding to slip into it gently.

'Oh yes. They were devoted to each other. Dad thought the sun shone out of Mum's eyes, and Mum.... Well, Mum was always very happy too. Although in a more pragmatic way, you know?'

Hillary cocked her head to one side. 'Your father was the dreamer, and she was the one who kept things together, sort of like that?' she hazarded a guess.

'Yes, exactly. She raised all three of us kids, kept the house spotless, made sure we were fed and clothed and didn't skive off school.' She smiled nervously. 'Whilst Dad worked, tended the garden and the allotment and went fishing. He was the one who always dug up a pine tree from the woods and helped us decorate it at Christmas. If we wanted a treat or something, we'd ask Dad first as Mum was more likely to say that we couldn't afford it. He'd bring home one of the farm sheepdog's puppies for us to play with, although Mum would never let us keep a pet of our own – not to live in the house, like. He'd build us a go-cart out of old crates and bicycle wheels but Mum wouldn't let us play on it until the homework was done. You know what I mean?'

Hillary smiled. 'I do. It sounds like you had an ideal childhood. Did you like living in Caulcott?'

'Oh yes. Well, as a kid, I did,' Mary Rose, after a moment's consideration, qualified her original statement. 'Of course, we never knew any other kind of life except life around the farm. After we all went to school in Bicester, it sort of opened our eyes a bit – you know, to how cut-off and out of the way the village truly was. My other sisters couldn't wait to leave. When you're a teenager, things suddenly change anyway.'

'Did your father ever look at other women?' Hillary asked

delicately, but Mary Rose didn't take offence. Instead she just laughed.

'Dad? Good grief, no.'

'And your mother? It couldn't have been much of a life for her, some people would say. Stuck at home; raising children, doing a series of menial jobs. It wouldn't have been surprising if she'd been tempted by the chance of some excitement or romance.'

Mary Rose shrugged her thin shoulders. 'I suppose not. But you never really think about things like that, do you? Not about your own parents, anyway. And who would they have an affair *with?* Have you seen Caulcott? It's pretty enough, but tiny. And everyone in those days knew everyone else's business. It's not like it is now, with neighbours hardly knowing each other's names. Besides, Mum and Dad were so ... well ... staid. Set in their ways. I'm sure she wouldn't even have thought about cheating on my dad. And just why are you asking this, anyway?' Mary Rose demanded. 'You don't think Mum was killed by some toy-boy she'd taken up with, surely? If you'd known her, you'd realize how ridiculous that is.'

Hillary smiled placatingly and held up a pacifying hand. 'I'm sure you're right: we just have to ask certain things.' She decided to change the subject before Mary Rose could get on her high horse. 'I expect you went over all this at the time, but had you noticed anything different in your mother's behaviour before she died? Had she said anything to you about anybody threatening her, for instance?'

'No. Nothing like that,' Mary Rose spread her hands. Her fingernails, Hillary noticed, had been painted a matching russet colour to match her sweater. 'In fact, Mum was more likely to do any threatening. Not that she was a troublemaker,' she added hastily, 'I just meant that she could stand up for herself. She always did. I remember once, my little sister had some trouble with bullies at school, and Mum marched into the school and read one of the teachers the riot act. We weren't sure whether to be embarrassed or to applaud.'

Hillary smiled. 'She sounds like a woman who knew her own mind.'

'Oh, she did.'

So if she'd found someone breaking into her house, she'd be the kind to rush in and challenge them, rather than play it safe, and run, Hillary mused, which was definitely something to bear in mind.

'I understand your mother blamed the local farmer for your dad's death?' she fished gently.

Mary Rose sighed. 'Yes. Dad should have retired long before he did, of course, but he had that old-fashioned work ethic, you know? If a man wasn't providing food for the family, he wasn't much of a man, that sort of attitude. Even though it was only him and Mum at the end, and they could manage perfectly well on their pensions, he still needed to go out every day and bring home the bacon. Until, one day, he just didn't,' she finished flatly. 'Come home, that is.' She stared for a few moments at her hands, as if surprised by the diamond and gold rings she found on her fingers there.

'You loved your dad,' Hillary said softly. 'His death must have been a big shock.'

'Yes.'

'And for your mum too?'

'Yes.'

'And she blamed Randy Gibson?'

Mary Rose sighed. 'She needed to blame someone, I suppose.'

'You didn't share her anger?'

Mary Rose thought for a moment. 'Dad was a mild-mannered sort of man, you know, easy going? But that didn't mean to say that he didn't know his own mind, and he could be stubborn at times when he wanted to be. Mum had been nagging at him for years to retire properly, but he just didn't want to. And I think, if he'd been given the choice, he'd have preferred to go the way he did, in the saddle so to speak. At least he was out in the fields he loved, in the fresh air. And it was sudden, and over with quickly. It could have been a lot worse, couldn't it? I mean, you hear so many dreadful things, about the way people can die. So....' Mary Rose shrugged helplessly.

Hillary nodded. Now for the tricky bit. 'Your son, Robert, inherited your mother's estate, I understand,' she said, careful to keep her voice utterly neutral.

Mary Rose stiffened visibly. 'Yes, he did. He was the eldest boy, and Mum's favourite. But he didn't kill her. I know that that other one, DI Jarvis, kept on and on at him, but he never went near Caulcott that day, and you can't prove that he did,' she ended mutinously.

Hillary nodded. Obviously there was going to be no leeway here and there was little point, at this juncture, in pushing it. 'All right, Mrs Gentley.' Hillary backed off with a brief smile. 'Is there anything at all that you can think of that could help us? Something that you didn't think of at the time, maybe? I understand that you might not have felt like talking about anything to DI Jarvis, but I can assure you that I don't have any preconceptions about your mother's death. And with the passing of time, sometimes, things can become clearer. Do you have any idea at all, no matter how tenuous or far-fetched you might think it is, about who might have killed your mother, or why?'

Mary Rose sighed heavily. 'No. I wish I did. There was some talk about another woman who went to the same old folks' club as Mum, and some rivalry over a man, but I think that's a bit far-fetched myself.'

'Yes, we know about that,' Hillary said.

Again Mary Rose shrugged helplessly. 'Then I'm sorry. I really can't help you. I wish I could. I hate it, not knowing what happened. Thinking of whoever did it, getting away with it. It makes me really mad sometimes, so mad I want to scream out loud. But I just don't know who on earth would want to kill Mum. She was a lovely soul and, as far as I know, never hurt anybody.'

And, Hillary thought sadly, who could ask for a better epitaph than that?

CHAPTER FOUR

A T A SMALL stand of farmhouses guarded by an ancient if still impressive Douglas fir, Wendy Turnbull turned off a country lane onto what she thought might very well be the site of an old Roman road, and headed towards the farming hamlet community of Caulcott. The smell of a pig farm was the first thing that hit her after she'd pulled over onto a muddy grass verge and climbed from the car, and she wrinkled her nose with a sigh. So much for the glamour of joining the police service, she thought with a brief grin. Cagney and Lacey it definitely wasn't.

Thanks to good old Google, she knew that the hamlet boasted a single pub, The Horse and Groom and one narrow ditch-lined lane. Along the length of this, were assorted farmworkers' cottages and a number of larger homes, which had quickly been snaffled up by the wellheeled who preferred to live the rural idyll – and who probably worked in London or Birmingham, which were both within an easily commutable distance, thanks to the nearby motorway. It made the real estate now spreading out around her very desirable, thank you very much, and completely out of her reach.

Not that she was seriously tempted. The water in the ditch, at this time of year, was high and looked perilously close to flooding, and she was glad that she'd had the foresight to stash her wellies in the boot of the Mini. A cold wind blew across the fields, and the overcast sky made everything look as if she'd somehow stepped into a black-and-white photograph. There was a sense of isolation about the place that made her shiver, and two crows, cawing raucously from a nearby denuded oak tree didn't do much to lighten the atmosphere. Mind you, as a Goth, it certainly had some pluses.

Making sure her camera phone was working properly, she zipped her black puffa-jacket right up to her chin and set off, snap-happily taking photographs as she went.

After about an hour, she'd gone from one end of the village to the other, and had been pleasantly surprised to find that a number of residents had actually been at home. These, perhaps not surprisingly, consisted mostly of the older contingent. A significant number of them had been original witnesses in DI Jarvis's investigation and, what's more, available and indeed eager for interview. Wendy got the impression that the murder of Sylvia Perkins was the one hot and favourite topic of conversation that would still be going strong in twenty years' time. Only one of Sylvia's nearest neighbours, an old woman by the name of Maureen Coles had passed on after having moved into a nearby nursing home.

Once back in the car, Wendy set off back to HQ, pleased to have a suitably impressive list of interview times lined up. Not that such a routine job would impress the boss of course. She wished she'd been given the Mary Rose Perkins' job instead, and wondered just what Sylvia's daughter might have had to say. Probably nothing new, she supposed realistically. But it was better than freezing her backside off in the back of beyond.

Still, she knew that Hillary Greene would play fair, and soon it would be her turn to have a proper bite of the cherry.

As she drove back towards Kidlington, Wendy hummed along softly with the latest pop tune playing on her radio, and with a slight pang, considered the woeful state of her love life. Barbara Lui, the beautiful oriental girl who was currently sharing her tiny flat in the village of Begbroke, was showing all the signs of having a wandering eye. Not hard, when you were a bodacious student like Babs, and had the entire pick of the female student body of Oxford to peruse.

Wendy shrugged off the slight pangs of heartache, and wondered if perhaps two shouldn't play at that game. Perhaps she should find herself a strapping male boyfriend, just to give Babs something to *really* think about. Being bi should have some advantages, after all.

With that sorted out, Wendy turned the volume up, and warbled along with more gusto.

Back at HQ, Superintendent Steven Crayle accepted a cup of coffee from Commander Marcus Donleavy's secretary with a smile of thanks. Once she'd given her boss his own cup and had withdrawn from the room, Marcus came straight to the point.

A tall man, with grey hair, grey eyes, and dressed in his trademark grey suit, Donleavy reminded Steven of a smooth, grey shark. He had the same dead-eye gaze and the same seemingly effortless and elegant hunting technique typical of that species.

'So, you've left Superintendent Sale in the computer room?' he said now.

'Yes, sir.'

'I know it hasn't even been a day yet, but do you have any thoughts about him that I should know about?'

Steven smiled slightly. 'As you say, it's very early days, but our initial impressions of him are favourable.'

Marcus nodded, not needing to be told whom Steven meant by the 'we'.

'Hillary's met him then? She seems happy about it?' he asked curiously. In truth, he'd chosen Sale mostly because he thought he was the best fit with Hillary. As far as Donleavy was concerned, there were any number of superintendents he could have chosen to take over from Steven Crayle, but Hillary Greene was almost irreplaceable. After all, the running of the CRT was mainly an admin job. Hillary was a detective right through to the marrow of her bones. And if there should prove to be any problems, it wouldn't be Hillary Greene who would have to go.

'She seems cautiously optimistic about him, sir,' Steven said a shade coolly. Like most of the rest of HQ, he wasn't entirely sure just how the professional relationship between Donleavy and Hillary actually worked. But everybody seemed to agree that she was in many ways his wing man, and that the two of them could, on occasion, be as thick as thieves. They certainly seemed to share the same ethos about their profession, but the scuttle-butt – maybe somewhat reluctantly – had it that it *was* strictly professional between the two of them.

Hillary herself had always talked about the man with a shade of wary caution teamed with a sort of wry respect that seemed to confirm that the scuttlebutt had it right.

Even so, Steven, no matter how much he told himself that it was ridiculous, couldn't help but feel a little bit jealous when it came to proof of the commander's interest in her, and felt himself tensing up.

'But she might not feel the same way after the two weeks are up and the CRT becomes the new super's sole domain,' he pointed out. 'It's going to take some time for Sale to settle in and begin to do things his way. This is all new to him, after all. They might have teething problems.' He shrugged, a shade helplessly. 'Who can say?'

He still felt a little guilty about accepting the new promotion, as if he was somehow leaving her behind. Of course, it wasn't the case. He didn't doubt that Hillary had meant it when she'd said that she was a hundred per cent behind him. And he was only moving a matter of five miles or so up the road.

Even so.

'Don't worry about that,' Marcus said abruptly, dragging

Steven's mind back from his morose thoughts. 'She'll soon whip him into shape.' He took a sip of his coffee. 'And if he does turn out to be a dud, she'll be perfectly capable of running that department on her own, and working around him.'

'Of that I have no doubt, sir,' Steven said blandly. And couldn't help but wonder. Had she ever thought of doing that when *he'd* been in charge? Then he angrily shook the thought off. No damned way would she have got away with it if she'd tried, and they both knew it.

Commander Marcus Donleavy eyed him briefly for a moment, but then nodded. Although he, like everyone else at the station house, wondered from time to time about the status of their personal relationship, Marcus wasn't about to pry into it. Besides, now that Steven Crayle was leaving the CRT it was hardly any of his concern. Hillary was, strictly speaking, a civilian now, and no longer bound by so many of the rules that governed serving officers.

He had no doubt that she still saw herself in her old role as his go-to DI, and, consequently, both of them behaved in exactly the same way as they'd always done.

'Right. Well, I just wanted to touch base with you about your new position,' Marcus swept on, draining his cup and putting it down on the coaster provided by his secretary. 'As you know, in two weeks' time you'll assume the title and the salary of Acting Chief Superintendent.'

'Thank you, sir,' Steven said crisply, placing his barely touched cup on a similar coaster.

'If all goes well, after a three-month trial period, that promotion will become permanent. And you'll be officially head of the new unit.'

'Yes, sir,' Steven said, hiding a grim smile as he contemplated the unspoken subtext.

So don't screw it up.

'As you know, your main priority will be breaking up the

sex-trafficking gangs, seeking out and prosecuting those who prey on vulnerable young women – and men – and groom them for the sex trade. After that bloody awful show a few years ago,' – he mentioned the name of an operation that had gained countrywide media attention after a gang of predominantly Asian men had been found guilty of sexually exploiting underage girls in council care – 'we're determined that nothing like that will ever happen again.'

'Sir,' Steven agreed, with feeling.

'So, a large part of your job will involve liaising with the Social Services, both Cherwell and Oxford Councils, schools and a number of charity groups set up to help the young and vulnerable. Communication is the name of the game when it comes to prevention. As well as this, you're going to need to recruit more than your fair share of female officers with expertise when it comes to dealing with the young and sexually exploited. With that in mind, I have a list here of officers who've also had special training in the areas of rape and domestic abuse.'

For the next hour or so they went through personnel files and pored over plans on the best way to liaise with the many disparate groups which all had their own agendas and operating procedures.

'And, finally, you'll need some kind of psychologist in place, perhaps civilian – we'll have to see what the budget can manage – to help the victims get through the court process, and at least provide some sort of rudimentary after-care,' Donleavy concluded. 'I've set up meetings and interviews for that as well as with other victim-support charity groups which will have to help you take the strain.'

'Sounds like I'm going to be busy,' Steven said, not unhappily. He was only just beginning to see the size of the task he'd taken on, but he was by no means daunted.

'I know. But if you want the promotion, you have to expect the workload that goes with it,' Marcus pointed out.

'I'm not complaining sir,' Steven said, a shade stiffly.

Marcus smiled. 'I never said you were. We chose you precisely because you're still relatively young and energetic enough for the task, whilst being seasoned and experienced enough at setting up and running your own show. And it's a good thing you're eager, because this is just the start of it. Now, it's time I introduced you to the main targets who will be your primary area of investigation. As you can image, there are no shortages of pimps and traffickers to choose from. You've got the Eastern Europeans to worry about, and that includes the Russians, as well as the domestic species of rat. And speaking of which, the biggest, worst, and most local villain of the lot is this chap.'

Donleavy punched up some data on his laptop and spun it around for Steven to see. 'Do you know him?'

Steven read the profile quickly, one eyebrow rising. 'I've heard of him, naturally. What copper hasn't? I'm not surprised that he's at the top of our hit list. I take it, sir, that this chat amounts to the "little word in my ear" that the brass want him to be our first priority?'

Donleavy nodded, and retrieved his laptop. He stared at the image of the man on the screen with a grim smile of disgust.

'Yes, you can,' he confirmed flatly. 'Dale Medcalfe.' He said the name as if spitting out poison. 'Born and raised in Blackbird Leys, back in the day when it really was the sinkhole of the county. Now aged thirty-four, six foot one, slim build, brown eyes. Never been married,' Donleavy continued, with a twist of his lips, 'which is perhaps not surprising. No woman in her right mind would have him, and anyway, why would you marry at all when you can have the pick of any number of prostitutes who come and go in your stable?'

'He runs actual brothels?' Steven asked.

'Oh yes, several. But that's not really why we want him so badly,' Donleavy said, eyeing the photograph of the man in the middle of his computer screen. With a strong jaw, fine nose, and high cheekbones, framed by almost angelic-like blond hair, it was only a few old acne scars that saved him from being too pretty, and made him, perversely, very attractive to women. Or so Donleavy had been told by any number of women who'd fallen foul of him over the years.

He sighed heavily. 'The brothels are really neither here nor there in the grand scheme of things. In fact, as you know, there's a growing argument for legalising them, like they do in Holland. It keeps the women off the streets, gives them a safe environment to work in, and, if run right, can even offer health initiatives and benefits. Not that our friend Medcalfe cares about any of *that*,' he snorted.

'Most of his girls are junkies, I take it?' Steven said flatly.

'Oh yes,' Donleavy greed grimly. 'If they are clean when they start working for him, they soon find cheap drugs on tap and don't stay clean for long. And if they resist, they're force-fed the stuff. But, as I said, it's not the brothels that will be your main target. Medcalfe's ownership of them would probably be impossible to prove anyway, since he employs teams of accountants and legal types to bind up his assets in so much red tape it's almost impossible for our people to unravel it all. As you know, officially, he earns his filthy lucre from a string of car showrooms. He sells the new Mini, and low-range sports cars for the most part. But that's just a front for all sorts of things: gambling, loan-sharking, extortion.'

'None of which will be in my unit's remit, sir,' Steven felt obliged to point out.

'No. But we know he's grooming underage girls for his stables, and that is. Like those other bastards, he's preying on young girls in care, girls from broken homes and families, those already at a disadvantage and desperate for love and attention. Girls and boys with no family or support system in place to look out for them. We've had any number of reports that he's selling girls as young as ten to paedophile rings, setting them up in a series of houses that he rents. We want the bastard stopped, and that's going to be the new unit's first and primary objective.'

Steven took a long, slow breath. 'It'll be our pleasure, sir,' he said. 'But I'm presuming it won't be easy. I take it we're not the first ones to take him on?'

'Hell no,' Donleavy confirmed grimly. 'Many have tried since Medcalfe first came on our radar ten years ago. But nothing sticks to the son of a bitch. He's careful and wily. He surrounds himself with a string of trusted lieutenants who take the fall for him, as and when needed. Some are family, and the others, if not related by blood, grew up with him in the Leys and are almost invariably loyal to him. Needless to say, they're well paid, and do their time without a murmur. Knowing they'll get kneecapped, or worse, if they don't, probably helps assure their co-operation. There are any number of brutal beatings that lead back to Medcalfe, not to mention one or two disappearances.'

Steven Crayle's eyes narrowed. 'How many do we suspect he's had killed?' he asked quietly.

Donleavy's grey eyes regarded the man opposite him steadily. 'You'll be getting the full dossier soon. Study it closely. You're going to have to be careful, Steven. This man is dangerous.'

Steven Crayle felt a small cold shiver snake up his back. 'Understood, sir,' he said quietly.

Hillary Greene, blissfully unaware of the nature of the conversation her lover was having with their commander, returned to HQ around lunchtime, and took her two young recruits up to the canteen, figuring that they might as well make use of it whilst they still had it. Once the latest round of budget cuts swept through the place, the canteen would probably be a thing of the past and they'd all have to make do with dry, supermarket sarnies and packets of crisps.

As they waited in the queue, Wendy eyed the vegetarian option with a forlorn look, whilst Jake Barnes was secretly amazed that anyone ate this kind of stuff anymore. Hadn't they ever heard about the new wave of British cuisine? He selected for himself the least of the evils on offer – a sort of ploughman's lunch option with a choice of fruit (he chose a rather wrinkled apple and a brown-spotted banana as the best of the bunch) and found an empty table at the back. As he poured out his glass of mineral water, Wendy sat opposite him with her plate of lacklustre salad. Hillary was the last to arrive, with a plate of some sort of white fish, swimming in what was alleged to be parsley sauce, with new potatoes and peas.

'Right, Jake, fill in Wendy on what we learned this morning. Then you can start the murder book.'

The murder book was the file that Hillary always opened at the beginning of any new case. It was everyone's job to keep it updated with everything they discussed; that way every member of the team could consult it whenever they needed to, and no clues, leads, or information was in danger of being lost or overlooked, because of a failure to communicate.

'Guv,' Jake said, and began to tell Wendy about Mary Rose Gentley. Hillary listened with half an ear as she ate her warm, tasteless fish, and wondered what Superintendent Sale was making of his new domain. No doubt the computer lads had him tied up in knots by now.

'So how was Caulcott?' she heard Jake ask, and listened distractedly as Wendy told them what she'd found out. When she had finished, the Goth handed Hillary her phone and she dutifully ran through the mass of photographs that had been taken.

In the grey November gloom, the small farming hamlet looked isolated, bleak and largely unlovely, but then, Hillary supposed fairly, nowhere looked its best in winter. Come spring, she could well imagine the little lane of cottages overlooking the fields would be a pretty enough place. Certainly their murder victim must have been happy enough living there, since she'd shown no inclination to leave after becoming a widow.

But as a place to commit murder, and not been seen whilst doing it, it did, she supposed grimly, have a lot to recommend it.

'I'd go barmy within a fortnight if I had to live there,' Wendy was saying. 'I know Begbroke isn't exactly city living, but at least being on a dual carriageway and only a few miles from Oxford, I don't feel as if I'm living on the edge of nowhere.'

'Some people must like it,' Jake Barnes pointed out.

'Must be mad,' Wendy said dismissively, and speared a pieced of wilted lettuce. 'Mind you, it *is* just the sort of place where you could get yourself murdered, and nobody *would* notice,' she said, somewhat eerily echoing Hillary's own thoughts.

'Well, let's hope that somebody, somewhere, noticed something that DI Jarvis overlooked, otherwise this is going to be a very short case,' Hillary said drily. 'Right, eat up. Next, we're going to see what Sylvia's middle daughter has to tell us. Wendy, you can drive. You have her address, right?'

'Yes, guv,' Wendy said eagerly. 'I think she lives in Milton Keynes.'

Hillary sighed. 'She would,' she said laconically.

'Somebody has to, guv,' Jake Barnes said with a cheerful smile, his grey-green eyes crinkling attractively at the corners.

Wendy grinned back at him. 'Got to be better than living on the edge of nowhere,' she shot back.

'You can keep your new towns,' Jake said.

'Not all of us can afford to live in swanky mansions in north Oxford,' Wendy pointed out sweetly.

Hillary shook her head. 'Play nice, you two. Anyone want dessert?'

With mutual shudders, Jake and Wendy declined. Hillary shook her head at them sorrowfully and went up to the counter to quickly select a jam sponge pudding swimming in a pool of glutinous custard.

That was the trouble with the younger generation. They had no stamina.

*

Lily Jane Barnard, nee Perkins, lived in a large estate of skinny, pale, stone-clad houses with eye-catching terracotta-coloured slate roofs that somehow failed to look even remotely cheerful, let alone Mediterranean. Each had a pocket-handkerchief-sized lawn, with a small shrub planted neatly in the middle. Lily's was a dwarf flowering cherry tree, Hillary noticed absently, as they walked up the paving-slab path to a front door that was painted a deep shade of blue.

'She has just the one child, Milly. Mrs Barnard was recently divorced, guv,' Wendy informed her helpfully as Hillary pressed the doorbell. 'She, Mrs Barnard that is, not her daughter, works at the local Sainsbury's as some kind of manager. The daughter's currently at uni in Birmingham.'

'Right, thanks,' Hillary said, and meant it. She'd spent the time on the drive though Buckinghamshire reading up on the forensic evidence again, such as it was, and going through the post-mortem results, and now found, to her annoyance that translating all that legalese and medical jargon had left her with a slightly fuzzy headache.

She shook the inconvenience of it away as the door opened, revealing an obese woman with a pretty face, dressed in jeans and a long, cream-coloured pullover.

'Hello, you're the police? I've just been speaking to Mary Rose, she said you'd just been over to her place. Come on in, I'll put the kettle on.'

Lily Barnard had a mass of dark curling hair that fell to her shoulders, and her face was free of make-up. In her mid-forties at least, Hillary gauged, she had the look of a younger woman, probably due to the fact that her chipmunk-like cheeks were too well padded to allow for any wrinkles.

She showed them straight through to a small but cheerful kitchen, done out in daffodil yellow and white and pointed them to a Formica table, surrounded by three ladder-back chairs. 'Please have a seat. Coffee OK?'

'Thank you,' Hillary said. She watched as the other woman set about making three mugs of instant, whilst Wendy sat down and got out her notebook, resting it unobtrusively on her knee, and out of sight under the table. Hillary had long since taught her that witnesses, when confronted with someone portentously taking down their every word, often struggled to talk freely or feel at ease.

Hillary smiled a thank you as Lily reached down for a cake tin, and produced what was obviously a home-made Victoria sponge. She got out plates and a knife and looked at them with an eyebrow raised in question. Hillary declined, but she gave the nod to Wendy to accept a slice, knowing that it would make the other woman feel better.

No doubt her parents had ingrained in her at an early age the importance of offering hospitality. And, unlike her sister, Lily had no reason to see the police as her adversaries. She knew from reading DI Jarvis's notes that all three of Sylvia's children had airtight alibis, and Lily, at least, had no son in the frame for her mother's murder.

'So, then, what can I tell you about Mum? Or that awful day?' Lily asked, taking the third chair and making it squeak slightly as she lowered her considerable bulk onto it. 'I'm sure I told the police all that I could right after it happened.'

'Just routine, really, Mrs Barnard,' Hillary said with a gentle smile. 'We're trying to build up a picture of how it must have been for your mum, and her way of life. My colleague here went to Caulcott this morning, and she tells me that it feels very isolated. Did your mother ever worry about living alone?'

Lily rolled her eyes and smiled. 'Tell me about it. I was glad to leave, I can tell you. But it suited Mum and Dad. And no, she never worried about that sort of thing at all. She always said that it was cities and towns that were dangerous, because that's where the people were, but that there was nothing out in the countryside to hurt you. She said she had nothing to fear from foxes and the dark. Just goes to show how wrong you can be, doesn't it?' Lily said grimly. 'But you can't really blame the village, can you? Bad things can happen anywhere, I suppose. And Dad was born there, you see, and Mum had always lived in a village as well, although not one as small as that. But they were both country-mice, no two ways about it. Mum never even liked it much going into Oxford.'

'She never felt lonely?' Hillary asked.

'She never mentioned it, no. But then, she had neighbours on either side of her who were always popping in, so I don't suppose she did feel lonely.'

'Oh? Which neighbours were these?' Hillary asked curiously.

'Oh, Freddie and Maureen mostly. Although I think Maureen, towards the end was going a bit....' Lily tapped her temple significantly. 'You know ... just a touch senile, like. Sad, but there it is. But Mum and Freddie looked after her, made sure she ate, did her shopping, helped her out with her housework and generally humoured her whenever she kept maundering on about the war, that sort of thing.'

'Freddie?' Hillary said, her radar picking up. She'd heard about the Forget-me-not Club Lothario, but this was the first time she'd heard about a second man in the case. 'He was your mother's boyfriend? Or this Maureen's, perhaps?'

'What?' Lily blinked and looked at Hillary as if she'd just grown another head, and then suddenly burst out laughing. 'Oh, sorry, no. Not that kind of a Freddie. Sorry, I meant Mrs de la Mare – Freda. She was the neighbour one door down from Mum on the right hand side.'

'Oh, I see,' Hillary smiled.

'I've got her down on my list of interviewees, guv,' Wendy murmured helpfully. 'Unfortunately, Maureen Coles has since passed on.'

'Oh no! Did she?' Lily Barnard said, sounding genuinely sad.

'She was a lovely old lady, I remember she used to make proper toffee apples. When we were kids, we used to bring her apples, and she'd make them for us. She was always dotty about her cat, I seem to remember. She never married – well, she was one of those maiden old ladies who you just could never imagine married, you know what I mean? But she always kept a cat – a big ginger tom, never any other sort – and doted on them like they were her children. I used to think it was the same cat until I realized that it would have to be about forty years old! Oh, I'm sorry to hear she's gone too.'

'Did your mother ever mention having any trouble with her neighbours?' Hillary asked.

'Oh no. They all looked out for one another, like I said. The only one in the village she had no time for was Randy Gibson, the farmer. And, by extension, his wife I suppose. You know how she felt about him, right?'

'Yes, your sister said. She didn't call you in the days before she died? She never mentioned anything that struck you as odd or funny?' she pressed on hopefully. 'Now that you've had so much more time to think, was there anything at all that she said that you didn't mention to DI Jarvis because it didn't seem relevant, but now strikes you in any way as being out of the ordinary for her?'

Lily frowned in concentration, then sighed. 'No. I wish there were. Believe me, I want to do anything I can to help. But the last time I spoke to her she was all excited about some up-coming trip or other with her old-folks' club. It was to see some sort of show. I can't remember what it was now – something to do with old-style music halls or something. Anyway, she seemed happy and cheerful, the way she always did. Oh, except that she did say something about Maureen's cat dying, and how she was taking on about it.'

Lily took a sip of coffee, then nodded. 'Oh yes. And that she was going to have to start thinking about buying a new car, because the old one was getting past it, and she wasn't looking forward to going through all the hassle and expense of finding and buying a new one. I told her that Dave – he was my husband at the time – would help her out if she wanted a man to go with her. You know, some garages see an old woman coming and think they can sell them any old rubbish, but they won't try that on with a man, will they?'

'No, not usually,' Hillary agreed drily. 'So you can't think of anyone with a reason to kill your mother?'

'No,' Lily said grimly. 'I still can't really believe it ever happened.' She twisted her mug of coffee restlessly about in circles on the table. 'Do you think you'll be able to find out this time around who did it?' she asked quietly.

'We'll certainly do our best,' Hillary Green promised gently.

Lily nodded, swallowed hard, and took a tiny sip from her coffee mug. Her lower lip was wobbling precariously. 'Good,' she said simply.

Once outside, Wendy shivered a little inside her puffa-jacket and rammed her hands morosely into her pockets. 'It never goes away, does it?' she said, walking slowly beside her boss back to the car.

'No, it doesn't,' Hillary said quietly.

CHAPTER FIVE

WHEN JAKE BARNES negotiated the Banbury Road round-about that evening, thankfully going against the rush-hour traffic queuing up to try and get out of the city of Oxford, he was feeling pleasantly tired. In spite of expectations, he was actually enjoying working for the CRT.

He drove a few hundred yards down the busy road, then indicated to turn into one of the many impressive big houses that lined this prestigious northern part of the city, his E-type Jaguar attracting the usual smiles or envious scowls from his fellow motorists.

Far from feeling particularly smug, Jake appreciated both the envy of his car and the desirable piece of real estate where he lived. Unlike others who'd been born with the proverbial silver spoon in their mouth, Jake had earned his own way in the world, and consequently actually enjoyed – and noticed – the good life he was living. After having grown up on a large estate in the poorer end of the nearby market town of Banbury, he was by no means blasé about what it now meant to live in a six-bedroom, white-painted, detached villa in one of the swankiest parts of Oxford.

As he parked and swung his lean, six-foot frame with ease from the low-slung car, he couldn't help but smile at the thought of how the little kid that he had once been would have been impressed with the iconic Jag. Ever since he'd seen the film, *The Italian Job* as a seven-year-old, it had been his dream to own one, and the car had been the first thing he'd bought with his new-found wealth.

Jake knew that he'd been lucky enough to be blessed with more than his fair share of brains, and although the comprehensive schooling he'd received had been no more than just about adequate, computers had come along at just the right time. Because he also had the kind of brain that had adapted well to the IT boom, and had the good luck to meet the right set of people, at the right time, they'd formed their own dot.com business on a shoestring budget.

Nevertheless, the company had managed to produce a few good best-selling products, including several popular apps for a mobile phone company, as well as that essential all-important one that had taken off and made them all multi-millionaires.

Unlike his fellow directors, however, he'd sold out his share just before the dot.com bubble well and truly burst and, consequently, had been the only one to come out of it ahead. Although he told everyone who asked that he'd seen the writing on the wall, and hadn't allowed himself to be blinded by greed, in reality, he'd simply never really believed his good luck could possibly last. Instead, he'd been beset by the typical, working-class boy's longing for financial security that only actual money in a real bank account could provide. Being a multi-millionaire in cyber-space or in a virtual reality had never been enough to satisfy him.

Since then, he'd invested that money very wisely, largely in buying up property like there was no tomorrow when the banks broke the economy and the housing market bottomed. So, now, he not only had a mass of long-term, safe-bet stocks to make the Chancellor of the Exchequer very happy, he also had a large letting business that others ran for him, and the revenue from which alone would see him through to his old age, even if he never touched his capital, or made another investment in his life.

He wished, sometimes, that his father had lived to see his only son succeed so well, but he'd died when Jake was just five and, in truth, Jake could now barely remember him. He only had old photographs to remind him of what he'd looked like. His mother, who now lived in a very nice part of Banbury, thanks to her son, had remarried a man named Curtis Paviour, a year almost to the day after becoming a widow.

Curtis had moved into their council house with them. He shared custody of his only child, Jasmine, with his former partner, Judy. They had broken because of Judy's drink problem, which in turn led on to a drug problem. So, by the time Jake was ten, the seven-year-old Jasmine had moved into their already cramped council house on a permanent basis.

But instead of feeling jealous or resentful, Jake had been won over by her – largely, it had to be said, because the little girl clearly worshipped him: vanity had always been his biggest weakness.

As Jake let himself into the pleasant hallway of his home, he noted absently that the original William Morris tiles on the floor had been buffed to a nice shine by his regular cleaning lady. Not that he'd ever have known what they were if it hadn't been for ex-wife, Tash, who'd been into design, and had taken it on herself to educate him in such matters, before leaving him for a personal fitness trainer.

The wooden panelling that lined the staircase smelled pleasantly of lavender furniture polish. He slung his briefcase somewhat carelessly down, and from the top of a reproduction Sheraton hall table, collected his mail where his daily had left it.

His heart picked up a beat as he recognized the logo on a large, padded, A-4 brown envelope, but he resisted the urge to rip it open there and then. Instead, he carried it through to the kitchen, and put on the coffee percolator for a much-needed brew. Like his boss, Hillary Greene, he was slightly addicted to good, well-made coffee.

He opened the fridge and surveyed the contents thoughtfully, selecting a cold chicken breast and making a Caesar salad with it, before sitting down on a stool at the marble-topped breakfast bar. He ate quickly however, all the time with one eye on the envelope. He finished his meal with a piece of brie, a slightly over-ripe pear and a handful of walnuts, and then took the envelope, along with a second mug of coffee, into his study. This room faced the back garden. In summer, the grounds outside became a lovely sun-trap, filled with flowering shrubs, and garden birds flocked to the feeders he'd put up whatever the weather.

He now pulled the curtains against the dark, dank November night and sank down in a buttoned-leather armchair. Finally he opened the envelope, taking out the latest, neatly typed report from Crimmins & Lloyd, the private investigators he'd hired to dig up all they could on Dale Medcalfe.

And tonight, in particular, on one of his employees named Darren Chivnor.

Jake read the report quickly but avidly, then went back to the beginning, taking it more slowly now, and making handwritten notes as he went. Normally, he'd use a computer, but he thought it wise, given that computers could be hacked, to do it the old-fashioned way just this once – even though a keyboard felt far more familiar to him than a pen.

As he worked, he glanced up at a framed photograph on his desk. In it, his 15-year-old self gazed back, his mother on one side, his stepfather on the other, and in front, her head tucked under his chin, a young Jasmine, at twelve, just blossoming from childhood to teenager.

When he'd left to do an IT course at a minor university near Birmingham, Jasmine had been a typical, gawky, 14-year-old adolescent, mad about some boyband or other, and typically rebellious. She'd just had a tattoo of a ladybird done on her shoulder, against the expresses wishes of both her father and stepmother, and was in the dog house, and vowing to have an eyebrow stud if they didn't get off her back.

Jake had, as usual, found himself the recipient of all her secrets and woes. She'd moaned about how unfair life was, and how nobody understood her, and how it was all right for him, he was escaping to Birmingham, which, whilst not London, had to be a vast improvement on where they were.

Jake, who secretly agreed with her, could only commiserate, and advise her to be patient. Soon she'd be sixteen, and could start doing the hairdressing and beautician course that she'd been raving about ever since he'd bought her her first Barbie.

And then he'd gone off blithely to uni with barely another thought about it. Or her. It wasn't until later, much later in fact, when he'd come home in his second year for the Easter vacation, that he'd realized just how off the rails things had become back on the home front.

He'd been aware, vaguely, for some time that whenever he'd asked after Jas, his mother had tended to become evasive, but it wasn't until he was actually back in the family home that he understood why.

The nearly 16-year-old Jasmine was totally out of control. He could still remember the moment when he'd realized, with a jolt of shock, that his baby sister was drunk.

It was the very day he'd come home, when he'd volunteered to make his world-famous macaroni cheese for dinner. He'd been in the kitchen boiling the pasta when his sister had grabbed him around the waist and welcomed him home with a smacking kiss on the back of his neck, and he'd smelt the waft of alcohol on her breath. Her words of greeting were slurred, and her giggles had far more to do with inebriation than the girlish good spirits he'd always associated with her.

Perhaps because of her mother's troubles, she'd always been a needy kid who craved love and attention, and Jake had never resented giving her both.

Later that night, when he'd angrily and self-righteously con-fronted Curtis and his mother about it, they'd confessed that Jas had been in trouble with her school for some time, both for being disruptive in class and for playing truant on far too regular a basis. The boozing was relatively new, however. They'd tried to keep her in at night, and monitor her friends and where she went, but she was growing to increasingly resent the curbs on her freedom and was threatening to run away if they didn't pack it in.

Appalled, Jake had demanded that they make her see a coun-sellor, and had been roundly told that that was already in hand. They'd also made sure that she was seeing a school guidance worker, and monitored her internet use and mobile phone time.

Their hurt anger had been enough to make him felt slightly ashamed of himself for trying to tell either of them how to be good parents, especially since he'd always known that his mother had done a fabulous job, under the circumstances, in raising him, and he never doubted that Curtis too, cared deeply for his daughter.

So he'd gone back to uni to finish his degree with a certain amount of optimism.

Optimism, it soon became clear, that was sadly misplaced.

The first hint that things were going from bad to worse was when his mother told him that Jas had left school without doing any exams or even applying for a place on the beauti-cian's course. Worse was to come when, at seventeen, Jas moved into a squat with several of her so-called 'friends' who were the despair of Curtis and his mother.

By the time Jake had got his degree and had set up the company and was beginning to make serious money, Jas had developed a drug habit.

Curtis, perhaps not able to cope with the guilt, furiously blamed Jas's problems on her mother, Judy. Growing up with an alcoholic junkie as a mother was bound to screw up a kid, he'd argued. And no matter how much they'd put their foot down, once they had legally lost control over her, their efforts to help her became all but impossible.

Just before her nineteenth birthday, she had defiantly told them that she was off, and had simply vanished.

Jake had finally tracked her down to a squalid bed-sit in Luton when she was twenty-one, and had paid for her to go into rehab, but it hadn't taken.

She became pregnant shortly after that, and perhaps that experience frightened her into sobriety for a while, because the doctors found several serious defects with the foetus during a scan, and had told her she'd probably miscarry, which she subsequently did.

This time, the second round of rehab worked. For a while.

By the time she was twenty-three, however, Jasmine was gone again, and this time Jake was unable to find her. Not that he'd ever stopped looking, since Curtis and his mother were both desperate for news of her. So he'd paid a number of PI firms to try and track her and, finally, a year ago, the last one had got lucky.

One of the PI's on her case had seen a photograph of her, taken with a group of working girls who specialized in S&M. The PI had then traced the girls to a stable belonging to Dale Medcalfe, whereupon the company had promptly thanked Jake for his custom, and told him that they would no longer be able to help him.

Which told Jake all he needed to know about Medcalfe and his reputation.

It had taken Jake a long time to find another company willing to take on his case, and even Crimmins & Lloyd, who had a reputation for being tough and well connected, were only willing to do the most careful and peripheral of investigative work for him. But it had been enough for them to find out that, though she had once been part of that circuit, and had indeed been one of Dale's girls, she hadn't been seen around for some time. Ten months at least, and nobody had any idea where she might have gone. Since girls weren't normally allowed to just walk away from Medcalfe to start out on their own, or go to a new pimp, it didn't bode well.

Now Jake tossed aside the report he was reading and tiredly rubbed his eyes.

He hadn't wanted to, but he'd told his mother and Curtis what he'd found out. And although they'd never spoken it out loud, he knew that they had the same grim, dark thoughts that plagued him.

Jake had promised them that he wouldn't let it rest, and nor had he. But the more he learned about Dale Medcalfe, the more he realized just how dangerous the man was, and just what he was up against. For a while, the sheer size of the task he'd set himself, paralysed him. He knew so little about that world, or how to begin to deal with it.

Clearly, a frontal approach was impossible. He could hardly march into one of the bastard's car showrooms and demand to know what had happened to his little sister. He'd either end up floating face down in the Oxford canal, or one of Dale's solicitors would sue him for defamation – depending on his mood.

And it was then that Jake had put his brains to good use, and had started to think laterally. If he couldn't take on Medcalfe, he had to find someone or some*thing* that could. So, after thinking about it, doing his research, and sweating not a little blood over it, he had told his mother to report Jasmine as a missing person officially, and had then answered the recruitment call to join, as a civilian consultant, the Thames Valley Police's CRT.

The timing had seemed almost miraculous. That the police service should be advertising for good-quality candidates for civilian work, just when Jake was looking for some sort of an 'in' into that world, had been like providence giving him not so much a sly nudge in the ribs, as a giant whack across the back of his head with a two-by-four. So he'd put himself forward, and quickly found himself just where he wanted, and needed, to be.

It was all taking time of course, but Jake was satisfied that things were coming together at last, and, as an added bonus, he found that he actually liked working for the police. Hillary Greene was not only a thoroughly competent investigator, with a history of bravery, she was a fascinating boss to have, and he was confident that he could win her around to his cause, given time. Until then, he was perfectly placed to take advantage of anything that might help him find Jas. He had already gained access to Hillary's computer, but it remained to be seen whether he could somehow wangle it so that Jasmine became a CRT priority. It might be that her case wasn't yet cold enough. A mere missing person might be too small-fry to attract Hillary's attention. But he wasn't deterred. If he could find other, older missing case profiles that were similar to Jas's he might be able to swing it, or, if he could make himself indispensable, he might simply ask her to do it as a favour.

He was sure, once she got Medcalfe in her sights, that she wouldn't rest until she'd taken him down. He knew her well enough by now to know that she wouldn't back down from a challenge. Or maybe, with Superintendent Crayle now off to work vice in some newly formed unit, *he* might be able to get Jas's case given a higher priority.

He just knew that, whatever it was that he had to do to find out what had happened to Jas, he would do it, and with Hillary Greene on board, his chances were so much better. She was as tenacious as a terrier with a rat once she'd been given a case, as he'd seen on their previous investigation. But if he had to work around her, he would do that too. So far he hadn't had to use her computer again, but when the time came, he would.

Right now, though, he had another lead to follow. He never did like to have all his eggs in one basket, and it hadn't taken him long to realize that, if he was to take on Medcalfe, somehow he had to find a way into the man's inner circle. And Jake, more than most, knew that money was the best way in that there was.

He had asked Crimmins & Lloyd to find out all that they could about those closest to Medcalfe. Slowly, and very carefully, they had, and for the past few months had been feeding him reports detailing particulars from the lowliest of pimps to his chief lieutenants. He studied these reports in minute detail, looking out for the weak link, for the slightest chink in the armour that would give him some kind of a starting point.

Now, with this latest report, he thought he might just have found it at last.

Medcalfe was protected by a brutal gang of men who were either related to him, or had grown up as his neighbours, and were, in some cases, even more fanatically loyal than his own blood. He rewarded them well, naturally, so now, instead of a life of unemployment and grinding poverty in the Leys, they found themselves driving souped up cars, living in nice houses in nice places, and pulling attractive women. There was always cash for booze or drugs, or the latest cinema-sized telly, and if they occasionally had to do time, they did it with a shrug and a swagger.

Then, Crimmins and Lloyd found one of his lieutenants who seemed to be just a little different from the rest.

He'd first come to their attention when they realized that, instead of spending his money on the usual bling and booze, he'd invested it. This led them to dig deeper. He had no police record – not even for juvenile offences like joyriding, shoplifting, and drunk and disorderly. This did not, however, preclude him from having a reputation as a skilled knife man, and he had inevitably come to police attention several times in cases where Medcalfe's rivals had been found slashed and bleeding. He'd never been caught, though, and nobody had ever testified against him.

He was also the youngest of Medcalfe's lieutenants, and trusted with both the near-legitimate financial aspects of the villain's empire, as well as the dirty end of it. So he was, to a certain extent, a cut above the rest of Medcalfe's usual gang.

Jake fervently hoped this meant that he might turn out to be just what he'd been looking for. He might be smart enough to want a way out, and greedy enough to take a risk if the price was right.

First of all, Jake had to figure out the best way to approach him – ideally managing it without ending up with a knife wound for his trouble.

Thanks to Crimmins & Lloyd's report he now knew where he liked to hang out, his family background and his financial dealings. The fact that he was accruing money in a secret bank account that his boss didn't know about, boded very well indeed. It smacked of a man making plans for his future; and a man like that was surely open to an offer.

But that didn't tell Jake nearly enough: he needed to know what made him tick, just what his dreams and aspirations were, and how far he'd be willing to go in order to achieve them. But in order to try and get some kind of psychological insight into the man, he had to get to know him.

Jake Barnes was no fool. He knew just what a dangerous game he was playing. Pulling a fast one on the police was nerve-racking enough, but this was in a whole different league. If Hillary Greene or Superintendent Crayle ever found out what he was doing, he might get his wrist slapped – maybe even be prosecuted and, worse-case scenario, end up doing some prison time.

However, if Dale Medcalfe ever found out what he was doing, he could end up dead.

He would have to be careful, very careful.

He picked up the report and studied the photographs which had been taken with a telephoto lens of Darren Chivnor. He knew from what he'd read that Chivnor was twenty-eight, five feet eight inches tall, a skinhead, the darkness of his scalp revealing that he would have had dark hair, had he allowed it to grow. He had dark, near-black eyes, and visible tattoos on his neck and forearms. He was skinny, but fit-looking, and reminded Jake of nothing so much as a vicious weasel.

All in all, not a character you'd like to meet in a dark alley late at night.

Nevertheless, he might just hold the key to what Jake needed. Now all he had to do was find a way to get him to hand it over.

If Jake Barnes had spent most of the night restlessly tossing and turning and thinking of ways to become best buddies with a knife-wielding thug, Hillary Greene spent most of *her* night wondering how long Steven would be willing to wait for an answer to his proposal of marriage.

Her own sense of fairness told her that she couldn't keep him waiting for much longer, but she found herself, unusually, dithering, incapable of coming to a decision.

Consequently both of them looked heavy-eyed and a shade pale the next morning. Jimmy gave her a quick report on his progress so far, tracking down his mugging and home-invasion cases. She agreed that a few of them warranted closer attention, but neither of them was particularly confident that they'd pan out or lead to anything.

She told him to take Wendy with him to interview the victims, since it would be good practice for her, whilst she and Jake went to the market town of Bicester where Sylvia's youngest, Marigold, lived with her husband. Their three kids, Rupert, Jeremy and Oliver, for some reason, had all chosen to emigrate, and now lived as far afield as Australia, Canada, and South Africa. It made her wonder what it said about their upbringing. If anything.

'Our murder victim must have had a fondness for flowers,

guv,' Jake said, as he pulled up outside a small semi-detached house in the Glory Farm area of the town. 'Mary Rose, Lily and Marigold, all the girls named after flowers.'

Hillary nodded. It might, of course, have been Sylvia's husband who thought of his girls that way, she mused, but didn't say it out loud. Instead, she contented herself with, 'Well, let's see what the youngest flower has to say about it all.'

Marigold Fletcher turned out to be a thin woman, with hair flamboyantly dyed the colour of her name. Wearing jeans and a multi-coloured knitted kaftan, she had applied her make-up with a liberal hand. She greeted them without surprise, indicating to Hillary that her sisters had pre-warned her about being interviewed. She immediately showed them into a not-too-clean kitchen, where she was, for some reason, boiling an enormous pot of pasta. Perhaps she was the kind of woman who liked to cook in marathon sessions and freeze it for quick, future use.

In between stirring the pot, she made them tea (bags) and provided biscuits (out of a packet) and lit up a cigarette, which she was careful, Hillary noticed thankfully, to keep well away from the pasta pot.

'I'm glad you're looking at Mum's case again,' Marigold said, blowing smoke industriously. 'I never thought it was right that someone wasn't had up for it.'

'Did you have any idea who that should have been?' Hillary asked promptly.

'Nah. Well, not unless it was that farmer, or more likely that wife of his. Mum never did like old man Gibson, and she was a good judge of character, was Mum.'

Hillary nodded. She saw Jake write something down, and, reading upside down, was pleased to note he'd written, *'Farmer's wife??? That's new.'*

It was exactly what she'd been thinking, and she was straight onto it. 'Mrs Gibson? I understand that your mother blamed *him* for your father's death, and that she'd gone out of her way a number of times to make life difficult for him, but what did she have against his wife, exactly?'

Marigold flushed a shade, and looked distinctly shifty. 'Well, nothing really. That is, *Mum* had nothing against her, as far as I know. But I saw her, Mrs Gibson that is, flirting with my dad once. Oh, it was yonks ago,' she laughed, a shade unconvincingly around her cigarette. 'And I was only a kid. I mean, I dunno, ten or eleven, maybe, and you don't always know what's what at that age, do you, so I might have got my wires crossed or something.' She thought about it for a moment, but evidently didn't give much credence to her own words, because she shrugged unconvincingly. 'Anyway, I went into the kitchen – this was up at the farmhouse, yeah, looking for Dad, one summer. I wanted money for the ice cream van I think, and I heard them laughing. When I looked in, she was sat on the kitchen table swinging her legs, and showing plenty of them and all, and Dad was in a chair with a mug of tea. The farm workers often popped in there for drinks, like, in the summer. Got to keep drinking plenty and all that, farming's a hard, physical job.'

She frowned, and prodded the pasta with a wooden spoon. 'There was just something about the way she was gawping at him. It made me mad, that's all.'

'You believe they actually had an affair?' Hillary pressed. 'Or did you get the idea it was just harmless flirting?' She was not convinced that it was relevant, but any new information was like gold in a cold case.

'Oh I dunno about that.' Marigold backed off quickly. 'I mean, I never saw them actually kissing or anything. And, like I said, I was a kid at the time, so who can say? I might have been overreacting. I know Mary Rose and Lily thought that Dad never looked at anyone else. And I don't think he did, not really. Mum certainly never did. That is, she never accused him of it, or anything like that. I mean, we'd have known if there had been any major rows going on in the house, wouldn't we? Kids have a way of knowing. It's just that....' Marigold sighed. 'I just never liked her after that – Mrs Gibson, I mean. And I still reckon she'd have been up for it, if he'd given her the nod, like. But then....' she shrugged. 'Perhaps it was just me after all. I was always Daddy's favourite, being the youngest.' She laughed at herself, and shook her head, scattering ash on the kitchen floor. Absently, she ground it into the lino with a trainer-clad toe.

Hillary decided to let the matter lie there for the moment. Two of the daughters thought their dad was the faithful type and one had grave doubts, but that was often the way of it: conflicting testimony was a way of life in her job.

If Marigold was right, it might just be relevant. Sylvia's murder could be linked to her long-dead husband having had a fling with the farmer's wife. What if she'd somehow only just found out about it, and confronted the 'other woman' with the knowledge? Suppose Sylvia had threatened to use it as yet another weapon in her on-going vendetta against Randy Gibson? It was just possible that Mrs Farmer Gibson might get it into her head to whack her old love-rival over the head with a poker to prevent her husband from finding out that she'd been unfaithful. But all these years later, would it really be so murderously bad? With Joe Perkins dead and gone, could Randy Gibson really be so jealous that his wife was that afraid of how he'd react? It was impossible to tell without gauging the man's character for herself, which had to be a matter of priority now.

As far-fetched as it might sound, it was certainly going to be interesting to find out what the lady in question had to say about it all.

'OK. When was the last time you spoke to your mother before she died?' Hillary asked, patiently going through the routine list of questions, taking the youngest daughter over the same ground as that of her sisters for the next half an hour.

Unfortunately, there were no more revelations, and when Hillary and Jake left, Marigold was on her fifth cigarette and was cooking a vast vat of tomato sauce to go with pasta.

'Next stop the farmer's wife, guv?' Jake asked with a grin, and Hillary smiled over at him wryly.

'Getting to know my methods well, aren't you, Jake?' Hillary mused mildly.

Jake smiled modestly. 'Doing my best, guv,' he said.

'Yes,' Hillary murmured. 'I noticed.'

Jake shot her a quick, questioning look, but she was looking blandly out of the passenger window. And with a mental warning not to read too much into it, Jake pulled away from the kerb.

Hillary Greene's lips curved into an enigmatic smile.

CHAPTER SIX

D S STEVEN CRAYLE had the usual difficulty in finding a parking space in Oxford, but since he'd factored it in, he wasn't late for his visit to the police station at St Aldates. Situated almost in the shadow of the famous college of Christ Church, it was an old building, but large and spacious, and the powers that be had decided that they wanted the new unit to based there, rather than at HQ in Kidlington, partly, he supposed, because the citizens of the world-renowned university city were still reeling about the revelations concerning the moral welfare of their young people, and the top brass thought that it would reassure them to know that something was being done about it. So, having the unit set up, very visibly, right in the heart of the old part of the city was bound to be a public relations triumph for them.

But Steven also suspected, far more cynically, that budget-based factors were concerned in the thinking somewhere. The unit would be a small one, but very dedicated, and therefore wouldn't need much space. Perhaps it was simply cheaper to have them operate out of, what some might think, an under-utilized police station. Not that he was complaining. It made a change to be able to look around and see the cathedral's stained glass windows, or the quirky and quaint moving parts of the clock tower in Carfax, rather than a somewhat ugly municipal-building car-park.

He walked into a foyer smelling just slightly of disinfectant, where a desk sergeant looked at him curiously. His beady eyes brightened and sharpened after he'd inspected Steven's ID. No doubt the locals were keen to get a grasp on the new high-flyer being thrust upon them. It was hard to say what the desk sergeant made of him, though he could sense the man pricing the cost of his suit as he assessed him.

'Yes, sir. Superintendent Inkpen is expecting you. Straight up the stairs, take the immediate corridor to the left, and go down almost to the end. You can't miss his office.'

'Thanks,' Steven said, with a friendly smile, and headed for the stairs. As he jogged up lightly, he wondered what Inkpen had made of Steven's appointment. After all, once the promotion became permanent, as DCS, he'd be the big cheese around here, with all the usual expectations that went with it, resting firmly on his shoulders, demanding that he get results. If the resident man was going to be hostile, it would only make matters harder.

As he tapped on the door, however, his mind was not so much on his new job, the new office, the new staff or the burdens or rewards of a new promotion: he was thinking, instead, about Hillary Greene. It was something that was becoming a very common, and not unpleasant occurrence in his life of late.

Just how long was she going to leave him dangling and waiting for her answer? It hadn't been easy working up the nerve to suggest marriage. Although she rarely spoke about it, he knew how much the disaster of her first marriage had scarred her. But he was sure he hadn't misread the signs – any of them – which had been there, almost from the first moment they'd met.

The attraction had been instant and mutual. They were well matched, and he'd never tried to hide from her just how much she meant to him. He simply felt it in his bones that they could be good together. And he was pretty damned sure that she felt the same way.

That, in itself, wouldn't necessarily have been enough to make him think that he was in with a chance with her. He was no green youth who thought that love could conquer all. And he was well aware of all the strikes against them – bloody Ronnie Greene being only one of them. There was the fact that he was six years younger than she was – not that it worried him, or her, he believed, but it was there. Then there was the fact that she was no longer technically in the job, and he was, and moreover, about to be promoted onwards and upwards. She must, at some level – if only subconsciously – feel a little resentment and envy.

But against all of that, he had just felt that she might at last be ready for a new start. That she might, finally, have managed to get out, emotionally and psychologically, from the shadow of her past traumas and feel capable of trust again. Be ready to admit that, at their age, this might be the last chance they'd get at finding some sort of lasting relationship that was worth the effort and commitment required.

But what if he'd got it wrong? What if she was just thinking of a way to let him down gently? As a voice called out, summoning him to meet his new colleague, Steven Crayle was not at all sure just what the hell he was going to do if that turned out to be the case.

But when Superintendent Ryan Inkpen rose from behind his desk to meet his new boss, he saw only a tall, good-looking, elegant man, with calm intelligent eyes, who smiled at him confidently and with his hand held out in greeting.

Hillary could see why Wendy had not been taken with the small hamlet of Caulcott, although she herself could see its charms. But then she was not a twenty-something, who thought civilization depended on traffic lights and street lamps.

'There are actually two farms within the settlement, guv,' Jake Barnes told her, as he drove his E-type down the narrow lane, trying not to notice the mud and muck that was probably being splattered up the sides of his beautiful baby's racing-green paint work, even as he spoke. 'But Gibsons' is the biggest. They don't do cows—'

'Cattle,' Hillary corrected absent-mindedly and automatically.

'... Cattle,' Jake repeated amicably, 'only sheep. And they're mainly crop growers – the usual wheat, barley and oil-seed rape. The other farm's a dairy outfit, but they also grow crops. Between them, they own pretty much everything as far as the eye can see.' He shot a quick glance around at the flat, winter-bleak landscape that seemed to stretch for miles, and probably did.

'Right – I've got the picture.'

'This is the Gibsons' place just ahead, guv.' He indicated to turn into the courtyard of a rather handsome, traditionally built farmhouse of the local stone which stood square and solid and dared anyone not to be impressed by its simple, Georgian-inspired proportions. Hillary looked at the front door painted a cheerful bright green, and placed squarely in the middle of the building, with a window on either side. A slate, inverted V-shaped porch perched over it, providing shelter when needed, from the prevailing wind and rain. An old black and white sheepdog was standing in one of the many outbuildings, watching them, its tail wagging spasmodically, as if it wasn't sure whether to bark at them, or come to them for some petting.

Chickens actually wandered about the courtyard pecking for who knows what it was that chickens pecked for. But there were no picturesque cobbles to complete the chocolate-box scene, only, for the most part, dirty concrete. One barn was full to the brim with straw, whilst another held rusting agricultural equipment. Hillary thought she recognized some sort of threshing machine, or flail, but wouldn't have bet money on it.

They walked to the door, unmolested by the dog, who'd disappeared back into the warmth and dry of the outbuilding, and knocked on the door.

The woman who answered their summons would have been classically beautiful when young, and was still very handsome even now, possessed as she was by high cheekbones, a fine nose and well-shaped mouth and jaw. She had a mass of platinum-silver hair, which she kept up in a classic and classy chignon. She wore warm black trousers and a tunic-style, gold top with some metallic threads in it that glinted even in the dull light of the November day.

She could have been aged anywhere from sixty to eighty, for she had that certain timelessness about her that Hillary could well believe caught the eye of men, and probably made most other women feel vaguely inadequate.

Perhaps even the young Marigold, all those years ago, had sensed that she would never be able to compete with one such as this, and had instinctively resented it.

'Mrs Gibson?' Hillary asked.

'Yes?' the older woman said, looking uncertainly from Hillary to Jake, as if trying to place them. Hillary noticed, without surprise, that her pansy-brown eyes lingered longest, and with definite feminine appreciation, on Jake, and it was his ID that she inspected first.

So score one for Marigold, Hillary thought, with amusement. The woman definitely had an eye for male beauty, and Jake, with his wide green-grey eyes, classically handsome, square-jawed face and lean build, was definitely worth any woman looking at twice.

'Police? Has something happened?' she asked, frowning a little as she looked over their shoulders, as if expecting to see flashing blue lights, or an ambulance, or some other harbinger of disaster, speeding up behind them.

'Civilian consultants to Thames Valley Police,' Hillary corrected and quickly explained what CRT was all about and what they were doing there.

As she spoke, she saw the other woman force a smile. 'Oh, so it's about Sylvia, I expect? I see, I thought all of that was over and done…. Well, never mind. Oh, please, come in. I'll put the kettle on. I hope you don't mind cats, only we always seem to acquire a plethora of them in this place. Randy keeps insisting that they're to keep the rats down in the silos, but I think he's just a cat man. They're always sitting on his lap, anyway. Personally, I can take them or leave them.' As she spoke, she led them past a narrow hall, where muddy wellingtons and raincoats lined both walls and through into a large, attractive farm house kitchen. It came complete with a black range, a square-shaped, well-scrubbed oak table in the middle of the room, and Welsh dressers lining the walls.

There were also five cats scattered about – two black ones, a lovely tortoiseshell, a mainly white one with a single patch of ginger in the middle of its back, and something that looked vaguely Siamese, which stared at Hillary arrogantly through slightly crossed, china-blue eyes.

None of them deigned to get down from the window-seats next to the room's radiators where they were curled up.

'Coffee?'

'Yes please,' Hillary said. 'Mrs Gibson—'

'Oh good grief, please call me Vanessa. I always think of Randy's mother whenever anyone calls me that. She was a bit of an old trout, though, to be honest, so it makes me shudder every time someone does it!' She laughed as she worked, but Hillary sensed a certain high-tensile edge to her.

She was nowhere near as relaxed or as nonchalant as she was making out which didn't necessarily signify anything sinister, Hillary knew. Some people, even the most innocent and blameless, seemed incapable of acting normally around police officers.

'Please, sit down. Would you like some cake?' Without waiting for a response, she produced a delicious looking fruit-cake from a tin, and placed it in the centre of the table, and cut large portions which she transferred onto china plates. Since it was nearly lunchtime, Jake accepted his with a genuinely happy smile and forked a bite immediately. 'Delicious,' he said, raising his fork in salutation. 'You can tell it's homemade. You cook wonderfully.'

'Thank you,' Vanessa Gibson said, giving him a radiant smile that revealed strong, white teeth. 'Here, let me cut you a piece of cheddar to go with that.'

Hillary watched the two of them flirting mildly, and thought that she could understand, now, what Marigold Perkins had seen, all those years ago. Vanessa Gibson was the sort of woman who was probably incapable of doing anything other than flirt with any man who happened to be in her orbit, regardless of his age or physical attractiveness. In fact, she would be surprised if sex, in any real meaning of the word, had anything to do with it at all.

She was not a psychologist, and wouldn't dream of consulting one without having her arm twisted behind her back, but Hillary would have bet anything that somewhere, probably in her childhood, something had happened to Vanessa Gibson that had made her come to rely on her looks and charm. Had she had very clever sisters who had made her feel intellectually inferior? Had her father or mother dressed her up as a princess from the age of three, and drummed it into her head that pretty girls, or good girls who acted nicely, got whatever it was that they wanted? Or had some man hurt her too badly, and at too young an age, leaving her determined that it would never happen again. How better to ensure that, than to always keep the upper hand by dazzling and controlling their libidos?

She caught Jake's eye, thought she read a hint of amusement, and realized he was playing up to Vanessa on purpose.

Hillary gave the slightest of nods back to acknowledge the ploy. There was, when she considered it impartially, quite a lot to like about her young assistant – he was bright, intuitive and helpful. Once she could figure out exactly what it was that he was up to, he might even prove genuinely useful. Providing she didn't have to nab him for something and have Steven arrest him, that is.

Once the farmer's wife had poured the coffee, Hillary got down to work.

'So, Mrs— Vanessa. What can you tell me about Sylvia Perkins? Were you surprised when you heard she'd been murdered?' She began with a general question, designed to get the witness talking; pinning her down to specifics came later.

'Well of course I was!' Vanessa Gibson sank down on a chair opposite them, cradling her own mug in her hands. It was a telling gesture, Hillary thought, indicating that her hands had gone cold and she was looking to warm them up, even though the room, with the range and radiators, was more than warm enough. Perhaps their arrival on her doorstep had come as something of a shock to her, especially when, as she'd already indicated, she'd thought the whole Perkins affair was over and done with.

On the other hand, Hillary mused with a mental smile, the woman might just have poor circulation.

As if sensing the direction of her thoughts, Hillary saw that Vanessa's hands were now busy working, restlessly turning the mug in circles on the table in front of her, another bit of body language that indicated stress. Although she wore several gold rings, each set with diamonds and either a ruby or sapphire, her rather knobbly knuckles gave away the truth of her advanced age. Hillary guessed that it was probably a cause of serious discontent that, short of wearing gloves, she couldn't hide this small distraction from her otherwise impressive charms.

'It was teatime of that day, I think,' Vanessa began to talk quickly. 'Yes, because Randy came in from the fields at his usual time, and told me that the police cars were swarming around

Sylvia's cottage like wasps around a jam pot. It didn't take long for us to find out why, of course. News gets around the village quicker than anything on the internet, I can tell you.' She gave what was supposed to be a mock-rueful laugh, but which came out as slightly bitter.

And Hillary could guess why.

How often must this woman have been the butt of the rumour mill around here? She couldn't see the lesser female mortals in the small hamlet taking kindly to Randy Gibson's attractive spouse.

'And you were shocked and surprised?' Hillary put in smoothly.

'Oh of course I was. You don't expect it, that sort of thing, do you?' Vanessa's wide brown eyes widened even further. 'I mean, in a sleepy, out-of-the-way place like this? In the cities, well…. You see the news and read the papers. But here? I mean, *here?* Of all the places you'd think it was boringly safe….'

Hillary nodded. She could have told the woman that nobody was safe, anywhere, anytime, but who liked a Jeremiah? 'Being such a very tight-knit community, I'm sure that everyone had a theory as to who could have done it. And why?' she said craftily instead.

'Well, yes. And no,' Vanessa Gibson said, shuffling a little uneasily on her seat. 'I mean, our cleaning lady was convinced that it was the same gang of thieves who were responsible for some thefts over Rousham way. That's another village, the other side of the valley. A couple of months prior to Sylvia … dying … a group of men in a big van were responsible for hitting several empty cottages and getting away with all sorts of stuff. Furniture, jewellery, televisions, that sort of thing. Rousham's a farming community like ours, and there were a lot of empty places about during the day, and nobody to see them at it, or stop them.'

Hillary nodded. She'd read about this incident in DI Jarvis's report. 'But that gang were later caught, and it was proved that they hadn't been anywhere near Caulcott at the time,' she reminded her gently.

Vanessa nodded a shade impatiently. 'Yes, we heard, but that all happened much later on. A few months later, I think it was. At the time it was the most popular theory around and we all thought it, pretty much.'

'Even though nobody had seen strangers around, or reported a strange van or car?'

Vanessa looked away uneasily from Hillary's enquiring eyes, and shrugged, taking a sip of her coffee.

Hillary let it ride, although she'd have bet a month's salary that Vanessa, for one, had never believed in the gang of robbers for one moment.

'But there were other theories too, I expect?' Hillary pressed on, careful to keep her voice light and pleasant, taking a sip of coffee and behaving as if they were two new friends having a chat at a coffee morning. 'Human nature being what it is, and all,' she added guilelessly.

'Oh yes, some of them more off the wall than others,' Vanessa agreed, again with an unconvincing laugh. 'The postman – I think it was the postman.... Or maybe it was Stan Barber ... anyway, the postman thought that a member of her family must have killed her. He said that nearly every murder victim turned out to have been killed by either their spouse or a close family member. Is that actually true?' she asked, her eyes giving lie to the throw-away nature of the question.

Unless Hillary was much mistaken – and she usually wasn't – there was a certain hint of strain in her voice, a shade too much tension as she spoke, that convinced Hillary that Vanessa was desperate to hear the answer.

'Statistically that's probably true,' Hillary agreed carefully. 'So called stranger-murders are rarer, and usually involve muggings gone wrong, or are the result of sexual attacks or drug-related, gang violence. The last two of those scenarios don't apply in this case of course, and since nothing was stolen from Sylvia's house …' She let herself shrug. 'The first doesn't seem likely either.'

'So it *was* one of the family?' Vanessa asked, again a shade too eagerly. Perhaps she realized it herself, for she flushed a little and took a gulp of coffee to cover it.

'We're not saying that, Mrs— Vanessa,' Hillary said, a touch sharply. 'But we're certainly not ruling out the idea that Sylvia knew her attacker. We're working on the assumption that Mrs Perkins let the perpetrator in, since there was no sign of a forced entry. And she'd hardly have been likely to let a stranger into her house, would she?'

'Oh, I wouldn't be too sure of that, if I were you,' Vanessa contradicted stubbornly. 'She never kept her doors locked, you know. None of them did. So anybody could have just walked in, if they'd thought to try the door.'

'None of them?'

Vanessa shrugged carelessly. 'All the old biddies who live around here. There were quite a few of them – Sylvia, that dotty cat woman, Freddie de la Mare, and so on. They're all much of that same generation, which grew up in an age when it was safe to walk alone at night, and you could just pop round to a neighbour's house for a cup of tea and leave your door wide open.'

'Ah,' Hillary nodded. 'Well, we'll be talking to her friends and neighbours soon enough,' she said peaceably. 'So, what did you think of Sylvia?' Hillary zeroed in suddenly and without warning. Beside her, she could sense Jake suddenly tense up. 'I understand she wasn't particularly fond of your husband,' she added quietly.

Vanessa Gibson didn't actually jump, but after a frozen moment, she gave a brief, slightly grim, smile. 'No. I know she wasn't,' she admitted openly. Then she sighed heavily, shot a quick glance at Jake, who pretended to be interested in his slice of cake, and shook her head. 'She blamed poor Randy for Joe dying in the saddle, so to speak. But everyone knew that was unfair,' she added, unable to keep the aggrieved exasperation out of her voice even now, years after the event. 'Joe practically begged Randy to let him carry on working. If you ask me, he just wanted an excuse to get out of the house. I mean, how could it be Randy's fault, really? Joe should have said if he wasn't feeling well. But he seemed fine that morning. And heart attacks are notoriously sudden, aren't they? They just hit you out of the blue and there's nothing anyone can do. But Sylvia just wouldn't have it.'

The tirade had been spoken more and more quickly and now she had to pause to take a deep breath. She also took the opportunity to take another half-hearted sip of her coffee and give a rueful smile. 'Not that I like to speak ill of the dead, or anything, but really, Sylvia could be the limit. And don't go thinking that Randy was the only one she had it in for either,' she warned them, all but shaking a finger under their noses. 'There were plenty of others as well. That poor woman who went to the same old folks' club for a start. Ruby ... something or other. Sylvia accused her of trying to get her claws into this man she was seeing. Really, she was quite vitriolic about it. I mean, how ridiculous, at their age, fighting over some ageing Casanova!'

'Yes, we know about Ruby,' Hillary said gently.

Vanessa Gibson flushed, as if sensing Hillary's censure, and her eyes glittered a shade malignantly. 'Then there was Maureen Coles. I know they'd been arguing, because my cleaning lady lives down the road from them, and she heard them and told me all about it.'

'Oh?' Hillary said. This was new. 'Did she overhear what the argument was about?' she asked curiously.

'Oh, her cat, I expect. With dotty old Maureen it was always about her cat,' said Vanessa unkindly. Then she held out a finger. 'Yes! That was exactly what it was about,' she nodded, in sudden remembrance. 'She was upset and accusing Sylvia of poisoning the poor thing because it kept going into her garden and stalking around her bird-feeders. Either that, or it kept scratching about in Sylvia's vegetable plot, unearthing her carrots or something. I know for a fact that Sylvia *did* complain about the dratted cat, because the postman used to tell me all about it. A regular old woman for gossip he was. We've got a new one now. Postman, that is. Nowadays they don't have time to chat.'

Hillary sighed, but kept on doggedly. 'And did *you* ever get on Sylvia's bad side?' she asked casually. 'It sounds as if almost everyone did, at some point or other.'

But for once, Vanessa was not quite so forthcoming. 'No, not really,' she said, a shade sullenly. 'I rarely saw her, especially after Joe died.'

'Did you get on with Joe? Was he a nice man?' Hillary switched tactics.

'Old Joe? Oh, he was a sweetheart,' Vanessa said, her voice warming up noticeably. 'Not much up top, maybe,' – she tapped her own forehead significantly, seemingly genuinely unaware of the unkindness of it – 'but he was the salt of the earth. Adored those girls of his, and had a gentle sense of humour about him, that just made you like him.'

'So you got on well with him?' she prompted.

'Oh yes. I get on well with all the farmworkers,' Vanessa said, as if surprised by the question. 'When you're a farmer's wife, you have to, don't you? Besides, I do the accounts, see, so I'm responsible for doling out the wages. And it's usually me who deals with any little piffling problems that come up. It helps Randy if I take as much of the load off his shoulders as I can, so I'm like the personnel manager around here. So it pays to get on well with the lads.'

'I expect you feed them too?' Hillary said with a smile. 'I mean, they drop in for cups of tea and cake.' She nodded towards the fruitcake still lying on the table.

'Oh yes. Like feeding the five thousand it is sometimes. They all eat like horses, but we regard it as being part of their wages, I suppose. Mind you, it depends on the time of year, how often they're popping in and out for grub. And where on the farm they're working.'

She sounded confident of herself now that they'd got off the subject of Sylvia Perkins, and Hillary thought that, probably, Marigold hadn't really had any reason to worry, all those years ago. Now that she'd met the lady, she couldn't really see Vanessa Gibson bedding her husband's farm labourers. Just enjoy making them wish that she would.

'Where is your husband, Mrs Gib— sorry, Vanessa?'

'Oh, probably ploughing somewhere. He'll be putting in winter barley I expect,' she said vaguely. 'Or mending the fencing. Something, anyway.'

Hillary nodded. She didn't particularly fancy traipsing around the fields trying to find him, so she knew they'd have to come back and hope to catch him another time. 'Do you know what your husband thought about Sylvia? I mean, about who might have killed her?'

Vanessa Gibson flushed again. 'He had no idea. Why should he?' she said defensively. 'Just because they didn't get on, it means nothing. Oh, I know there were some who pointed their fingers his way,' she said hotly, 'but I don't think it's fair to still be picking on him now. People think that running a farm is easy, and that we're sitting pretty, living in a big house and with all that land. But if you knew anything about farming, you know that it's getting harder and harder to make ends meet. Poor old Randy's been working his fingers to the bone for the last twenty years or so to keep this place going, and Joe Perkins and the rest of them know it. That's another reason why Joe kept on working, I think. Out of loyalty. Not that that wife of his would know anything about it. So for her to accuse poor old Randy of being responsible for him dying ... I tell you, it shook Randy, when old

Joe died. He felt guilty enough about it as it was, even though he didn't have any reason to, without Sylvia going on and on about it. Pouring poison into the ear of anyone silly enough to listen. Not that many did,' she finished, smugly.

Hillary wondered what had triggered that particular diatribe, but thought that until she'd had a chance to interview Randy Gibson, now wasn't the time to explore it.

But there was definitely something worrying the beautiful, uptight farmer's wife, and it didn't take a genius to figure out what it was.

'Well, I think that's all for now, Mrs Gibson,' Hillary said, pushing her empty coffee mug aside and getting up.

Vanessa looked slightly surprised that it was all over so soon, and rose a shade uncertainly. 'You won't go talking to Randy, will you?' she asked urgently.

'We'll have to interview him, Mrs Gibson,' Hillary said firmly.

'Oh yes. I know you have to do that. I mean, you won't go upsetting him with nonsense, will you? I mean, it's not as if he knows who murdered Sylvia. None of us does.'

Hillary smiled, but didn't offer any promises.

'None of you?' she echoed hopefully.

'I mean the village. It wasn't us. It simply couldn't have been one of us,' Vanessa insisted.

'Oh I see,' Hillary nodded. 'Well, it's mainly all a matter of routine,' she lied reassuringly. 'And, as I said, we'll be talking to all of Sylvia's friends and neighbours in the village. Your husband is just one of many on our list.'

'Oh. I see.' Vanessa Gibson nodded and gave them a reluctant smile as she showed them out, but she didn't look, it had to be said, particularly reassured.

CHAPTER SEVEN

ONCE IN THE car, Hillary buckled up her seat belt, and turned to Jake as he slotted the key into the ignition. 'So what did you make of all that?' she asked him, curious to see how much he'd picked up.

Jake, realizing that he was being tested, paused before starting the engine and thought about the last half-hour or so. This was a chance to show Hillary Greene that she wouldn't be wasting her time in taking him under her wing, so he couldn't afford to blow the chance to impress her.

'She seemed uptight and nervous,' he began cautiously.

'Yes. Go on.'

Jake stared through the windscreen thoughtfully. 'She seemed to be a bit all over the place. One minute talking a mile a minute, most of it clearly of no use to us, so why bother saying it? Then the next minute being very careful about what she said, whilst trying not to let on that she was. Once or twice, she seemed genuinely nervous about something – something that went beyond a mere case of nerves, I mean.'

'What do you conclude from all that?' she encouraged, amused by his obvious anxiety not to give her a wrong answer.

'I think she was hiding something,' Jake finally committed himself to an opinion.

Hillary nodded. Finally. 'Did you notice that she was

contradictory as well?'

'Guv?' he frowned. What had he missed?

'One moment she was saying that anyone might have done it – Sylvia's family, the old lady with the cat, Ruby Broadstairs, hell, at one point I was even expecting her to dob the postman in it, if she'd thought about pointing the finger at him in time. And yet, as we were leaving, she was insistent that it couldn't be "one of us" who did it – that nobody in the village or close to Sylvia could be in the frame.'

Jake slowly nodded. 'Yes. I see what you're getting at. She needs to make up her mind. What do you think it all adds up to?' He turned to look at her, his eyes sharp and shining with a glint of excitement. 'Do you think that she did it?'

Hillary smiled wryly. 'I'm not psychic, you know. I can't just look at a suspect and know if they're guilty or not. Or very rarely anyway,' she added with a laugh. 'You have to take the stance that anything's possible and work from that.'

'Come on, guv,' Jake cajoled. 'Everyone knows you've got the experience needed to make good guesses.'

Hillary grunted, and tried to imagine all her bosses' faces, if she'd ever gone to them with just her best guess. 'I've been known to play my hunches from time to time,' she admitted carefully. 'But a hunch is nothing without evidence, proof, or witness testimony to back it up. Remember that.'

'Yes, guv,' Jake said with mock humility. Then shot her a grin. 'But if you had to guess?'

Hillary's lips twitched. 'If I had to make a guess, I'd say that *she* thinks, or at least suspects, that her husband did it.'

Jake glanced back up at the house, his lips rounded in a silent whistle. 'So that's why she was acting like a cat on hot bricks. Well, you would, wouldn't you, if you thought your old man had killed someone?'

'Or she could just be the nervy type,' Hillary pointed out laconically. 'But until we know more, it doesn't really get us any further forward, does it?' she mused, more or less speaking her thoughts out loud now, rather than in any attempt to educate Jake. 'It depends, really, on just *why* it is that she suspects him. Was it something specific, for instance? Did he come back that day with some bloodstains on his clothes, telling her that he'd cut himself on some barbed wire or something? Or had he told her that morning that he was going to call in on Sylvia to give her a piece of his mind, and Vanessa got scared that they'd had a slanging match that had escalated out of all control?'

'In other words,' Jake said, 'something that would provide us with some actual proof. Or, at the very least, some solid conjecture – if there is such a thing.'

'Right,' Hillary agreed. 'And, by the way, there is no such thing.' She looked over at the farmhouse pensively. 'Or was it more nebulous than that for her? Had she just got the feeling that he'd had enough, or that something had set him off, the proverbial straw that broke the camel's back. Did she just sense a change in his behaviour and put two and two together to make twenty-two instead of four? In which case it might mean nothing at all. He might just have been in a bad mood that day, or had indigestion.'

'You mean she might have been worrying all these years for nothing?' Jake said, and shook his head. 'Man. As the Yanks would say, what a bummer.'

A bummer indeed, Hillary thought. 'Like I said before, anything's possible.'

'So do you think she had an affair with Sylvia's husband?' Jake asked, changing the subject slightly. 'I certainly got the feeling that she wouldn't have said no if I'd offered. I swear, once or twice, I could feel her foot, nudging against my calves under the table.'

Hillary glanced across and looked at him thoughtfully. 'Naturally you're irresistible to all women, Jake.'

Jake laughed, but was clearly a little annoyed. 'Wouldn't that be nice?'

'So what do you think?' She put the ball firmly back in his court. 'If you had to guess, that is? Did she or didn't she sleep with Joe Perkins, and any number of others for all we know?'

Jake turned the key in the ignition and, as the engine purred into obedient life, he snorted. 'No chance, I reckon, guv. That woman's all bark and no knickers, if you ask me. Or rather, she keeps her knickers very tightly pulled up.'

'What a charming way with imagery you have, Jake,' Hillary complimented him.

They were still laughing when they finally pulled out of the farmyard. It didn't, however, stop either of them from noticing that Vanessa Gibson watched them leave from behind one of the curtains, her face a pale, anxious oval against the glass.

That afternoon Hillary had a meeting with Rollo Sale, since Steven was still at St Aldates, and she briefed him on the case so far. She was pleased that he seemed to grasp all the salient points quickly and didn't feel the need to put his oar in point-lessly, just for the sake of making a suggestion. Instead he'd simply indicated that she should get on with things and wished her luck.

Wendy and Jimmy reported back on their interviews with the muggers who targeted old folks, both of them thoroughly disgusted with the state of humanity, but also convinced that none of them was in the frame for Sylvia's death.

She told them to keep at it and file their reports in the murder book, then, after five o'clock had come and gone, hung around the station for a while longer, until it was clear that Steven wouldn't be back any time soon. Then, she left reluctantly and drove back to her narrowboat, which was now permanently moored in the nearby village of Thrupp.

Once on board the *Mollern*, she made a salad, big enough for two, and put a bottle of white wine in the fridge to chill, but in truth, she didn't know if Steven would be coming over that night or not. They hadn't made any firm plans, and she found the uncertainty unsettling.

As Hillary Greene restlessly attempted to read a Hardy novel, Jake Barnes, who'd left HQ dead on time, most definitely had plans.

Standing in front of the full-length mirror in the dressing-room of his spacious master-bedroom suite, he scrupulously checked his appearance. It was important, because tonight he needed to make sure that he'd got his image just right.

But, for once, it was not a woman that he was dressing to impress.

He was aggressively dressed in designer-everything, from the Calvin Klein jeans to an Armani jacket. The watch on his left wrist was gold, huge and about as in-your-face as it could get, as was the diamond pinky ring on his left hand. As if that wasn't enough a thick rope of gold chain was just showing through the silk shirt, where he'd left two buttons undone, just for that purpose.

Privately, he thought that the bling made him look like an escapee from one of those disco-dance films of the eighties. Even the Gucci loafers looked as if they could tap out a John Travolta dance step on their own.

But everything about him screamed one thing: money.

He looked like a man with more money than sense – and certainly taste. But then, Jake supposed with an apprehensive shiver, subtlety would be lost on a man like Darren Chivnor.

According to his PI's report, the Dog and Duck was just one of the many pubs on the edge of the notorious estate where Medcalfe's employees (for want of a better word for them) liked to hang out. Although the man himself had long since left Blackbird Leys behind him, and lived in a very upmarket, mock-Tudor des res well to the north, his workforce seemed to remain fairly loyal to the place.

Jake was very well aware that his car looked distinctly out of place in this area. Not that he'd brought his beloved E-Type, of course. Instead, he was driving a near-classic Porsche, painted in metallic sky-blue. It was the car he used when the Jag was in the garage for any reason, and was well insured. Although it was, in its own right, still a very desirable automobile indeed, he didn't have the emotional attachment to it that he had for the E-Type, so if it was nicked, he could live with it.

He parked the machine in the rear car-park and walked casually inside. The pub was a pleasant enough sort of place, right on the outskirts of the estate, and therefore practically rubbing shoulders with a neighbouring area that was fast gentrifying. So, along with the criminal element, there was a mix of recent locals who didn't know better and a few lost tourists. Most of the pub's customers, however, were the local regulars, consisting of old-timers who knew who Medcalfe's boys were, but had nothing particularly to fear from them, since they kept well out of their way, and their own law-abiding lives seldom overlapped or clashed with theirs.

Three such were sat supping beers at a table, from time to time warily watching a young lad in baggy jeans and a hoodie, who was playing a slot machine, and swearing viciously but without any real anger, every time he inevitably lost.

A young obviously married couple were seated at a table laid for food, and were perusing a menu, seemingly oblivious to their surroundings. The bar was pleasant enough, clean, but not well lit.

Jake felt his shoulders tense as he spotted Darren Chivnor through an open archway to the left, leaning over a billiard table with a wooden cue.

So he'd got lucky first time. He'd been prepared to keep coming to the pub for as long as it took, but he was glad that he didn't have to. Being so far outside of his comfort zone, he'd never felt so vulnerable, and he didn't like the sensation one little bit.

He made his way to the bar and ordered a vodka and orange juice. Making sure that when he opened his wallet, the barman would notice the wad of cash inside it. Like most people nowadays, Jake usually used plastic, but whilst flashing an American Express Platinum Card about might actually say more about how truly wealthy he was, it just didn't have the impact of cold, hard, sterling.

He took his drink to a table and sipped it, but barely imbibed any of the liquid. Since he was driving, the last thing he needed was to be pulled over and lose his licence. From time to time he saw the barman watching him curiously, and Jake, with an inner satisfied smile, thought he could understand why. For the bartender, a middle-aged, balding man with an enormous beer gut, was finding it hard to place him. He was not a regular, that was for sure, not when he was wearing more on the little finger of his left hand than the cost of the average semi-detached around here. Nor was he one of Medcalfe's lads. And he didn't look like the usual tourist – although he might have been one of those crazy Americans who liked to splash their cash.

Jake just hoped, a shade uneasily, that he didn't smell of cop. He didn't know how true it was that hardened criminals could spot a cop a mile off, and had always been inclined to regard that as something of an urban myth that should be taken with a good pinch of salt. Nevertheless, he consoled himself with the thought that, since he wasn't a cop, not even technically, he couldn't possibly look like one. Could he? Unless hanging around the Thames Valley HQ for the past few months had somehow rubbed off on him?

He was spared further pointless worry when Darren strolled through to the bar, folding a wad of his billiards winnings into his back pocket as he shouldered up to the bar. Jake heard him ask for the barman for the same again, and noticed the older man dip his head and say something quietly into his ear as he handed over a pint.

Darren sat casually on the nearest barstool and took a gulp and, sure enough, casually turned to glance Jake's way.

Jake took a sip of his drink, let his eyes meet those of the skinhead for the briefest of seconds, then casually looked away again. He hoped he'd judged it just right. He didn't want to come across as a rival gang member off his turf or – worse still a gay man, hopelessly out of his depth and trawling for love and affection in all the wrong places. That would get him a certain part of his anatomy quickly handed back to him on a plate.

On the other hand, he'd needed to do just enough to be sure that he'd made contact. To have Chivnor clock him, check him out, and wonder about him. And that, Jake was pretty sure, he'd managed to do.

That was all he needed, for now. He was in no rush, but it meant that, the next time their paths crossed, Chivnor would remember him, and Jake intended their paths would cross again in the very near future.

He left his drink almost untouched on the table, and got up. That gesture alone ensured that several pairs of eyes turned his way in surprise. Jake would have been willing to bet a four-figure sum that no customer of the Dog and Duck had ever failed to sup up before, and he wondered which of the room's drinkers would snaffle his glass first.

As he walked to the door and passed through, he made sure that he glanced at the bar again. Yes! Chivnor was still watching him, his eyes curious and slightly mocking. His gaze, however, quickly dropped to the gold chain around Jake's neck and Jake clearly sensed the envy in the quality of the narrow-eyed look that returned to his face.

Jake allowed himself to give the merest fraction of a nod. It could have meant anything. A vague hello, or merely an acknowledgement that his bling had been clocked and duly respected.

He saw the wiry young thug's eyes narrow, then he was through the door and gone. His heart was thumping deep in his chest and he felt slightly sick. When he got in the Porsche, his fingers shook just a little as he turned the ignition key. He pulled away a shade too fast, making sure to rev the engine as he did so. He hoped the throaty roar of the sports car had been audible inside. He wanted Chivnor to know that he had a classy ride.

His mouth felt dry as he signalled left, and in the driving mirror he saw himself give a definitely shaky smile. Hell, if just being in the same room as one of Dale Medcalfe's goons was enough to give him this many jitters, he needed to toughen up and grow a backbone fast.

As he drove back to the familiar safety and civilization of his north Oxford mansion, Jake Barnes couldn't help but think that Hillary Greene would almost certainly have been able to out-stare the skinhead thug without even breaking a sweat.

The next morning, Wendy Turnbull was definitely feeling the effects of the night before. Usually she didn't go out much on weekdays, and certainly didn't push the boat out enough to have to need to take a taxi home, but when she'd got home from work the previous evening, Barbara had been all dolled up and with somewhere far more special to go than the impromptu student mini-rave, which she'd claimed to be her destination. Wendy herself certainly wouldn't waste a glamorous turquoise onesie on a wind-blown gig in some out of the way barn or skanky warehouse. No, that number just begged for a little one-on-one action.

Did Babs really think she was that dumb?

Instead of calling her on it as she should have done, she'd chickened out and let her go off, blithely spouting her lies and promises to be home by one. Which she hadn't been of course.

Wendy had tossed and turned till gone four before the little madam had wandered home, smelling of a perfume that had somehow miraculously morphed into a different brand from the one she'd been wearing when she'd left.

Wendy, of course, had pretended to be sound asleep when the Chinese girl had slid ever so carefully into bed beside her.

Now, as she drove into work, she was still berating herself for being an emotional coward. At some point there'd have to be a showdown. She just couldn't have Babs thinking she could two-time her whilst at the same time living rent-free at her place, using her like a sugar-mommy. Wendy was far too strapped for cash herself for that! Love was one thing; keeping a dolly bird was another thing altogether!

At least she'd had enough self-respect not to stay in all night pining for her, Wendy thought now with some satisfaction. She had, in fact, ventured into Oxford to paint a few nightclubs red and, as a result, just might have picked herself up an admirer.

Trev Ballantyne. A nice name, Wendy thought now, recalling his face through something of a wine-blunted fuzz. A student from Brasenose College, or so he claimed. Mind you, Wendy hadn't been so sozzled that she'd just taken *that* claim at face value. Around Oxford, a lot of low-lifes pretended to be some-thing they were not, and all of them with an eye to the main chance. On the other hand, he had been in with a bunch of mates, all around his age, whom he claimed were his rowing buddies. And when Wendy had checked with some of the waiters, they'd confirmed their bona fides.

Now, as Wendy parked her Mini in a careful spot near an end row, thus diminishing her baby's chances of picking up any dings or dents from other careless parkers, she shut off the engine with a world-weary sigh.

Tall, strapping, Trev Ballantyne certainly had a rower's upper body strength, with a mop of attractive blond hair to top it off. He spoke with something of an upper class accent, true, but then, Wendy supposed with a sigh, it *was* Oxford. What else could she expect? On the plus side, he was studying jurisprudence, and had seemed genuinely interested in her job working with the police.

Of course that might have been just a come on, a bit of mindless flattery to butter her up with an eye on a mere one-night stand, but Wendy hoped not. At least he'd been gentlemanly enough to see her into a taxi, and had asked her for her telephone number, which were all good signs.

She just wished she could remember whether or not she'd given it to him. By the end of the evening, things were becoming a little vague.

Still, she realized, with a spurt of sudden practical thinking, she knew where she could find him if she wanted to make the first move. Brasenose wasn't a college that she knew particularly well, but with a bit of luck, she soon might. It had been quite some time since she'd bothered with some boy-on-girl action, so it was high time she got back into the swing of it. And a hunky, blond Sloane-Ranger rower was just what she needed to show Babs that two could play at that game.

She was still smiling gently around her slightly thumping head when she walked down the stairs and into the rabbit-warren of a basement, where the CRT hung out. When she walked into the communal office however, everyone was already there ahead of her, and Hillary Greene was standing in the doorway, chatting to Jimmy.

Wendy shot a panic-stricken glance at her watch. She'd not been too drunk to remember to set her alarm, but perhaps the hangover had slowed her down? She felt a brief rush of relief when she saw that it was not yet nine.

Jake Barnes grinned at her over Hillary's shoulder, making the boss look around and make room for her.

'Guv,' Wendy said brightly, as she slipped by, hoping her gold-and-black eye make-up had successfully hidden all signs of last night's ravages and excesses from her face. She'd pulled on a heavy leather studded jacket over a pair of black leggings, patterned with tiny crucifixes, and a red and black lace bustier. She'd dyed the tips of her spiky hair red to go out last night, and she was confident that it still looked good.

Hillary eyed the Goth in full regalia and smiled. Given the girl's outfit, the following few hours should prove very interesting indeed. 'Ah, Wendy, just the woman I was looking for. Fancy going to prison?' she asked brightly.

Wendy drove happily through the Berkshire Downs towards Hampshire, her mind teeming with images of what a Victorian prison should be. She knew that the place they were going to wasn't one of the really high-security places, as Robbie Grant was in for robbery, not murder. But the penal place down by the coast *was* one of the older specimens, and therefore must still retain some of the brooding menace of her imagination.

Think Sherlock Holmes on Dartmoor with an escaped convict on the loose, or Bram Stoker's mental institution in *Dracula*, she thought happily, as she urged the Mini on towards the south coast.

Beside her, Hillary was far more prosaically reading Robbie Grant's rap sheet. As DI Jarvis had reported, he'd started off with the usual petty stuff – shop-lifting, mugging, before, not long after his sixteenth birthday, progressing to burglary and then robbery.

He was currently inside for holding up a post office in Swindon. His sawn-off shotgun, however, had proved to be unloaded, which had resulted in him getting a three year stretch instead of the ten she, and everyone else in law enforcement, thought that he should have got. He'd been inside for six months, and, with the over-crowding situation in prisons being like it was, she wouldn't have been accused of undue cynicism if she expected him to be out sometime in the middle of next year.

Next time, the shotgun might be loaded.

'Sometimes I despair.'

She only realized she'd spoken the thought out loud, when Wendy said curiously, 'Despair of what, guv?'

'Our judicial system,' Hillary said shortly. 'You need to turn off the main road up here.' She'd had to visit this particular example of Her Majesty's Pleasure on a number of occasions before, and vaguely remembered the way. And she'd rather trust her memory than the satnav, any day.

About half an hour later, Wendy found herself pulling up to a set of chain-link gates. Suddenly, she felt unaccountably nervous, her hands on the steering wheel becoming damp with sweat.

Beyond her, the prison was everything that she could have hoped for. The dark brooding November sky was filled with threatening rain-clouds, and the mammoth, brick-built building, with its rows of anonymous, small, barred windows, gave her the delicious shivers. But there was something far too normal and banally realistic about the modern guardhouses and barriers, and the uniformed prison guards, which ruined the experience for her.

The whole place seemed to reek of dispirited realism, rather than Gothic grandeur.

After they'd been thoroughly vetted, and had their IDs checked and been allowed to park the Mini in the requisite carpark, Wendy could feel her heart begin to thump unpleasantly. She tried to tell herself that it was just the result of her lingering hangover, but she knew it wasn't. There was definitely an air of institutionalised apathy and hopelessness about the place that dragged her down.

Inside, the feeling of unease grew worse. The old, bulging, cream-plastered walls should have radiated cold menace, but instead radiators made it pleasantly warm. Too warm; she felt herself beginning to sweat. The floors of undistinguished grey

113

lino smelled cleanly of Flash floor liquid, and the men who were pushing mops about, and looked up at them curiously as they passed, looked less mad, bad, and dangerous to know, as merely listlessly bored. Nevertheless, Wendy could feel them watching her. Without realizing it, as they followed their escort down to the day room, where the prisoner was expecting them, Wendy moved a little closer to Hillary in a subconscious plea for protection. Her heart thumped a little harder, and she felt the beginnings of an itch of panic creeping up her spine.

Hillary, who hadn't missed the girl's growing unease, glanced across at her sympathetically. 'Feeling a little claustrophobic?' she commiserated quietly.

Wendy shot her a thankful look. 'I suppose I am, guv. A little bit sick, too, if I'm honest.'

Hillary nodded. 'Don't fret it. Everybody feels the same way when they first come to one of these places. I know I did. You can't help but get the notion in the back of your head that perhaps some kind of really hideous mistake will be made, and they won't let you out again.'

'Yeah.' Wendy breathed out explosively, and managed a not-quite amused laugh. 'Like there'll be the giant computer cock-up of all time, and my name will somehow jump from the visitors' section to the inmate section. And then some female warden who looks like Ernest Borgnine will welcome me to a cell and tell me that I'll be collecting my old age pension before I see the light of day again.'

Hillary grinned. 'Don't worry. This place is still currently men only. So even if some mad hacker with a grudge against you somehow managed to fiddle the system, somebody would smell a rat.'

'Yeah. Unless they think I'm in drag,' Wendy muttered, her eyes still on the back of the prison officer in front of them. He was a tall, fifty-something man who had a bearing so military, that he might just as well have had 'old soldier' tattooed on his forehead. Although she was only speaking in a whisper, she had the feeling that he was listening to their conversation, and probably laughing up his sleeve at them.

They passed through several barred, locked gates, and every time the prison officer had to use one of the keys in the vast bunch that was chained to his belt, Wendy flinched.

The further they went inside, the more she felt the panicky feeling threatening to overwhelm her. Knowing that she wasn't the only one who'd ever felt this way, did little to comfort her. So when they stepped into a square, brightly lit room, scattered about with tables and chairs, and with daylight streaming in on two sides, she felt a little better. There was table tennis set-up in one corner, and a large, wide-screen television was going in another. Several men, with women and children who were obviously visiting family members, sat around the tables, chatting. It reminded Wendy vaguely of any sort of day room at either a hospital, or a college, or some other public building. The prisoners weren't even wearing any kind of a uniform, but normal clothes. There was the smell of coffee in the air, and several kids were playing in an area that had obviously been specially designated for them, and kitted out with simple plastic toys in bright, primary colours.

Only the presence of several men dressed in black trousers and white shirts with black epaulettes, standing at the doors and keeping a watchful eye over the people within, told the true story of where they were.

'Grant is over there.' The prison officer spoke and led them to a table where a lone male sat watching them approach. He was in his late twenties, Hillary gauged, and looked nothing like his mother. No doubt Mary Rose was thankful for that now, and remembering the woman living her respectable new life in her swanky new house, she couldn't see her ever visiting here.

'Robbie Grant?' Hillary asked, nodding a 'thank you' to the prison officer, who turned and strolled casually towards a hatch area set back in the far wall, no doubt to have a cup of coffee and keep an eye on them. She held out her ID to Robbie Grant, who stirred himself enough to actually look at it. Not easy, when he looked almost terminally bored.

He had lanky brown hair and vaguely brown eyes, and was draped over the hard-backed chair as if he was boneless. Dressed in faded jeans and a black T-shirt, he was one of those men who looked as if they were constantly smirking at the world, the sort that made you just itch to kick their shins to get rid of that couldn't-care-less attitude.

His eyes shifted to Wendy, and widened at little at the Goth outfit. Then the smirk was back.

'I was told you wanted to see me. About my gran, yeah?' He absently scratched his chin, which needed a shave. 'You still trying to find out who done her in then? I thought you lot had given up. On account of it was too much for your poor coppers' brains.'

Hillary sat down and indicated for Wendy to do the same. 'No murder case is ever closed, Robbie. I'm a retired DI, and I work cold cases. I'm going to do my best to get justice for your grandmother. Do you care about that?'

She looked across at him steadily. He managed to rouse himself out of his terminal lethargy enough to actually shrug one shoulder. 'I s'pose,' he drawled.

Hillary knew why he'd agreed to see them of course. A visitor, *any* visitor, relieved the monotony of their day-to-day existence, so she didn't pay his Oscar-winning performance of indifference much mind. Inside, he was as alert and interested as a cat at a mousehole, of that she had no doubt. Their visit was probably as much entertainment as he'd had since arriving here.

'Did you do it?' she asked flatly. 'Did you kill your old gran?'

For a second his eyes flashed, then he smirked again. 'Nah. I liked the old bird, didn't I? She always gave me money for fags when I was a nipper.'

'Had you seen her recently? Before she was murdered?'

'Nah. Hadn't been around … dunno. Might have seen her the Christmas before. She usually bought me something nice, Christmas and my birthday, like.'

Hillary's smile twisted a little on her lips. 'I can see you really thought a lot of her.'

Robbie Grant shrugged.

'On the day she died, you told DI Jarvis, the senior investigating officer, that you were home all day, alone. Not much of an alibi, was it?'

Robbie again shrugged, and again smirked. He was lounging so far back in the chair now that he looked almost in danger of sliding off it and under the table. 'She couldn't prove otherwise, could she? Your DI Jarvis. How is she, anyway? She was a bit long in the tooth, but not a bad-looking bird. Do tell her I said hello. I think she quite fancied me, you know.' He picked between his front teeth with a fingernail. 'I could tell. She was so hot to pin it on me, see? Got real mad when she couldn't have me up for it. That's how I could tell she wanted me bad, see. Sexual frustration.'

He nodded solemnly, and Hillary wondered where he'd picked up the poppsychology terminology. From a packet of cornflakes, most likely, she mused.

'I felt almost sorry for her,' Grant continued with his little fantasy, still industriously picking the breakfast out of his teeth. 'I told her, I wouldn't mind giving her one, anyway. Like I said, she was an older bird, but still fit. I told her I wouldn't tell on her, see, if she wanted to slip around to my place one night.' He winked lasciviously.

'I'm sure she was flattered,' Hillary said drily.

Grant smirked again. He was almost as good-looking as he thought he was, Hillary thought, but his looks would be much improved with a broken nose.

'Yeah, well, you lot couldn't pin it on me 'coz I wasn't there,'

Grant taunted. 'Nobody saw me, did they? And believe me, in that dead-end hole where Nan lived, someone would have, if I'd been there. 'Sides, why would I want the old girl dead? Like I said, she was my nan.'

'You were her sole beneficiary,' Hillary pointed out flatly, and when he looked at her blankly, said, 'You got all her money.'

'Oh yeah! Good old Nan.' The smirk was now so wide it was in danger of splitting his face. Beside her, she saw Wendy Turnbull's hands clench into fists and knew she was probably fighting a similar desire to punch him.

'You spent it all, of course,' Hillary went on. 'All that old lady's lifetime savings.'

'Too right!' he admitted with unrepentant glee. 'Had a holiday to Benidorm. Got a new motor. Spent it on the birds. Even went to a casino in London. First time ever in one of them places.' Grant's voice grew dreamy now. 'You ever been to one of them? I felt like I was in a James Bond film. Carpet up to your ankles, and the birds…. Talk about glamorous.'

'Did your grandmother ever speak to you about any of her neighbours? People she didn't like, or who had a grudge of some sort against her?' Hillary interrupted his day-dream ruthlessly.

'Nah. And if she did, I sort of tuned her out, you know. She'd start to go on about something and I'd just' – here he mimed flicking a switch against his temple – 'tune her out. Old people are dead boring.'

He looked around, careful not to catch the eye of any of the guards, and then looked back at Wendy. 'You got a boyfriend, darlin'?'

'A girlfriend actually,' Wendy said sweetly.

Robbie Grant looked momentarily surprised, then disgruntled. 'Oh great. Just my luck. Two female cops come visiting and one of 'em's a dyke.' Then his gaze turned to Hillary. 'Now you, I wouldn't kick *you* out of bed. Like good ol' DI Jarvis, you're a bit long in the tooth, but I wouldn't hold that against you.'

'You're not going to get the opportunity to hold anything else against me either, Mr Grant,' Hillary assured him. 'Do you have any idea who might have killed your nan? Don't you want to see the bastard inside for it?'

'Course I do,' Robbie Grant said. 'Bugger deserves it. If I have to be in here, so should he.' Since Hillary wasn't quite sure that she could follow the logic of that argument, she let it pass.

'But you have no idea who might have done it?'

'Nah. I'd'a said if I did. Like I said, she were me nan, weren't she?'

And with that, Hillary knew she had to be content.

Like DI Jarvis before her, she was inclined to keep Robbie Grant high on her list of possibles, but if he had murdered the old lady for his inheritance, there seemed little chance of proving it now. Especially all these years later.

Hillary sighed.

Wendy sighed.

And, after another token smirk, Robbie Grant sighed as well.

Which at least made it unanimous.

CHAPTER EIGHT

HILLARY DROPPED WENDY back at HQ with orders to write up their report on the Robbie Grant interview for the murder book, and then beckoned Jake to follow her out.

'You have Wendy's list of Sylvia's neighbours and the times that they stated that they're likely to be available for interview?'

For reply, Jake patted the little electronic tablet that he kept with him at all times. Hillary sometimes wondered if anyone with a pacemaker inserted in their chest could actually keep it closer to his heart than Jake kept that electronic gizmo. She wouldn't have been surprised if, when the time came for an to upgrade, it would have to be somehow surgically removed from his person.

Not being a particularly avid fan of technology herself, she couldn't see the attraction of being constantly hooked up to the Internet, or of being perpetually electronically linked to a swarming mass of faceless humanity via Facebook or Twitter. Emails were as much as she could cope with, the majority of which, according to the rare times when she bothered to dive into her spam, were either trying to sell her penile erectile systems, or a time share in Barbados.

She sat back in the passenger seat as Jake revved the engine lovingly, and offered up a passing mental apology to Puff as they passed her old Volkswagen, since she knew she was becoming used to being chauffeured around in such a spectacular beast as this.

Jake headed out into the sticks with barely a glance at his sat nav, and let his mind wander instead to the details of his second planned encounter with Darren Chivnor.

If Hillary noticed his abstraction, she didn't let on. Not surprising, since her own thoughts nowadays seemed invariably to lead her into the should she/shouldn't she funk that surrounded the conundrum of what to do about Steven's marriage proposal.

Damn it, what had possessed the man to ask her?

Once Jake turned down the remote country lane leading to the small hamlet of Caulcott, however, both of them brought their minds firmly back to the business at hand.

The first on Wendy's list of Sylvia's contemporaries lived three doors down on the left from where she'd once lived, in a charming stone and thatch cottage that was probably the devil to keep warm in winter.

The cottage's owner, Phyllis Drew, turned out to be almost a caricature of a cartoonist's version of a little old lady, possessing as she did, a riotous mop of snow-white hair, twinkling blue eyes set in a deeply lined and seamed face, and rosy pink cheeks. She even had the slightly stooped, hump-back walk that needed the aid of a walking stick, and came complete with a little Jack Russell terrier that danced in excitement around her feet. She was wearing a flowered apron over a warm dark-blue track suit, and incongruously hefty, modern-looking white and pink trainers on her tiny feet.

Myopically she studied Hillary's ID card, and then smiled and shrugged, as if giving up on it, and invited them inside cheerfully.

'Call me Phil, my lovey, everyone else does,' she informed Hillary breezily. 'And come into the kitchen – it's the only warm room in the place. Don't mind Charlie – he'll be asleep by the range, but we won't disturb him. He does snore a bit, I'm afraid, so you'll just have to ignore him.'

Jake Barnes, expecting to see another, much more elderly Jack Russell curled up asleep on a chair, gave a little start of surprise to see an old man asleep there instead. He too possessed a lot of white hair and pink cheeks, but in his case, his wrinkled face was dwarfed by his gaping mouth, through which, every now and then, came a sudden, snuffling snore, which made his dentures rattle. There was no regular pattern to his snoring, though, Jake soon realized, as long moments of silence stretched between a variety of snorts, whistles and assorted lip-smacking.

Hillary gratefully accepted the use of one of the battered, faded chintz armchairs that were grouped around an old-fashioned Aga, and noticed Jake pull out a straight-backed kitchen chair which he placed out of the way in the corner, where he could take notes without being obvious about it.

'This is about Sylvie, I expect?' Phil Drew began. 'An extraordinary looking young girl came around…. Was it yesterday or the day before? I forget' – her husband gave a sudden thunderous snore and shuffled about on the chair, but didn't wake – 'my memory isn't what it used to be I'm afraid. Anyway, she said we'd be getting a visit from the police about Sylvie. Cup of tea, lovey?'

Hillary accepted for both herself and Jake, and smiled down as the Jack Russell sniffed her ankles suspiciously and then, canine curiosity apparently satisfied, settled down by her feet and rested his head on her shoes with a heartfelt sigh.

'What can you tell me about the day she died, Mrs Drew?' Hillary asked, as the old lady set about making the hot drinks.

'Phil, lovey. Call me Phil. And I'm not sure that I remember anything in particular. Time goes by so fast, doesn't it? I can't believe it's been five years since she went.'

'Yes, time's a funny thing,' Hillary said patiently. 'And I wouldn't ask you to try and remember specific things that happened on specific days. But when you look back, what do you remember most about Sylvia around the time that she died?'

'Oh well, there was that bit of a to-do about that man she was seeing at the old folks' club. They say she got into an argument with some other woman, but I can't see it amounting to much myself. Sylvie had too much sense, if you ask me, to go making a fool of herself over a man at her age. I reckon the gossips blew it up out of all proportion. Some people have nothing better to do than make their own entertainment at other people's expense.'

The cups of tea dispensed, the old woman settled herself down beside her husband's chair with a bit of a creak and a groan. Beside Hillary's feet, the Jack Russell gave a corresponding groan, as if in sympathy with his mistress, and rolled over onto his side with another sigh.

'Then there was Maureen Coles making that fuss over her cat, and Sylvia had—'

'What cat?' The voice that interrupted was male and totally unexpected, and Hillary suddenly realized that she hadn't heard any snores for a little while. She glanced across to look at Charlie Drew, who wasn't looking at her, but at his wife, one shaggy white eyebrow raised in query.

'Old Maureen Coles's cat. You know, the last one she had before she had to go into that home; the one that was poisoned. What was his name now? Maureen always did give her ginger toms such funny names. She said they deserved something unusual. A funny woman, you know, she always was a bit dotty, but especially towards the end, but harmless enough, the poor old soul.'

'Sputnik,' Charlie Drew said.

Hillary blinked. 'Sorry?'

'The name of her cat. The one that got poisoned,' the old man said, looking at her with some puzzlement, and clearly wondering who she was.

'Oh,' Hillary said. And although she just knew that she was

going to regret asking, she couldn't resist. 'Why did she call it Sputnik?'

'Cause it shot off like a rocket whenever you looked at it,' Phil provided the punch line without a modicum of humour, and nodded emphatically. 'That moggy had a touch of the feral about it, if you ask me.'

'Who are you?' Charlie Drew said, looking at Hillary with mild curiosity.

'I work for the police, sir,' Hillary said.

'Oh,' the old man said. 'Then you won't mind if I go back to sleep?'

Hillary could sense Jake grinning over in his corner, and fought to keep her own face straight. 'No, sir. Please don't let us interrupt your nap.'

Charlie nodded and closed his eyes.

'Course, there was her grandson,' Phil went on. 'Foulmouthed layabout if ever there was one. Never liked him. I told Sylvie so, too, never kept it a secret from her or spoke about her behind her back,' Phil said. 'I like to be up front with people. I wouldn't be surprised if he wasn't behind it all.'

Hillary nodded. 'Yes, we've spoken to Robert Grant,' she said. 'You told the original lady who investigated Sylvia's murder that you didn't see any strangers hanging around that day?' she prompted gently.

'Then I didn't,' Phil said uncompromisingly. 'Nothing wrong with my memory back then. If that's what I said, then that's what I meant.'

'But did you see someone whom you might have expected to see perhaps, going past the window that day, visiting Sylvia?' she put in casually. 'Say Vanessa Gibson or her husband? Or someone else who lived in the village?'

'Well, I might have done,' Phil agreed cautiously, taking a slurping gulp of her tea. 'I wouldn't have paid no particular mind about it, if I had.'

Over in his chair, her husband gave a muffled snort. Then a distinct snore. Then silence. Jake found himself fascinated by the very random nature of the man's performance actively waiting and anticipating what the next noise might comprise, and consequently almost missed what Phil was saying.

'You always see the farmers and their workers coming and going, either in the tractors, or moving the sheep about.'

'So you wouldn't have paid particular notice if any one of them turned in at Sylvia's gate?'

'Shouldn't think so, as I already said, lovey. You get used to seeing the same old faces, don't you? Oh, I get it.' The old lady suddenly sat up a bit straighter in her chair. 'You think Randy Gibson might have got fed up with Sylvie's snarky ways and bashed her with the poker?' Phil cocked her perky little head to one side, looking momentarily like a curious cockatoo, and evidently thought about it for a moment, before shaking her head. 'Nah, I can't see it myself, lovey. Want a biscuit?'

'Love one,' Charlie said from his chair.

Beside her feet, the Jake Russell, obviously responding the word 'biscuit' perked up and whined hopefully.

Hillary reminded herself that patience was a virtue, and accepted a Garibaldi.

Over on his chair, Jake chewed his bottom lip and industriously scribbled in his notebook.

If Jake Barnes was manfully fighting the urge to laugh, Steven Crayle, had no such problem. Sitting in his office, he'd spent the morning going over the CRT's operational procedures with Rollo Sale. But now that his fellow superintendent had left to chair a meeting with the computer techcicians, thus getting the chance to become better acquainted with the majority of his staff, he had time to check out the dossiers that Superintendent Ryan Inkpen had given him during his St Aldates' visit.

And he was currently studying Dale Medcalfe's list of known

associates, and contemplating just how many of them he would be crossing swords with, once the new unit was up and running.

Like Commander Donleavy he was looking forward to putting many of them away, with Medcalfe himself being the main prize. But there were several of his lieutenants who needed bringing down almost as much as their boss: Darren Chivnor being chief among them.

Unusually, Chivnor had no official police record, but there was a long list of his suspected victims in their files. Mostly members of rival gangs, who, for obvious reasons, had refused to name the person who'd given them knife scars and other brutal warnings in equal measure. But there were also, on the list, a number of female victims, no doubt prostitutes in Medcalfe's stables who had somehow incurred the big man's wrath, and had needed bringing into line. Perhaps they'd been holding back more of their punters' money than Medcalfe had thought reasonable. Or maybe some of them had even contemplated going to work for a rival outfit. Whatever the problem, it was clearly part of Chivnor's job to see to that end of things. And although he'd been very careful not to mark the merchandise where it showed or mattered – i.e. their faces or breasts – a number of girls had been taken into A&E by Chivnor with injuries that ranged from fractured ribs to wrenched arms, elbows and shoulders.

As Steven stared down at the photograph of the tattooed skinhead, he felt his skin begin to crawl. Once he'd got the new unit up and running, he was going to look forward to meeting Mr Chivnor in a formal interview room, and then, arising from that, in a court of law. His days of running around without a police record needed to come to an end. Which, Steven acknowledged grimly, would probably require some sort of a sting operation, and those were always notoriously chancy. After the spectacular and very public failures of several other such operations in the past, he knew that the top brass wouldn't exactly be keen to authorize many more.

So he'd have to be careful. This new job held out the offer of big rewards indeed, but he wasn't unaware that with the big rewards came big risks. Just one mistake could see his career in tatters.

Steven shifted uncomfortably on his chair as he realized that, in future, he might have to send in undercover operatives, and mostly *female* undercover operatives, at that, to infiltrate Medcalfe's world. He could feel the thought of that responsibility weighing him down like a ton of bricks.

He sighed and shuffled the folders around, selecting one on Medcalfe which had come in from one of their financial experts. In the past, they'd tried to get Medcalfe on tax evasion or fraudulent accounting, but it hadn't panned out. He'd been far too wily for that. Steven couldn't help but think that that approach had always been too tame. In his experience, someone who liked to keep men like Chivnor close to him, had to have a personal taste for violence as well. In the past, his predecessors seemed to have assumed that Medcalfe liked to keep his hands clean, but what if, in fact, he had a taste for brutality?

Steven smiled grimly. If that were the case, then who was to say that Chivnor, or someone like him, wouldn't be able to place Medcalfe himself at the very heart of some of the worst of their crimes? Maybe even place him at the scene of one of the several murders for which they were almost certainly responsible?

He sighed, realizing that he was fast getting ahead of himself. The likelihood of getting one of Medcalfe's thugs to grass on him had to be infinitesimal. He'd ask Hillary what she thought about it later on tonight. He'd long since come to value her insight and experience with all manner of villains, and didn't doubt that any success he might make of the new job would be down largely to her help and input behind the scenes. Nor was he the sort of man who was afraid of taking good advice when he was given it.

But he also knew that the buck stopped with him.

He felt a familiar feeling of pleasure wash over him as he contemplated an evening together with Hillary. He'd cook something – salmon perhaps, and bring a bottle and a romantic DVD for them to watch. Then he wondered if, tonight, maybe she'd finally have something more personal to tell him than how to set about clearing out the scum from their city.

He leaned back in his chair and gently twisted it around, staring up at the narrow, high window that just about reached ground level and gave him a view of people's passing feet as they accessed the car park. Then he thought of his new office overlooking Christ Church and felt guilty that he was leaving here, and she wasn't. Was that part of the problem? Was that why she hadn't given him an answer yet?

He turned back restlessly to the Medcalfe dossier.

The next witness on Wendy's list was out, and the third was a rather deaf old man who thought that they were from the council. Hillary indicated to Jake that they should call it a day for now, and they began to trudge back to his car.

It was as they passed Sylvie's old house, that the door of the next house down opened, and a curious woman moved out onto her doorstep and watched them approach with the clear intention of hailing them.

Hillary slowed down and paused at the end of the garden gate.

'You the police?' the woman called boldly. She lifted a cigarette to her mouth as she spoke, and squinted at them through the smoke. She had the stick-thin, emaciated look of a dedicated smoker, to whom food meant very little. Her thinning hair was dyed an uncompromising red, and she regarded them with thoughtful blue eyes that seemed to miss very little.

Hillary estimated that she was probably in her late sixties, maybe early seventies, but there was nothing of Phyllis Drew's little-old-lady about her.

'Yes,' Hillary acknowledged simply.

'Thought so. Well, come on in then. I'm Freddie de la Mare.'

She showed them into a cottage similar in size to the Drews', but vastly different in every other respect. New double-glazing and doors, along with a modern oil central heating system kept the whole of the interior pleasantly but not overwhelmingly warm.

The front room to which she showed them had a thick carpet and an obviously well-used but comfortable leather settee with matching armchair combo, and a wooden coffee table in the centre of the grouping. As Hillary approached and took one of the chairs offered, she saw that the coffee table had a glass top over a poster of a pastoral scene by Constable. It was in odd contrast to the vibrant and far more modern-looking landscape paintings on the walls, by an artist Hillary didn't know.

Freddie de la Mare seated herself on what was obviously her favourite spot on the settee, having as it did the best view of the flat-screen TV in one corner, and stretched out her long legs under the coffee table. She was wearing a pair of stretch leggings in a vibrant shade of blue, and had a long knitted jumper that reached far below her hips, in horizontal stripes of rainbow hue.

Her face, however, was all but colourless, making the dark cherry red of her lipstick stand out in odd contrast.

'I saw that young girl who was around the other day. She said someone would be coming around to interview us about Sylvie. So when I saw you go into old Phil's place, I knew it must be you. Not that you'll have got much out of Phil and Charlie,' Freddie said with a wry laugh, and promptly lit up another fag from the dog-end of her old one.

Hillary resigned herself to an interview in the fug. She could hardly ask the woman to stub out the cigarette in her own home, and in November, with a cold wind blowing outside, she could hardly ask if she could open a window. Knowing her luck, Hillary thought grimly, she'd probably catch pneumonia and sue the police service.

Quickly summing up the individual in front of her, Hillary doubted that any offer of tea or coffee would be forthcoming, not so much out of miserliness, or even out of defiance or absent-mindedness either, unless she missed her guess. No, Freddie de la Mare simply looked to her like a woman who clearly had other matters on her mind.

'So, why are you opening Sylvie's case now, after all this time, if you don't mind my asking?' Freddie got straight down to the point. 'Has something new come up? There's been nothing about it in the papers.' As she spoke, she puffed industriously, and the half-full ashtray that was residing on the edge of the table quickly became the recipient of yet another long, delicate tail of ash.

'I'm afraid I'm not at liberty to discuss that, Mrs de la Mare.'

'It's Ms, actually, but for pity's sake, just call me Freddie.'

'Freddie then,' she agreed peaceably. 'Any relation to the poet by the way?' Hillary couldn't help but ask. She hadn't taken an English degree for nothing. Opposite her, she could see Jake cast her a quick, uncomprehending look. She sighed heavily. It would no doubt do him good to read something other than computer manuals once in a while, she thought, a shade sourly.

'Not that I'm aware of,' Freddie drawled. 'My side of the family were more artistically bent,' she admitted, and cast a hand over the vibrant landscapes. 'I don't sign my works,' she added, with a vague sort of embarrassment that came with acknowledging that the paintings were hers.

Hillary took another look at the artwork. 'They're all yours? You must be proud of them. I know I would be,' Hillary said truthfully.

Freddie gave a shrug and puffed on her fag. 'Oh they sell well enough to the tourists,' she said gruffly. 'There's a gallery in Oxford which takes my work, and one in Woodstock, and Stratford. These are all oils – I hang them on the walls till they're dry. This lot will be dispatched next month, and then the canvases I'm working on now take their place.'

'It must be nice to earn a living from your own creativity,' Hillary said. 'Did Sylvia buy any of your work?'

Freddie gave a dry, hacking laugh, that promptly turned into a dry, hacking cough. When she'd finished, she turned bright blue eyes on Hillary. 'No fear. Sylvie thought them far too high-priced. She preferred flower prints anyway,' she added, with a dismissive shrug that silently acknowledged that there was no accounting for taste. She stubbed out the poor remains of her dog end, and contemplated the packet of cigarettes and lighter next to the ashtray.

Before she could reach for another one, Hillary tried to distract her. 'Did you see Sylvia the day she died?'

'No. That would have been the day before,' the artist corrected. 'She was going out in her car somewhere, and I was in the garden. I waved. Never saw her alive again after that.' Although Freddie stated the words flatly, and there was certainly no sentiment detectable in her expression, Hillary was sure that she could detect a true sense of sadness behind the matter-of-fact delivery.

'You'd known her long?' she asked gently.

'Been neighbours for more than forty years,' Freddie said abruptly and reached for and lit another cigarette.

'It must have come as a great shock to you when you heard that she'd been murdered.'

'Hell yes.'

'She didn't seem the kind of woman to be murdered, did she?' Hillary said, in a slightly whimsical way. Jake shot her a keen-eyed glance: he'd worked with her long enough now to know that she never did anything – but anything – by accident. Quickly he turned towards the chain-smoking artist and his eyes narrowed thoughtfully.

He couldn't see it himself, but something about the woman had obviously triggered on Hillary Greene's radar. What the hell was it? Freddie de la Mare had a sort of gruff and abrupt manner of speaking, but he didn't believe it was that.

'No. When you put it like that, she wasn't, was she?' Freddie concurred, looking at Hillary with suddenly near-hostile eyes. 'Sylvie was the sort to give you the shirt off her back if she thought you genuinely needed it more than she did.'

'A lot of people seemed to think, at first, that a gang of robbers was responsible,' Hillary said casually.

'DI Jarvis didn't arrest anyone,' Freddie said uncompromisingly. 'And I can't believe that nobody would have seen them around and noticed them if they'd been here that day.'

'Vanessa Gibson seemed to like that idea.'

Freddie puffed on her cigarette, eyeing Hillary through the haze of smoke like a cautious cat that was contemplating a creature that it hadn't encountered before. A snake perhaps, or a stoat.

Was it predator or was it prey?

'Vanessa's shit-scared that Randy did it, that's why she's so keen to put the blame elsewhere,' Freddie surprised them both by stating flatly. 'I could tell that the first time I met her after we'd all heard the news about Sylvie.' Freddie grunted another dry, hacking laugh, and tipped her ash into the already burdened ashtray. 'I could have told her that she was worrying about nothing, but it wouldn't have made any difference. Women like her were born to worry. Besides, she'd never gone out of her way to be friendly to me, so why should I bother?' The artist shrugged one bony shoulder indifferently under the vast, multi-coloured sweater that hung over her like a tent.

Hillary nodded. Yes, she couldn't see Vanessa Gibson and Freddie de la Mare ever being friends. They were too catastrophically different.

'So you don't think Randy was to blame?' Hillary said, allowing herself to sound as curious as she felt. The artist, as she'd just ably demonstrated, observed much, and had the brains to form her own interpretations of what she saw, and if she didn't think Gibson was guilty, Hillary wanted to know why.

'Not the type,' Freddie said flatly. 'For all that Sylvie tried to make his life miserable, most of it was water off a duck's back to him. The only thing Randy really cares about is keeping the farm going, and trying to please that wife of his. He just about manages the first, but he'll never manage the second. So he had no real time for Sylvie's accusations or bile, since it didn't affect either of those two goals.'

'But she did make trouble for him.' Hillary wouldn't let it go that easily.

'Oh yes. She was a little bit unhinged on the subject of her Joe, I have to admit,' Freddie agreed glumly. 'She loved him you see, and his loss really devastated her.'

'So she needed someone to blame,' Hillary put in.

'Exactly.'

'But if she touched a nerve,' said Hillary, deliberately playing devil's advocate, 'he might have snapped. Someone said that she had encouraged ramblers to cross Gibson's land, for example. Now if that affected his crops, and thus the future of his farm—'

'It didn't,' the artist interrupted quickly and emphatically. 'There's always been a right of way there; it skirts one of his wheat fields. The ramblers always kept to the hedges, and didn't do any damage, and Randy knew it,' Freddie said, contemplating the glowing tip of her cigarette thoughtfully. 'Besides, like I told you, Randy's not the type to pick up a poker and bash an old lady's head in. If he was going to do something like commit murder, it would have to be at some remove. Mow her down in his tractor one dark night, maybe. Or push a lighted, petrol-soaked rag through the letterbox and scarper. But face to face? No way. If he *had* visited her that day, Sylvie would have made mincemeat out of him and sent him on his way with a proper flea in his ear. Believe me, he's not the type for personal confrontations.'

She puffed on the fag, her yellow, nicotine-stained fingers competing for colour with a magenta and emerald-green paint stain on her right hand.

'Have we disturbed your painting?' Hillary asked gently.

'What? No. Well, yes, but no.' Freddie contemplated her stained hand with a slightly bemused look. 'It was time I took a break, I mean. I paint upstairs, in one of the bedrooms. I was thinking of coming down for a coffee anyway.'

Hillary nodded, thinking that the usually straight-talking older woman was protesting just a little too much.

So, she'd been looking out of her studio window and had seen them, Hillary mused. And had needed to sound us out so badly, that she'd abandoned her latest canvas without a qualm.

Interesting. Very. In fact, Freda de la Mare was interesting Hillary a great deal.

'So if it wasn't robbers, and it wasn't Randy, who was it?' she mused, almost teasingly. 'DI Jarvis, the original investigator was very much in favour of the grandson, Robbie Grant. We've just visited him in fact – he's currently doing time for violent robbery,' Hillary said. 'So perhaps she was right. All we need now is to place him in the vicinity at the time. He inherited Sylvia's estate, so we have motive. Who knows, we might be ready to make an arrest before the end of the week.'

Freddie nodded, took a long haul on the fag, and once again slowly blew out a stream of smoke whilst watching the glowing amber end of her cigarette.

'He was a wrong 'un, right enough,' she agreed gruffly. 'Not that Sylvie would have it, mind.' She smiled grimly, showing, for the first time, the full extent of her own misshapen and yellow-stained teeth. 'For a bright woman in every other way, she had a blind spot where he was concerned. But it won't do, you know,'

Freddie said, shaking her dyed red head sadly.

Hillary, who had anticipated some such rejoinder, went very still. 'Oh? Why not? The young man didn't strike me as having anything even remotely approaching a conscience. And for all his protestations of loving his old nan, his own creature comforts were clearly far more important to him. I could see him killing the old lady for his inheritance very easily.'

'Oh yes, I dare say all that's true,' Freddie agreed, still contemplating the tip of her cigarette as if it could give the Sphinx a run for its money in providing enigmatic interest. 'He's a total little shite, and no mistake. But he wasn't here that day – the day Sylvie died. I knew the sound of his car, see. It had something wrong with the exhaust, which gave it a distinctive, throaty sort of roar. So I always knew when young Master Grant had come calling on his granny to touch her up for some cash. And I didn't hear or see his car that day.'

'Oh, I don't think that's too much of a problem,' Hillary said casually, wondering just how much out on a limb the woman was willing to go. 'He could have borrowed a mate's car, for instance.'

Freddie de la Mare slowly raised her fag to her lips and looked across at Hillary. 'But I didn't see him. And since I was upstairs painting that day, I would have noticed him.'

'But according to DI Jarvis's notes, you didn't see anyone entering Sylvie's house that day. And yet, evidently, *someone* did.'

Freddie shrugged, unwilling to be phased by the clever little riposte. 'Unless they came in the back way,' she countered instead with superb elan. 'And that little scrote had no reason to. It would involve walking all of twenty yards more. He was too lazy to do that when he could just park outside the gate.'

'Unless he came prepared to kill her,' Hillary argued reasonably. 'Then he wouldn't want to be seen.'

'Rumour has it that Sylvie was killed by her own poker.' Freddie tossed the ball neatly back into her court. 'That doesn't

135

smack of pre-meditation somehow, does it?'

Hillary smiled gently. 'Perhaps not. A member of the family then?' she mused.

'What? One of her girls?' Freddie scoffed. 'No way. Sylvie's girls all loved her to bits. And why not? She was the salt of the earth. She loved those kids, and looked after them, and gave them the best damned start in life that any kid could possibly want or reasonably ask for. And they all loved her back, in their own unique way, believe me.'

Hillary nodded, abruptly changing tactics. 'Well, thank you, Miss— Sorry, Freddie. You've been very helpful, and we may have to come back and speak to you again soon, but for now, I think that'll be all.'

She got up, her abrupt departure catching Jake as much by surprise as their witness, and pausing on the way to the door, Hillary stopped before one of the oils hanging on the wall. It depicted a cold, wintry scene, with snow-capped bull rushes lining a frozen-rimmed pond. A pair of grey cygnets paddled about in the middle, one stretching out its neck and wings prior to take off. A lemon-coloured sun cast a wintry light over the bare, skeletal trees. It was distinctive and competent, whilst at the same time dripping with a near natural-Gothic atmosphere.

It made her shiver appreciatively.

'Which gallery in Oxford did you say sold your canvases?'

Freddie named a well-respected establishment in St Giles. Hillary nodded thoughtfully. She would look out for them. If they didn't blow the budget totally, she might treat Steven to one. It was his birthday soon, and she knew he'd appreciate Freddie's stark view on the natural world.

'Sorry about the smoke,' Freddie said, noticing, as she opened the door to the hall that a vapour trail of grey miasma was being sucked out. 'I've been on the cancer sticks for so long that I just don't notice it anymore.'

'That's quite all right,' Hillary said, nevertheless glad to know that she'd soon be stepping out into the bracing, clean air. 'Your home, your rules.'

Freddie shot her a quick, uncertain look, then gave a wry smile and a brief nod. Although exactly just what it was she was acknowledging, perhaps neither woman would have been able to say.

Outside, Jake took an ostentatious lungful of cold November air and pulled his coat closer around him. Hillary walked down the lane towards his E-Type, her mind feeling far more lively than it had when she'd left the Drews' place.

'She's a character, isn't she?' Jake said cautiously, once they were seated inside the Jag, and out of the cold wind.

'Oh yes. She's that all right,' Hillary agreed amiably.

'I thought … once or twice, guv,' he began tentatively, 'that you had your gimlet little eye cast her way?'

'Oh yes.'

Jake grinned. 'I think the lady noticed.'

'Of course she did. She doesn't miss much, our Ms de la Mare.'

Jake waited. He knew there was more to come, and he was right. 'You notice she didn't offer us tea or coffee?' Hillary offered as an opening gambit.

Jake nodded solemnly. 'Very suspicious behaviour, guv.'

Hillary's lips twitched. 'In a way it was. It meant that she had a lot more on her mind than merely observing the rules of hospitality. And when you come across a witness with a lot on their mind, you pay attention.'

'Noted.'

'And did you notice her hands?' Hillary asked.

'Nicotine stained? Of course – they were practically glowing yellow, the amount of fags that she goes through…. You're not interested in that. What else?'

'They were paint stained. With recent paint,' Hillary said.

'Yeah? So what, guv? She told us she'd just been painting upstairs.'

'What did you think of her pictures?' she asked him, turning a little in the bucket seat to better look at him.

Jake, a little surprised by the seeming change of topic, suddenly frowned warily, as if scenting a trap. 'Well, I'm no art expert guv but you don't have to be, to be able to tell quality when you see it, do you? Although they're not my thing, and I wouldn't hang 'em in my house, I could tell they had merit. You liked them, didn't you?'

'Yes. And you're right – they're the real deal. I think, when you start researching our Ms de la Mare you're going to find she's an artist of some renown.'

Jake nodded, already resigned to hours of research. 'So what's the significance of the paint on her fingers, guv?' he asked patiently.

'She was painting, saw us, and left her work to come down and waylay us,' Hillary said. 'Why? Most artists are so wrapped up in their work that they wouldn't hear a fire alarm going off. And I suspect that Freddie de la Mare, if she did hear a fire alarm go off, would rescue her artwork long before she'd even give her own safety a passing thought. But for some reason, she had to talk to us instead. Why?'

Jake nodded slowly. 'OK. I can see that might be a little out of character, but perhaps she just wanted to get it over and done with.' He tested the theory carefully. 'She did seem genuinely fond of Sylvia Perkins, after all. Maybe the thought of having it all raked up again gave a her a fit of the blues, and she just wanted it finished. Psychologically, that hangs together, right?'

Hillary smiled. 'Perhaps. So she leaves her work, beckons us in, doesn't offer us refreshments, and proceeds to tell us … what exactly? What was it that she was so keen to tell us, do you think?'

Jake, catching something in Hillary's voice, suddenly had the frustrating feeling that he was missing something obvious. That he was, in fact, being exceedingly dim about it. But what was it that Hillary had deduced that he hadn't?

'I dunno, guv,' he was finally forced to admit.

Hillary sighed gently. 'No need to beat yourself up about it, Jake. I wouldn't have spotted it either if I hadn't been interviewing witnesses for over twenty years. Tell me, when I suggested that it was robbers who killed Sylvie, what was her response?'

'She thought it was a daft idea, and, as it turns out, she was right, wasn't she? That gang that hit the other village around the same time were nowhere near here the day the old lady was murdered.'

'Not the point, Jake,' Hillary said helpfully. 'When I moved on to Randy Gibson, another prime contender, what did she do?'

'She didn't think he had it in him,' Jake said, still clearly puzzled. 'And she sort of struck me as someone who'd be a good judge of character,' he added, a shade defiantly, but willing to back his own judgement.

Hillary smiled. 'No need to be so defensive. As it happens, I agree with you. I think she's probably got her neighbours well sussed out too – which was why I was so keen to hear what she thought about Gibson. But again, that's not the point. What happened when I suggesed it might be one of Sylvie's daughters? As we know, statistically your nearest and dearest are the most likely ones to do you in. Freddie's intelligent enough to know that.'

'But she didn't think so in this case,' Jake pointed out quickly. 'And she watched all three of Sylvia's daughters grow up, so would be in a good position to know. Why do you think one of Sylvia's own daughters did it?'

Hillary sighed. 'I don't as it happens. Not that I'd let that keep me from having an open mind on the subject. Once again, you've missed the point.' Her lips twisted into an amused smile at Jake's obvious and growing anger.

'What did she say when I put the best suspect of all in the frame, Robbie Grant?' she persisted.

'Oh, she really didn't like him, guv,' Jake said at once. And then blinked. 'But she was very clear that he hadn't been around that day, wasn't she? That thing about his exhaust? Being so positive that she would have seen him?'

Hillary nodded. 'Now you're getting it.'

'But, guv, if the vicious little bastard really hadn't been there, then that's that, isn't it? I don't think Freddie de la Mare is the type to lie. Even if she was, why would she lie to save the neck of someone like Robbie Grant? If she'd seen him at Sylvie's that day, why not just say so?'

'Oh, I'm sure she would have.'

Jake looked at her helplessly. 'I still don't get it, guv.'

'No. There's only one reason why Freddie de la Mare abandoned her painting and waylaid us the way she did. What was the first thing she wanted to know? What were more or less the first words out of her mouth, once we'd settled down?' Jake frowned, she carried on. 'She wanted to know why we'd opened the case again. She wanted to know if we had any new evidence,' she reminded him.

'That's right, she did. And you told her you couldn't comment on it,' Jake nodded. 'Guv, do you think *she* did it?' he asked, a shade wide-eyed now.

'I've told you before,' Hillary said in exasperation. 'I don't have a crystal ball. But what I do have is the ability to listen. And what I just listened to was a woman who, in direct contrast to Vanessa Gibson who tried to tell me that anyone and everyone could have done it, went to great pains to tell me the exact opposite. That *nobody* I cared to suggest could have done it.'

Jake took in a long, slow breath. 'You're right! I see it now. She did.' Then he let out his breath in a slow whistle and slowly frowned. 'But I still don't get it, guv,' he moaned. He hunched over the steering wheel and frowned out at the glowering

November sky. 'Because, unlike Vanessa Gibson, she hasn't got a husband who might be in the frame for it, or, like Mary Rose, a son who's a prime suspect. So why would she do that?'

Hillary grinned and gently punched him on the top of his arm. 'Congratulations, Jake. *Now* you've got the point.'

CHAPTER NINE

A T HQ, HILLARY told Jake to type up the de la Mare interview for the murder book, then set about learning all he could about the artist as his next priority. Then she caught up on some of her own paperwork, and touched base with Jimmy, who promptly told her about Jake Barnes's curious and inexplicable short stop at a certain pub.

'The thing is, guv, I can't figure out what he was doing there,' Jimmy said in conclusion. 'It's hardly his local, and I can't see why an up-and-comer like our Boy Wonder would bother with a place so close to the Leys. It's not as if there was anything special on that night – no live music or anything to attract him there.'

'He might just have arranged to meet an old friend,' Hillary pointed out thoughtfully. 'It might have been a convenient halfway place to meet. You couldn't see if he met up with anyone, I suppose?'

'No, guv, I didn't dare go inside. And it's the sort of place that would probably have lookouts for anyone peering in through the windows. But if he was meeting someone, it was a very short meeting, like I said. He didn't stay long.'

'Not likely to be social thing then.'

'No. And he didn't take that flash Jag of his with him either, but a nearly-as-flash Porsche instead.'

Hillary frowned. She was not sure she liked the sound of that.

'Is the Porsche registered to him?' she asked, sharply, and it was a measure of her respect for the man, that it didn't even occur to her to ask if the old ex-sergeant had thought of checking.

'Yes, guv, all legal and above board,' Jimmy concurred. 'He's got five cars registered to him as a matter of fact.'

'OK. So whatever it was he was up to, he didn't actually care if anybody else took notice of his number plate and tracked him down that way then. In many ways, that's something of a relief. Perhaps he just didn't want to risk the Jag in that neighbourhood. I know I wouldn't,' she added, a shade enviously. 'If I owned a baby like that, I'd keep it wrapped up in cotton wool.'

Jimmy grinned. 'The Porsche wasn't exactly a junk heap, guv. If it had been lifted by some light-fingered tea-leaf it would have to have hurt.'

'The rich live in a different world from you and me Jimmy,' Hillary said drily. 'And I dare say it's insured up to the wazoo. Still, it is odd. Anything happened that tweaked your radar?'

'No. Nobody followed him out or showed any undue interest in him. I'd have taken a snapshot of them if they had. I've got one of those camera gizmo's on my mobile. And I didn't see anybody in particular that put the wind up me.'

Hillary nodded. 'OK. He drove straight home you say?'

'Yes, guv.'

Hillary shrugged. 'Well, keep at it. He's got to do something to tip his hand sooner or later. And it's beginning to look as if he's definitely got something specific in mind, doesn't it?'

'I reckon, guv,' Jimmy said shortly. Then his old eyes looked at her curiously. 'We gonna tell the new boss about this? What do you make of our Rollo then?'

Hillary sighed. 'Early days yet, but he seems OK. And no, I don't think we share our doubts about the Boy Wonder with him just yet. Jake is still the top brass's golden boy and we aren't exactly swimming in proof that there's anything to worry about yet, are we?'

Jimmy thought that the fact that Jake Barnes was helping himself to Hillary's computer and her access codes without her permission was more than enough, but wisely kept silent. Besides, like her, he was curious as to what the boy was up to. He didn't think it was anything seriously criminal, but he wasn't willing to bet anything on it either. And if it *did* turn out that he was doing something very naughty indeed, then, like Hillary, he'd much rather that they were the ones to catch him at it. At least that way the CRT would get some of the kudos, and maybe avoid the worst of any political fall out.

Yeah. Right.

Contemplating such unwarranted and rare optimism made the old man smile.

That night, Hillary sat in front of the small wood-burning stove in the front, V-shaped living room of her narrowboat listening to the sounds of Steven busily cooking in the small galley. Every now and then, the delicious smell of poaching salmon wafted her way.

She sipped a glass of white wine as, outside, the darkness that was often so complete on the canal, pressed against the *Mollern's* porthole windows.

When Steven came in with a tray of beautifully prepared fish, salad and new potatoes, she pulled out the small table that was affixed to the wall and helped him lay the cutlery.

He'd taken off his jacket and tie and was dressed in just his white shirt over dark blue trousers. His hair was slightly mussed, and there was just the faintest of shadows on his chin. He looked incredibly sexy.

'You are staying the night, aren't you?' she said softly, and, as he sat opposite her and shook out his napkin, he met her gleaming sherry-coloured eyes with a soft smile.

'I thought I might.'

Hillary nodded in satisfaction. He kept a spare suit and

all the usual accessories in her tiny wardrobe, but she didn't begrudge his belongings the space, which on a narrowboat, was always paramount.

'Hmm, this is good.' Although she could cook well enough to ensure that she didn't starve, she was not into food in the same way that he was. 'Can I taste dill?'

'Yes.'

'Herbs are beyond me. Too much hassle,' she said with a grin.

'I find cooking relaxing,' he said, tasting his freshly made mayonnaise. 'There's something about measuring and mixing and creating the dishes that allows me to relax, detox, and relieve some of the stress. And if this new job is going to pan out how I think it probably will, then I'm going to be of Masterchef standard before the year is out.'

'Oh?' She was, naturally, dying to know what his new job really entailed, and was secretly very glad that he was willing to share the load with her.

It saved her having to find out behind his back.

Thus encouraged, he told her everything that had been happening, and when he'd finished, listened quietly to her thoughts on it. 'And you're right. You might well have to run a few undercover operations. You ever done much of that type of thing before?' she finished.

'No.'

'Then ask for help,' she advised flatly. 'You're setting up your own team, they've given you a wide scope. Make sure you pick someone with experience in that area. It's not the sort of thing you can pick up as you go, not when other lives are at stake. Don't be afraid to delegate power, and don't be afraid of learning stuff from people with less rank. Do you want me to put out a few feelers for you, see who might be interested in joining your team? Sort out those who are actually good from those who just think they are?'

Steven leaned back in his chair, his stomach full, his mind

feeling more and more at ease with every passing moment. 'Would you?' He knew that Hillary had a vast network of old pals who owed her favours. 'That'd be a great relief. And speaking of which … I really think we should tell Rollo Sale about Jake Barnes.'

Hillary sighed. 'I know you do. And I understand why it sticks in your craw to keep him in the dark. But just give it a bit longer, yeah?' Thinking of what Jimmy had told her, she added softly, 'I think Jake might be about to show his hand.'

Steven looked down into his half-empty wineglass. 'It's just that I know, if I was coming into a new job, I wouldn't appreciate being kept out of the loop.'

Hillary nodded. 'Fair enough. But we've got a few weeks yet before you leave, you can always tell him then. And who knows, by then we might have something solid to go on. And don't forget, Rollo Sale knows as well as we do that the top brass were crowing all over the media when Jake Barnes joined the CRT. It was the biggest PR scoop for them for years, and he won't want to be the harbinger of bad news on his first day on the job so to speak. So we'd be doing him a favour if we can clear it up and keep it in house. Not to mention, getting it all sorted out while it's still officially your watch, and not his.'

'And if we can't?' he asked, a shade moodily.

'Then *you* can tell Donleavy his golden boy has feet of clay,' Hillary grinned at him.

'Gee, thanks a lot.'

'One of the privileges of rank,' Hillary pointed out sweetly. 'At which point, you smile sweetly and swan off to your swanky new office in St Aldates, and leave the rest of us to clean up the you-know-what.'

Steven forced a smile. 'Now *that* sounds good to me.' He finished the last of his wine and looked at her gently. 'So….'

Hillary quickly reached across and took the now empty glass from his hand. 'So,' she echoed, guessing what it was he wanted to talk about, and determined to steer him well clear of the subject. 'Since you're staying the night ... what say we make it an early one?'

Steven's dark brown eyes softened. 'It's barely eight o'clock,' he said, then blinked in surprise as, outside, there was a loud bang and a prolonged whistle, and through the dark windows, a fountain of green and red lit up the sky. 'I forgot, it's Bonfire Night.'

Hillary looked at the fading firework and laughed. 'How appropriate,' she said, getting up and reaching for his hands. Not that he needed much encouragement in getting to his feet and being led to her narrow little bedroom. 'Whenever a couple got together in the old films, didn't the camera always cut to fireworks, or waves crashing to shore, or some other old chestnut like that?' she asked archly.

'Hoorah for Hollywood,' Steven Crayle said wryly, his heart rate, as it always did whenever Hillary looked at him as she was now, sky-rocketing far above those of the fireworks outside.

The firework displays were also in full swing when Jake Barnes drove to a piece of waste ground in the Leys, where one local display set for that night had been advertised on the surrounding telephone poles for quite some time. He did not, however, get out of his Porsche right away, but drove slowly along the streets until he spotted Darren Chivnor's car pull up, the driver parking blatantly on a double yellow line.

He knew from his PI's report that this was Chivnor's local 'park' and that he could usually be counted on to take his younger siblings to such events. Jake wondered, cynically, if Chivnor was just grooming his little brothers to go into the family 'business' and if treats like this were all part of the bribery and buttering up process.

He made sure that Darren, and two younger lads who bore a striking family resemblance to him, were just climbing out of the car, before driving past, very slowly, and revving the engine ostentatiously.

He saw one of Chivnor's brothers, a lad of about thirteen or so, spot the Porsche and say something to the other lad with him, who looked to be about eleven. He pointed at the Porsche and probably said something both foul-mouthed and appreciative, because Jake saw Darren Chivnor start to look his way.

Even though it was a cold November night, Jake had the window wound down and had one elbow casually hanging out as he drove past. There was plenty of street lighting about and he saw Darren clock first the Porsche, then the driver.

He didn't exactly do a classic double take, but Jake was in no doubt that Chivnor had recognized him from the pub last night, and must immediately have started wondering on what the chances were of them coming across each other again so soon, which was fine by the multi-millionaire. In fact, Jake was relying on the thug to have just that cockroach-like sense of caution. It was bound to make him curious, and his own sense of self-survival would make it almost certain that he'd have to try and find out what Jake's game was.

Satisfied that he'd done enough, Jake drove on and found a legal parking spot a little further down into the estate and quickly jogged back down toward the fireworks display. He was in a residential area, and the streets were full of families and excited kids dancing about and waving sparklers around and, in spite of their parents' dire warnings about the consequences, letting off bangers at the feet of their squealing, dancing friends.

All the mayhem was one of the many reasons why he didn't spot his old colleague and pal, Jimmy Jessop, walking a hundred yards or so behind him. Of course, Jimmy was dressed in a long raincoat and had an old woollen bobble-hat pulled low down over his ears, so that he looked like any other anonymous old-age pensioner simply out to enjoy the entertainment.

When Jake fetched up on the bit of waste ground, the display was just starting with an impressive line of Catherine wheels that were busy spiralling out lines of blue, white, red and green circles. He stood and watched them, making no effort to look for or approach Darren Chivnor and his younger brothers. If all went as he hoped it would, he would have no need.

Instead, he stood on the edge of the crowd, and watched. Some Roman candles came next. Jimmy Jessop, stationing himself behind and just to the right of Jake, glanced around casually.

They were not a quarter of a mile from the pub he'd visited yesterday, and Jimmy doubted very much that the boy wonder was here for the fireworks. After all, when you're worth millions you could afford tickets to the vast displays that the city usually put on. Either that, or he could attend the private parties put on by his well-heeled friends. Hell, if you were Jake Barnes, Jimmy thought with a silent grunt of laughter, you could pay for your own display in your own back garden that would far outstrip this effort, and not have to resort to anything more than raiding the petty cash box.

So when, after about ten minutes, a very likely looking lad indeed began to edge towards Jake, Jimmy began taking snaps of the pretty fireworks with his camera phone. And if said camera just happened to point Jake's way, none of the excited kids or happy families around him, munching on burgers and baked potatoes, seemed to notice.

Jake himself said nothing as he felt a man's presence by his side. He didn't even look around as Darren Chivnor moved up to his elbow. Both men looked up as a rocket whooshed into the sky, spitting out a fountainhead of lime green, blue and red sparks into the air above them.

'Nice Porsche,' Darren said.

'Thanks. I like it,' Jake responded. His heart was thumping, and his throat felt constricted, but he was pleased with the way he sounded. Casual. Confident. Unworried.

'Cost a packet, I expect.'

'It's a classic,' Jake agreed modestly. 'Not a bathtub Porsche, but then it's only my third car.'

'Third car? You've only ever had three cars?' Darren asked, clearly puzzled and caught out by the response.

Jake tensed. He didn't want to laugh, or put the thug's back up. Nothing, he assumed, could make you an enemy faster than making someone like Chivnor think that you were insulting their intelligence or talking down to them.

'No. I meant I keep a collection, and the Porsche is only my third-best car,' he explained, trying to make it sound as throw-away and easy going as possible. The last thing he needed was to sound as if was trying to start a pissing contest. He shrugged inside his sheepskin-lined, caramel-coloured coat and managed a self-mocking laugh. 'I'm a bit of a sports-car freak, I suppose.'

'Oh, got it. You only drive the Porsche when you're slumming it,' Chivnor said, a shade sullenly.

Jake, not sure how best to answer that, merely shrugged again and said nothing, on the basis that, when you found your-self in a hole, it was usually best to stop shovelling. For, just as Jake had worried he might have, the skinhead had clearly taken offence.

Darren shot a sideways glance at him, then unexpect-edly laughed. 'No worries, mate. My kid brothers were well impressed, third car or not.'

Jake smiled a shade warily, and watched the path of another rocket.

Chivnor lit a cigarette. 'Saw you in the pub yesterday.'

'Yes.'

'What you after then? You a journalist?'

'Hell no,' Jake said, genuinely surprised by the question. Apparently, the spontaneous surprise of his words seemed to reassure Medcalfe's lieutenant, because he grinned again and nodded his head in approval.

'Good. Because there ain't no story for the meee-deee-ah here,' Chivnor said flatly, making a sarcastic sing-song out of the word 'media'. 'They tend to end up very discouraged whenever some hot shot out to make a name for himself as a crime reporter starts snooping around. 'Sides, haven't they heard? The Leys has cleaned up its act, so we don't want no bad pub-leeec-eeety around here.'

'I know what you mean. I've been the victim of media attention myself from time to time,' Jake said, truthfully enough. 'Trust me, I'm no friend of reporters.'

'You ain't a player,' Chivnor said flatly, making it a statement rather than question. 'I'd know you if you were. And so would my boss.'

'No, I'm not a player,' Jake confirmed, 'nor do I have any ambitions to be,' he added, careful to keep his voice amiable.

'You out to score? If so, you've got the wrong bloke,' Chivnor said, sounding rather amused now. 'Been a long time since anybody mistook me for a dealer. Not that I can't point you in the right direction like—'

'Please, do me a favour,' Jake interrupted. 'Do I look like a mug?'

Chivnor shrugged. 'OK. You ain't a journo, you don't want to score, and you ain't looking to make trouble. I admit it, you got me curious. So who are you then?'

'I'm a very rich man,' Jake said simply. 'My name's Jake Barnes. Look me up. I expect I'm on Google.'

'Who isn't nowadays?' Chivnor said, massively unimpressed. 'I expect my old mum's mongrel Mutley, is on there. What do you want?'

'I want to make you rich too.'

Chivnor laughed. 'Do I look like a mug?'

'Nope,' Jake said flatly. 'And there's nothing stupid about becoming rich. I should know. I grew up on an estate just like this,' he said, nodding around him. 'Now I've got holiday homes in the Caribbean, Gstaad and Sydney. I drive what I like, wear silk in bed if I fancy it, and enjoy a certain class of lady. Like I said, look me up. And if I want to spread a goodly amount of money your way, you'd have to be a mug not to at least listen to what I have to say. Right?'

Chivnor watched another rocket light up the sky, and for the first time, Jake dared to turn and look at him.

From his vantage point, Jimmy Jessop took a quick photograph of the two men. He had no idea who the skinhead was, but if he wasn't in the police data base somewhere, then he'd eat his bobble-hat.

Bobble and all.

'Maybe,' Chivnor said flatly, and then just turned and walked away, calling to his two kids brothers to join him at the burger stand as he did so.

It was only then that Jake realized that his knees felt like jelly and his chest was hurting, because he'd forgotten to breathe out. He let out his breath in an explosive whoosh, and left before the fireworks display had finished.

Jimmy Jessop, however, waited until the very end, and then followed, at a carefully calculated distance, the skinhead and the two younger kids with him. He jotted down the licence plate number of the car that they got into, then slowly walked back to his own vehicle.

It wouldn't take him long to upload the photographs onto his computer. He'd made sure he knew how to engage the night-time gizmo on his camera so he was reasonably confident that they'd give him a clear enough image.

But he had a bad feeling about this. Something about the tattooed skinhead gave Jimmy a bad case of the shivers. Whatever it was Jake was up to, he was already sure that the kid was in way over his head.

He only hoped that between them, he and Hillary Greene would be able to make sure that the boy didn't actually drown.

*

The next morning Jimmy got in early and was already working through his list of possible muggers-turned-home-invaders when Hillary strolled past the open door.

'Guv,' he called her into the doorway, then solemnly handed her over the photographs and gave her a run down on what he'd been doing last night.

'I expect to have a positive ID on our friend there sometime today guv,' he finished. 'Maybe tomorrow, if the computer boys are backlogged.'

'OK,' Hillary said, eyeing the tattooed skinhead in the photographs with a sigh. 'It's not looking good for our Jake, is it?' she added morosely. 'You sure you didn't see him score?'

'No, guv,' Jimmy said firmly. 'Nothing was exchanged between them except for a few words. Besides, I think we'd have spotted it by now if our boy was a user, don't you?'

Hillary nodded. She didn't think Jake had a habit, but he might still be using. Or just starting out. But she hoped not. Even more, she hoped he wasn't setting up shop as a dealer himself. But then, why would he? He sure as hell didn't need the money.

'OK, let me know the moment you've ID'd our charmer here,' she said.

Jimmy coughed a warning, and Hillary slipped the photographs discreetly back into the brown paper folder and held it down by her side before turning casually and smiling at Wendy, who had been hiking energetically down the corridor towards them and now appeared just behind her. If she'd noticed Hillary's actions, she gave no sign, and Hillary moved to one side to let her pass.

'Jake pulled in just behind me in the car-park, guv,' Wendy greeted her cheerfully. 'So, first come, first served, right? If you've got any plum assignments in mind that is?'

Hillary agreed cheerfully that that sounded about right to

her. 'So Jake can stay in the office and give Jimmy a hand when he's finished doing his own assignments, and we get to visit Caulcott again,' she said, laughing as Wendy groaned and theatrically rolled her extravagantly black-lined eyes.

'I'm not sure I actually got the good end of the bargain there,' she moaned, but with a happy smile. Today she was wearing an old black-lace blouse, with an intricate cameo tight around her throat, and a long black skirt, with black granny boots. Her face was ghostly pale, contrasting with her panda-like black eyes and cherry-red lipstick.

'If you want to stay here instead of learning how to interview witnesses—' Hillary began, but Wendy was already shaking her head. 'Right then, follow me.'

As they passed Jake coming down the corridor, Wendy shot him a cheerful finger, and Jake mussed her orange-tipped spiky hair in passing. Just what the Goth thought about that was unprintable and still echoing along the corridor when they started to climb the stairs back into the meagre grey daylight.

Graham Teign and his wife lived at the end of the row of cottages where Sylvia, Freddie de la Mare, and the now deceased Maureen Coles had once lived, and were obviously a little excited and pleased to see Wendy again.

'Come on in, love,' Graham Teign said, not unsurprisingly perhaps, recognizing her at once as he answered the door, and stepping aside to let them pass. He was a tall, thin man with greying hair and large, knobbly hands that had perpetually dirty fingernails from all the gardening that he no doubt did. Even in November, his garden, front and back, was a riot of shrubs, artfully mixed, with attractive foliage and late-blooming Michaelmas daisies.

'Visitors, darling,' he called through to the front room, where a plump woman of similar age was busy knitting on a pair of outsized needles. A multi-coloured scarf lay gathering pace on her lap as she looked up, her eyes eagerly seeking out those of first Wendy and then Hillary.

'My wife, Gill,' the man of the house introduced her with obvious and touching pride.

Hillary showed them both her ID, not that they seemed all that interested in it, and Gill Teign nodded. 'Well, sit you down then. Gray, why don't you put the kettle on. Tea? Coffee?'

Hillary accepted coffee, Wendy opted for tea, and they both chose a chair each from the mismatched ones on offer in the eclectically furnished room. A small fire blazed away merrily in the grate, occasionally making a popping sound as the flames hit some resin in the wood.

'This is about poor Sylvie, of course,' Gill Teign said, nodding her head. She had an untidy mop of brown curls, heavily shot through with grey, and a slightly sagging face, as if she'd recently lost a lot of weight. 'I still can't get over that. You any nearer to finding out who did it?'

'We were hoping you could help us with that,' Hillary said, just as her husband came back with a laden tray. It didn't take long for everyone to sort themselves out and soon they were all sipping from mugs and the Teigns were talking about their old friend.

'Course, we knew all about that ding-dong about some Maurice Chevalier look-alike down at that old folks' club Sylvie used to go to,' Gill Teign said, somehow managing to keep on knitting whilst drinking her tea at the same time. Her needles clacked at lightning speed too, and Wendy found it fascinating that the woman didn't ever seem to have to look down to see what her hands were actually doing. 'Me and Gray had a laugh about that, didn't we?'

'Yerse,' her husband agreed, examining his dirty fingernails. 'Mind you, I don't think Sylvie thought it was that much of a laughing matter, Gilly.'

'Oh tush.' His wife tossed her head dismissively.

'Tush nothing,' her husband insisted. 'I got the feeling that Sylvie was serious about the fella, you know.'

Gill Teign sighed heavily. 'Well, you might be right at that,' she conceded eventually. 'She'd been a widow for some time. Perhaps she had hoped that something might come of it. She had to be lonely, don't you think, living all by herself?'

'What did the man in question think about that?' Hillary asked, deliberately stirring the pot a little. 'Was he as keen, do you think?'

'Oh, couldn't say. We never met him, did we, Gray?' Gill said at once.

'No, we didn't go to the club. Still don't. Reckon we're a long way off needing the services of the Forget-me-not Club just yet,' her husband said fervently.

Hillary nodded. It was interesting. Ideas as to how serious Sylvia had been about her love-rival were definitely mixed; some of her friends and neighbours sure that it was nothing more than a storm in a teacup whilst others, like the Teigns, thinking that it might genuinely have been important to Sylvia.

If it had been, she needed to know about it. She was going to have to talk to Ruby Broadstairs and the man in question soon and see if she couldn't sort out, once and for all, just how things had really been between them. A love triangle was a potentially explosive bit of geometry, no matter what the ages of the three sides.

After all, neither of the other two involved, according to DI Jarvis, had had an alibi for the time of Sylvia's death.

'What can you tell me about Freda?' Hillary asked casually, making Wendy look up from her notebook and give Hillary a curious look. She'd read Jake's report on the Freda de la Mare interview the moment that he'd finished it and he'd made it very clear that Hillary, for some reason, had found the talk more than interesting.

Now here was proof that she was definitely digging for dirt

on the artist. Wendy wished that she'd been the one sitting in on that interview, and hoped she didn't miss anything else that good.

'Freddie? Oh, she and Sylvie were great chums. Had been for donkey's years,' Gill said.

'Oh yerse, thick as thieves those two. Maureen as well. The three musketeers we called them,' Graham Teign said. And then laughed. 'Or the three must-get-beers, as Freddie renamed them when she heard about it.'

'Oh Gray! That sounds awful,' Gill said, but she was smiling. 'Well, Freddie likes a glass of wine, and she might get a bit merry in the Horse and Groom at Christmas time and so on, but she's hardly a heavy drinker.'

'Did Sylvie like to drink?' Hillary asked, slightly surprised. There had been no report in DI Jarvis's investigation that indicated anything like that.

'No, no, that was just Freddie's joke, I think,' Graham said. 'Being an artist, she sort of marches to her own tune, like. No, Sylvie liked the odd glass or two on special occasions, as do we all, but nothing more than that. The same for Maureen, although towards the end, I don't think she drank at all. You know, she started to go gaga.'

'It's called Alzheimer's, Gray,' his wife said reprovingly. 'Freddie was one of the first to notice it. Her memory started going. Then Sylvie, who lived right next door, started hearing odd things – like the vacuum going in the middle of the night. Apparently Maureen had woken up, saw that it was two-thirty or something, and thought it was in the afternoon instead of the middle of the night, and started doing the housework.' She sighed and shook her head. 'It was sad. But between them, Freddie and Sylvie took care of her. Saved her from having to go into a home until right to the very end. Or almost. Like I said, they were thick as thieves those three. Had been ever since they were all young women.'

'They'd all lived next door to each other for some time then,' Hillary said.

'Oh yes.'

'It was sad to see Maureen towards the end. Got really bad, she did,' Gill said regretfully. 'She started thinking burglars were watching her house. And then she accused Sylvie of killing poor old Sputnik.'

'Huh. Everyone knows that was down to Paul Quinlan. I always said that daft sod would do some real harm one day, and he did,' Graham Teign said complacently, draining his mug. 'More tea?'

'No, thank you,' Hillary said. 'Who's Paul Quinlan?'

'Him opposite.' Gill nodded vaguely across the road. 'Lives in the cottage facing Sylvie's old place. Keeps chickens,' she added, somewhat cryptically.

'And you think he was responsible for killing Maureen's cat?' Hillary said, trying to keep up.

'Oh yerse,' Graham answered for her. 'Keeps chicken, see.'

Wendy clearly didn't, but Hillary Greene suddenly saw the light. 'Oh. Got you. He laid poisoned bait to keep the foxes down?'

'Right. I told him and told him, you just can't do that. Other things eat it, see. Wild birds, and then they die. A neighbour's dog that gets out of the garden. Badgers. Nobody with two brain cells to rub together puts down poisoned bait. But would he be told?'

'Or in this particular case, a neighbour's cat,' Hillary said.

'Exactly.' Gill nodded, and added a bright red ball of wool to her needles. It contrasted and clashed nicely with the emerald green she had been using. 'It broke her heart, poor old soul. She really doted on her cats, see. And what with her not being herself … it really sent her loopy. Not even Freddie could console her.'

'Who do you think killed Sylvia?' Hillary threw the question out casually, but for once, the Teigns had little to say. Gill looked at her husband, who looked back at her, and then they both looked at Hillary.

'Sorry, we've got no idea, love,' Gill finally admitted sadly.

'But I hope you catch the sod,' her husband added emphatically. 'She was all right, was Sylvie.'

CHAPTER TEN

Paul Quinlan's chickens were audible from the moment they opened the garden gate and walked up towards the house. His was a more substantial building than the cottages opposite, being both detached, and taller, with dormer windows and an uncompromisingly solid appearance. It also sat in a larger plot, and around one side was clear evidence of a substantial vegetable patch. The contented clucking of the poultry came from the rear of the property, and Wendy could have sworn that she also heard a goat bleating just as Hillary rang the doorbell.

Paul Quinlan, so the Teigns had informed her, was a bachelor, although apparently 'not that way inclined' who worked in the banking industry during the week somewhere in High Wycombe, but liked to live the good life at the weekends. Country-dwellers born and bred probably found the thought hilarious.

'Makes his own cheese,' Graham Teign had informed them knowingly, as he showed them out. He might just as well have said that he knitted his own jumpers from dog hair and ate dandelions in his salad, from the way he shook his head.

But the cheese-making probably accounted for the sound of goats, Wendy thought now. Then she had the absurd mental picture of herself attempting to milk a billy goat and tried hard not to start giggling as the door opened, and a dapper little man with a neat moustache and goatee beard looked out at them. He couldn't have been over five feet tall, and had a patch of bright red on each cheek that told them he'd only very recently just come in out of the cold air.

'Yes?'

Hillary Greene explained who they were, and Paul Quinlan very carefully inspected both of their IDs before smiling and letting them in. He was dressed in very clean denim dunga-rees underneath a warm-looking black wool sweater, and was wearing what looked like army-issue boots.

'You'll have to come on through to the back if you don't mind. I was just seeing to the wine.'

Hillary assured him that they didn't mind at all, and followed him out through a well-appointed kitchen to an out-building, where he obviously made not only his own wine, but brewed his own beer as well.

'I've got the elderberry on the go at the moment,' he said, going over to a plastic vat and proceeding to stir it with a steam-cleaned wooden paddle. The aroma was heady and Hillary took a step back from the potent blast of alcohol that emanated from the dark, claret-coloured brew. She could only hope that some of the rawness of the alcohol came out during the fermentation period, otherwise one glass would knock you off your feet.

'This is about Syliva Perkins, I take it?' Paul Quinlan asked, as he stirred gently. He looked to be in his early fifties, and couldn't have weighed more than nine stone. Wendy thought that if he ever lost his job in the banking industry, he could always hire himself out as a garden gnome and, again, had to fight back a fit of the giggles.

'Yes. According to DI Jarvis, you weren't at home the day she was killed?' Hillary got straight to the point.

'No. I was at the bank. I didn't hear the shocking news until I drove home and saw all the police cars milling about in the road,' Paul said. 'It gave me quite a turn, I can tell you. I mean, you don't expect that sort of thing to happen in a little place like this do you?'

It was a lament Hillary heard too often to comment on.

'According to your neighbours, you regularly put out poisoned meat?' she said instead, and the banker stopped in mid-stir. He shot her a quick, penetrating look that slowly turned into a scowl.

'Yes, that's true. Since they banned fox hunting, I needed to do something to protect my hens. If you ask me, they should bring it back. But might I ask what on earth that has to do with anything?' he demanded, his scowl turning more and more belligerent.

Wendy, who'd been wondering the same thing, thought how sweet the little man looked when he was flushed with anger.

'I understand, around that time, that a cat in the neighbourhood died of poisoning.'

'Sylvia didn't keep a cat,' Paul Quinlan said defensively.

'No, but her good friend and neighbour did: Maureen Coles.'

'Oh. Right, the poor lady with dementia? Yes, I heard something about her cat dying. But I thought that it was natural causes,' Paul said implacably. 'It was old, I think.'

'So Sylvia didn't confront you about it then?' Hillary said, sounding surprised. 'Only I heard that Maureen thought her friend was to blame, and since it was common knowledge in the village that it was only *you* who were in the habit of laying down poisoned bait, I thought Sylvia might have tackled you about it.' Hillary eyed the banker with a steady gaze. 'And from what I've learned about Sylvia Perkins, Mr Quinlan, she wouldn't have shied away from making her feelings known and felt. She would have been quite capable of taking you to task for it, on her friend's behalf.'

Paul Quinlan flushed even more. 'Well, be that as it may, she certainly never said anything to me about it. And, what's more,' he continued, working up a proper head of steam now,

'I'd have given her a piece of my mind if she had tried to. I lay meat down on my own land, on my own property to protect my own domestic fowl. And if anyone has or had a problem with that – not that anyone ever has, I might say – then that would be their problem, and not mine,' he finished grimly. And had he not been stirring a vast pot of stewing elderberries with a paddle, he'd probably have crossed his arms across his chest and nodded his chin emphatically just to underline the point.

'I see,' Hillary said, then smiled sweetly. 'So Sylvia never talked to you about it?'

'No, she did not.'

'Well, in that case, thank you, Mr Quinlan. I think that's all for now.'

The banker huffed and puffed a bit, but then seemed to twig that it was now all over, and quickly showed them out before Hillary could change her mind.

Once outside, Wendy couldn't restrain herself any longer, and began to giggle helplessly. Hillary, walking beside her back to the Mini, let her.

'You really showed him, guv,' Wendy chortled at last, slumping behind the driving wheel and wiping the tears of laughter from her eyes.

Her mascara and eye-liner, Hillary noted vaguely, had to be the expensive, waterproof kind, or she'd have smeared it everywhere by now, and would look like a demented panda.

'He was so cute, I wanted to pick him up and take him home,' the Goth added. 'I'll bet he's worth a bob or two as well.'

'Fancy a sugar-daddy, do you?' Hillary asked archly.

Which only set the girl off into another fit of giggles.

'Come on, sober up,' Hillary said, smiling herself now. 'I'm going to interview the scarlet woman next, and you've got to write up your notes for the murder book. That should bring you back down to earth.'

Wendy sighed, and asked wistfully, 'The scarlet woman?'

'Sylvia's love rival,' Hillary said briskly. 'It's about time we heard what Ruby Broadstairs had to say for herself.'

'Oh right, guv. But can't I come?'

'It's Jake's turn,' Hillary heard herself say, and wondered why she was suddenly sounding like someone's mother. Good grief, she thought, just a shade hysterically, has it really come down to that? Was she nothing more than a glorified babysitter now?

'Where does she live?' Hillary asked briskly.

'She's in a care home now, guv. Witney.' Wendy named the small market town about twenty miles away, and turned the key in the ignition. With a last, wistful look at Paul Quinlan's house, she nosed the Mini out onto the muddy lane and drove back towards Kidlington.

Whilst Hillary and Wendy were on their way back to HQ, Jake Barnes was taking an early lunch, and driving to the local branch of his bank.

When he got there, he had to go through the usual checks and rigmarole in order to draw out £20,000 in cash. He'd thought about this long and hard, and in the end, had chosen this amount very carefully. In this day and age, it wasn't such a huge sum of money that it could actually turn anybody's head – and certainly not someone like Darren Chivnor. You could hardly retire on it, or buy a house with it.

On the other hand, it was nothing to be sniffed at either. It represented a new car, a modest caravan, a luxury holiday, or a really fancy piece of jewellery. It was, in effect, a nice little sweetener.

Presented in a sea of orange-coloured ten-pound notes and purple twenties, it looked impressive – way more impressive than mere words on a cheque, or computer printout. There was something about slightly smelly, in-your-hand currency that brought out the greed in almost everyone. Or so Jake hoped.

The cashier very helpfully put it into a padded brown

envelope for him and he drove straight back to his house in order to deposit it in his safe.

If all went well, once he'd handed it over to Chivnor, he'd never see it again, writing it off to expenses. Its express purpose was to sharpen Darren Chivnor's mind and get it firmly focused on what he was offering.

And as an opening gambit, he hoped it would do the trick.

Now the only thing he needed to do was to arrange for a way to hand it over without him getting a knife in his ribs for the trouble. At the same time, convincing Darren Chivnor that telling him what he wanted to know would be well worth the risk he'd undoubtedly be taking.

Probably much easier said than done, Jake acknowledged grimly and ruefully, as he drove back to work, swallowing hard around a throat gone suddenly dry.

But there was no turning back now.

If Jake Barnes was feeling less than comfortable as he went back to HQ, the man occupying his thoughts had no such worries.

Darren Chivnor, also in a manner of speaking at his place of work, was standing outside an-end-of-terrace house in Botley, watching as a grey people-carrier pulled up beside him. He nodded at the driver and glanced around once again to make extra sure that everything was all clear. It was. No one was paying them the slightest bit of attention.

A shaven-haired cockney, the driver stayed firmly behind the wheel, leaving it to Darren and the muscle-heavy man who'd been sitting beside him in the passenger seat, to offload the merchandise.

The girls were all in their mid-teens, Darren thought, running an experienced eye over them, and more or less fresh off the boat from the Baltics. One or two looked petrified enough to bolt, and these he kept a very keen eye on as he ushered the string of seven girls to the front door. Most of them looked merely curious and wary, and shied away from the big, silent man who'd travelled down with them. Darren knew him vaguely, and thought he probably worked as a bouncer in one of the seedier clubs where Dale had a half-share, up Leeds way. Not that many of the women found Darren's presence much more reassuring, but several of them smiled when the door was opened to reveal a slightly chubby, middle-aged woman dressed in faded jeans and an old red sweat-shirt, who welcomed them to their new home.

Darren knew they wouldn't be deceived by 'Ma's' maternal-like appearance for long though. It was her job to 'train' the girls for their proper jobs, and learning to be waitresses or cleaners had nothing to do with it.

Once they were safely handed over, Ma nodded at him with her usual flat-eyed stare, and Darren nodded back mutely. The bouncer climbed back into the van beside the cockney, and the van drove away, keeping carefully within the speed limit.

Dale didn't like it when his boys broke the law and brought the cops down on their backs, no matter how minor the mis-demeanour might be.

Darren walked a few streets away to where he'd parked his own motor and slipped inside. Dale liked his right-hand men to drive good, middle-of-the-range, and therefore anonymous, cars, and Darren's was no exception. He was careful never to park it anywhere near any of the knocking shops or chop shops, just in case some nosy neighbours were inclined to make notes of number plates and make anonymous phone calls to the cops.

Not that the area he was in now was populated by people likely to do that. It had been chosen too well. Most of the houses were let to students. This created ideal cover – who was going to notice more teenaged foreign girls amid a multitude of other teenaged students of mixed ethnicity? Perhaps far more impor-tantly, students came and went with monotonous regularity, and could usually be relied upon to be too interested in their own lives to pay much attention to those of their neighbours. And if most students could also be relied upon to regard the police with suspicion anyway, and therefore be less likely to get involved in anything than the usual average member of Joe Public, well, all the better.

As Darren turned the key in the ignition, he reached for his phone and texted the usual message to the usual pay-as-you-go phone to confirm that the consignment had been safely handled.

After shutting down that particular phone, he reached for yet another one, this one his own personal model, but before texting his girlfriend, he paused and stared blindly out of the windscreen ahead of him. His thoughts were not so much on arranging to meet up for a bit of noonday nookie with Lisa, but on Jake Barnes.

Last night, after dropping off his brothers back at his mum and dad's house, he'd driven back to his flat and promptly hit the Internet. Just as Jake Barnes had predicted, the dot-com millionaire-turned-property-dealer had been well represented.

Darren had to admit, he'd been well impressed. His new mystery friend had hit it big young, but, what's more, he'd had the good sense to get out before the bubble had burst. He'd seen the writing on the wall with the economic crash, and bought up real estate like it was going out of fashion, and consequently now owned property that would be worth it's weight in gold bricks now that house prices were on the up again. And with the dearth of letting properties, he must be raking in millions in rental alone.

Darren knew that his boss, Dale Medcalf, who fancied himself more as an entrepreneur than a criminal, would have been impressed with Barnes's c.v. as well.

Far less impressive, of course – not to mention, far more worrying – was the news that Jake Barnes had joined the Thames Valley Police Force, as a civilian consultant bringing his experience and expertise in order to help solve cold cases.

Dale would not have been impressed with that. And he certainly wouldn't like it, not one little bit, that the plod's flavour-of-the-month golden boy had been talking to him, Darren.

'What's the tosser playing at?' Darren snarled at the windscreen of his car, and when a woman pushing a baby stroller passed by and glanced inside at him, his scowl sent her scurrying on.

Darren leaned back in the comfortable leather seat of his mid-range saloon car and forced himself to take long, slow breaths. He couldn't, however, get out of his mind the image of the Porsche Jake Barnes had been driving last night.

The playboy had told him that he owned other sports cars too. A Ferrari for sure, Darren thought now enviously, a bright red one probably. And an Aston Martin maybe – a James Bond special. If he'd had Barnes's dough, Darren thought dreamily, he'd own an Aston Martin.

He sighed, then rubbed a hand across his bristling scalp. Just what was the tosser's game? Surely he was smart enough to know that he was playing with fire? If they were seen, if any one of Dale's other boys saw them together.... The skinhead broke out in a sudden sweat. He wouldn't even be able to tell the boss just what it was all about because he didn't know himself. And that was definitely not on.

The smart thing to do now was to drive to Dale's place and tell him everything that had happened. Admit that Jake Barnes was sniffing around for some reason, explain who he was, and ask him what he wanted Darren to do about it, but there were two problems with that. Darren hadn't worked for Dale Medcalfe for so long without learning something about how the bloke thought. Dale was a meticulously tidy thinker. Anything or anyone that remotely threatened either his money or his safety, was dealt with ruthlessly. Even if he did come clean about Barnes and offer to tidy up the problem for him, it might not be enough to save his own skin.

Dale might start thinking that there was more to it than there was. That maybe he was being played. That he, Darren, might have something cooking with Barnes. Maybe even that they were planning some sort of a coup together. The trouble with top dogs, Darren knew, was that they were always paranoid about other top dogs trying to take away what they had.

So going to Dale and having to tell him something he didn't like, was never a good idea. Especially when he didn't know what Barnes's game was.

Then there was a second thing to consider: Jake Barnes had said that he wanted to make him rich. Darren now knew that Barnes wasn't talking out of his arse. He had more than enough money to spare to keep such a promise. What kind of a fool would he be if he didn't at least find out what the man had in mind?

Darren shifted a little in the seat. Outside, it was the usual shitty grey November day. Damp, dreary, cold. Like most of the rest of the population, he wanted to be in the sun, where the sky was blue, and the sea – a warm, clear blue sea – was only a short walk away.

Since he'd risen high in Medcalfe's empire, he'd had the opportunity to take Lisa away with him on some prime holidays. Not just to Spain either, or naff places like that where every tosser could now afford to go. Last year they'd gone to St Lucia. Now *that* was the life all right – living on an island in the Caribbean. They'd loved it – both of them. The food, the way of life, the people. 'Course, he knew they had hurricanes and shit like that, but if you had the right amount of money, you had fancy architects build you stuff that was windproof, right?

Ever since he and Lisa had begun to get a taste of the good life, Darren hadn't been able to stop himself from dreaming about getting away from Oxford. It was why he'd begun to save every penny he could, why he'd set up the secret bank account, why he was careful to use every ounce of his muscle and cunning to cream off every last penny that he could. Not that he wasn't careful, of course. Dale would know exactly how many 'perks' he was helping himself to, and he was very careful not to overstep the mark.

At the rate he was going, he'd maybe have enough money to buy a small beach bar somewhere by the time he was forty, but he wanted more; so much more than that. And he wanted Lisa to have more, too. She was already talking about having kids. Hell, they'd been together nearly five years now. They'd met at school, and Lisa Soulsbury had been the prettiest girl there, long blonde hair and blue eyes. The lot.

When they'd left school, and he went to work for Dale, their school romance had cemented into something good and solid. A girl from the neighbourhood, she knew that Medcalfe represented their best shot at the good life, and he didn't want to let her down.

So far they were doing OK. They had the flat they shared in Osney, the respectable 'company' car, the holidays, the high quality booze and clothes, but they weren't doing *great*. They weren't about to be able to go and set themselves up in the sun, far away from Oxford, and the bloody English weather, and the prospect of being able to do just that before they were both too old to enjoy it, had been very low. Except now there was Jake Barnes, and his offer to make them rich.

Darren turned the ignition, but sat for a few minutes before driving away. He was no fool: nobody offered to make you rich for nothing. There were always going to be risks. He knew, far better than most, just what could happen to those who were stupid enough to underestimate or cross Dale Medcalfe.

But Darren wasn't about to underestimate him, was he? Or cross him, either, until or unless he knew for sure that the rewards would be worth it, and that the odds in the gamble of taking on Medcalfe were firmly stacked in his favour, and he couldn't make up his mind about that until he knew just what game Jake Barnes was playing.

From the moment he'd Googled the self-made multi-millionaire, there had been one burning question plaguing him. Namely, why would someone who'd made so much, so young, suddenly interrupt his playboy lifestyle to go and work for a pittance as a civilian consultant for the plod? Darren, who'd spent most of the previous night tossing and turning beside his lovely blonde Lisa, hadn't been able to come up with any definitive answer. He just knew that Jake Barnes must have done it for a reason. He had to have some sort of an angle. Clearly, he had something in mind, just as he'd made contact with him, Darren, for a reason.

The sooner he found out what it was, the sooner he'd know whether his dream of a new life for himself and Lisa was just a pipe dream, or whether it was actually within his grasp.

But he'd have to be careful. So bloody careful. One wrong move, and Medcalfe would do for them both, but somehow the thought that at least Jake Barnes would share the same fate – with a cement block tied to his ankles as he was tossed into the Thames – wasn't particularly comforting.

The care home in Witney where Ruby Broadstairs now lived, had been built less than ten years ago, and was a substantial, pleasant-looking building with red roofs and walls of yellowish brick. On the outskirts of Witney, David Cameron's own constituency no less, it had a small but pretty set of gardens, and was clean and pleasantly decorated throughout.

Just inside a set of automatic doors, they signed their names in a ledger to satisfy the fire regulations and buzzed the intercom to be let in.

A cheerful woman, rotund and red-cheeked, led them through a series of doors towards a residential area called Spindlewood, and there they were taken to a lounge, where a number of flowering pot plants livened up the atmosphere. An enormous flat screen television was on in one corner, but most of the residents were nodding off in their chairs. Only one old man seemed to be actually watching it. Double French doors let in a lot of light, and in the summer, would open out onto a pleasant garden, with benches for seating, and wide, paved paths for wheelchair access. Now, in November, the bird feeders were full of hungry blue tits and chaffinches, which one old lady seemed to find far more entertaining than the television.

Hillary was with her on that.

'This is Ruby,' the care worker said, leading them to the far corner, where upright lime-green chairs had raised legs, to allow old bones to more easily sit down and get up again.

'Ruby, visitors for you. Isn't that nice?' The care worker gently woke the old lady who'd been dozing, and Jake found himself surprised by a pair of beautiful dark-blue eyes that were suddenly turned on him. Ruby Broadstairs had obviously just recently visited the on-site hairdresser, for her white hair was a dandelion-head of newly washed and set white curls.

'Hello. You're not my grandson,' Ruby Broadstairs accused him.

Jake gently admitted that he wasn't. He sat down in the chair beside her, leaving Hillary to pull out a chair to face the old lady. She carefully showed her their ID cards and explained who they were and why they were there. After a moment, Ruby sighed but nodded, and smiled at the care worker. Whereupon their escort, satisfied that Ruby wasn't upset and seemed happy enough to talk to them, tactfully left them alone.

'I remember Sylvia,' Ruby said thoughtfully. 'Nice woman. We went to the same club. Oh, years ago now.'

'That's right,' Hillary encouraged gently. 'You and she were rather fond of the same man, or so I've been hearing. Bit of a looker, was he?' she smiled.

'Oh, Maurice. Maurice, yes. A very nice man. Dead now, they tell me.'

Hillary, who hadn't known that, looked at Jake, surprised. Jake frowned, then shrugged. The latest information showed him still alive and living in Thame with his daughter.

'Perhaps she's a bit confused, guv?' he murmured.

'I'm not deaf, young man,' Ruby said sharply. 'Nor, unlike some of my friends here, am I losing my mind. It's my legs that have gone,' she admitted with another sigh, 'which is why I'm in here. I couldn't manage any more, even in an assisted living place. But this is a nice home – I like the people. In the summer they have trips out to the garden centre, and things like that. A nice young man wheels me around.'

Ruby sighed, and glanced around at her fellow residents.

'I'm sorry, Mrs Broadstairs,' Jake apologized, feeling both embarrassed at having been caught talking about her as if she wasn't there, and uneasy and slightly absurd that they could actually suspect this lovely, feisty old lady of murder.

'That's all right, I'll forgive you,' Ruby said, reaching out to pat his knee. 'Thousands wouldn't, mind. Maurice died a couple of days ago. An old friend of mine, Rosie, comes visiting now and then, and she'd just heard the news.'

Hillary nodded. 'In that case then, we won't be able to interview him, will we? Unless we hold a séance, that is.'

Ruby laughed. 'I like you. You're much more fun than that other woman policeman who came to interview me. Oh dear, you can't be a female policeman, can you? Oh well, you know what I mean.'

'Yes I do. Her name was DI Jarvis,' Hillary smiled. 'So, what can you tell me about Sylvia? I understand that, on the day she … er … died, you were alone at home all day.'

'Yes. But I couldn't prove it, as DI Jarvis pointed out to me,' Ruby said, with some spirit. 'Thinking I'd kill the poor woman over Maurice. I mean, really. He was a lovely man, mind, I'm not saying he wasn't,' Ruby admitted with a defiantly flirtatious sigh of remembrance. 'And I'm not saying that he wasn't a bit of a charmer and a rogue. Funny how those two things often go together, isn't it?' she interposed wistfully. 'I mean, I thought he and I were coming to an understanding, so it was a bit of a shock when Sylvia and I got together, and we learned that she thought so too.'

Ruby paused, and then reached into the sleeve of her cardigan to pull out a tissue and gave a delicate lady-like cough into it. 'Sylvia was very angry with him. More so than with me, really. I suppose I forgave him more easily. My husband, dear man that he was, was something of a rogue too, on the sly. I had to turn a blind eye more than once. But I don't think Sylvia ever had to. Not to hear her talk, anyway. Her Joe was as faithful as a spaniel, apparently.'

Ruby's big baby-blue eyes suddenly twinkled. 'Mind you, with Sylvia as a wife, he probably wouldn't have dared to stray. Ah well.' She shrugged one painfully thin, bony shoulder. 'That's life. In the end, neither one of us got him. Maurice, I mean. He moved away from the village not long after that awful business with Sylvia. I think one of his daughters took the view that he should get well out of it. I think your DI Jarvis made his life pretty hot for a while back then.'

This time her blue eyes were definitely twinkling.

'Do you think Maurice might have had anything to do with Sylvia's death?' Hillary asked, but she was smiling too. 'Rogues and charmers have been known to turn nasty when they don't get their way, after all, and according to DI Jarvis's notes, Maurice had no alibi either.'

'Oh not him,' Ruby said at once. 'If anything, I'd have said it would be the other way around. Had Maurice called on Sylvia, the mood she was in in those days, she'd probably have brained him. Oh! Now that sounded heartless, didn't it? And I didn't mean it to. I keep forgetting what really happened to poor Sylvia. It's horrible.' The old lady looked and sounded suddenly genuinely distressed now.

'Please, don't upset yourself, Mrs Broadstairs,' Hillary said quickly, shooting a quick look over her shoulder to see if they'd attracted the attention of any of the carers. 'We won't take up much more of your time,' she promised.

'Oh no, dear, you carry on,' Ruby said robustly, stiffening her shoulders visibly. 'It's my duty to help the police, I know that. I want you to catch whoever killed poor Sylvia. It's not right that he should still be running free, is it?'

'No,' Hillary agreed flatly. 'Did Sylvia ever say anything to you that now strikes you as odd? Was she worried about getting threatening phone calls, or was someone pestering her? Following her, maybe spying on the house, or anything like that?'

'Oh no dear. I'd have remembered if she'd said anything like that. Besides, your DI Jarvis asked me the same thing at the time. And I can tell you, as I told her, Sylvia seemed totally normal. Her behaviour was just the same as ever. She didn't seem worried about anything in particular.'

'All right. Well, thank you, Mrs Broadstairs. I don't think we'll keep you any longer,' she said, and over in his chair, she saw Jake nod silently in relief.

They had to find a care worker to punch in the access codes to let them out, and were reminded to sign themselves out in the register. Once in the car park, Jake took a long, slow breath.

'Places like that always give me the creeps,' he said, a trifle shame-faced.

'Oh, I don't know. I thought it was a nice place. Well run. You hear such horror stories sometimes about old folks' homes, but everyone there looked happy and well cared for,' Hillary pointed out.

Although she understood exactly what he meant.

'I know, I know. It's not that,' Jake said, a shade helplessly.

'It's just the thought that you might end up in such a place yourself someday, if you're unlucky enough to live so long,' Hillary said drily. 'That's what's really giving you the heebie-jeebies.'

Jake smiled uncertainly. 'Maybe. But for me, unless disaster strikes, I'll still be rich enough to be able to afford to stay in my own home and hire a whole bevy of hot and cold running nurses to see to my every whim, and allow me to grow old disgracefully, thank you very much.'

Hillary laughed. 'Sounds like a plan to me.'

'So, are we ticking old blue eyes back there off the list of suspects?' Jake asked, nodding his head back towards the building that they'd just left.

'You know my methods by now, Jake,' Hillary said. 'No one get's ticked off unless we've the proof in hand to clear them. But she goes to the bottom of the list, certainly.'

Jake laughed. 'That's a relief. If we'd had to arrest her, I'd have felt like.... Like ... I don't know. Like the biggest bastard since....' But words failed him.

Hillary smiled. 'Yes, I get the picture. Still, if it *does* turn out to be Ruby after all, it won't be me or you has to arrest her, will it? We don't have the authority. I think we'll let the new boss have the honours instead. See what Rollo Sale makes of that.'

Jake grinned. 'Welcome to the CRT,' he drawled.

CHAPTER ELEVEN

A FTER JAKE HAD typed up his report for the murder book, he decided to take off early. Since Hillary was still closeted in the new boss's office with Steven and Rollo Sale going over the monthly review, he told Jimmy, who merely grunted.

'S'long as you've worked your hours,' Jimmy said unconcernedly, and apparently deep in his perusal of computer print-outs of all known muggers who targeted the elderly. But the moment Jake had collected his gear and left, the older man stood up and stretched.

To Wendy, who was helping Jake with his research into Freda de la Mare, he said casually, 'I'm off to the canteen for a bite. I missed lunch.'

Wendy, who was studying a critic's favourable review of one of the artist's shows, barely heard him and vaguely nodded her head in acknowledgement.

Once outside the office, Jimmy picked up his pace, and was not far behind Jake, when he reached his E-Type in the car park.

At least, Jimmy thought happily as he got into his own humble Ford, an E-Type Jag was an easy vehicle to follow. It wasn't as if it could blend in with the crowd.

When Hillary finally finished wrangling with budgets and the latest, unhelpful memos from head office on how to do her job, she found the small communal office oddly empty. Only Wendy looked up when she poked her head around the door.

'I'm off to interview some of the other members of the Forget-me-not Club. Want to come?' she offered.

'Sure,' Wendy said with enthusiasm. Although Freda de la Mare was an interesting study, she wasn't so fascinating that Wendy would pass up the chance to watch Hillary Greene in action.

Jake had no difficulty in finding the smart, mock-tudor house in Aylesbury, since the private investigators had been very clear in their directions. It was just that somehow the destination was not what he'd been expecting.

As per his other instructions, Jake had bearer bonds in his briefcase to the tune of £50,000 and he turned off his mobile phone. His other various electronic gadgets he also locked away in the car's glove compartment. The man he was about to meet was certainly very careful about not leaving any footprints – electronic or otherwise – that might lead to his front door.

As he climbed out of the car and looked around, he didn't see the small, anonymous runabout that was Jimmy's own modest pride and joy pull up in a gap in a line of parked cars. The area was strictly residential, and in the middle of the afternoon there was both a lot of parking and a lot of cover to be had. Most families nowadays had to two cars, and Jimmy was confident that the Boy Wonder hadn't spotted him.

He stayed in the vehicle though as Jake glanced around, and was relieved to see that he was just checking the house numbers. So, it wasn't so much as if he suspected that he was being watched, as that he just hadn't been here before and wasn't sure of his surroundings.

Jimmy too, looked around curiously. The road was wide and lined with lime trees and horse chestnuts. The houses were all fairly large and detached, of mixed styles, with garages and large gardens. All of them had that casually prosperous look that screamed comfortably off, upper middle class.

Jimmy waited until Jake had selected his house of choice and disappeared inside a garden gate – in this case, a black, wrought-iron double gate, that allowed access to the drive and garage. When he was confident that enough time had passed, he got out and followed, wincing as a niggling little bolt of pain shot down his lower back. It was becoming a more and more common occurrence for him nowadays, and he could only hope that it wasn't an omen of bad things to come. Was it lumbago when your back started to go like that, or something else? Jimmy couldn't remember. And didn't much care.

As he walked along the pavement, the little bit of exercise soon put it right, and when he got to the gate in question, all thoughts of his health had disappeared. He made a note of the number, then carried on walking, until he found a street sign that told him that he was on Lime Avenue. He then walked back to his car and opened up his own laptop, typed in his password, and then the name of the street and number.

Before long, he was looking at a stream of information on the owner of the house.

And very interesting it was too.

Inside, Jake Barnes was shaking the man's hand. Gordon Tate was about Jake's age, but with a heavy spare tyre of fat around his middle, and sandy-coloured hair that was already thinning on top. He had very round, wide, hazel eyes and a slightly fleshy, sensuous mouth; the way he looked Jake up and down left him in very little doubt as to his sexual orientation.

'You come highly recommended by Crimmins and Lloyd,' Gordon said, nodding to a sofa, 'otherwise, I don't usually do business with strangers. Well, you can never be too careful, can you? But I trust Peter,' – he named one of the lead investigators with the PI firm – 'we went to school together. Winchester. Want a drink? I've just had some fine Mumms come in.'

Jake turned down the offer of champagne with a gracious smile. 'Normally I'd love to, but I'm driving.'

'Oh, of course. The curse of modern living. I always wish that I'd lived about two hundred years ago, myself. Then I'd have a dashing coachman to take me everywhere, and so would my guests.'

'Were they making Mumms back then though?' Jake asked.

Gordon Tate laughed. 'Good point! So. Did you bring the bearer bonds? No cash and no cheques; I hope Peter made that quite clear.'

He had. Jake nodded and reached into his briefcase. He pulled out the bonds, wondering vaguely why the 'facilitator', as Peter Lloyd had referred to Tate, didn't want cash. Still, that was none of his business. Perhaps Gordon was afraid that the serial numbers on them could be tracked or something.

'Lovely,' Gordon said, counting the bonds with a deftness and dexterity that left Jake feeling deeply respectful. He doubted that even a minute had passed.

'It's all here.' Gordon reached into a drawer in a sideboard and handed over a brown paper envelope. 'The photographs were a bit of a challenge, though. Did I detect Peter's work with a telephoto lens?'

Jake looked back at him blankly and the other man smiled and held up a hand. 'OK, pax. None of my business. As I said, it was a bit of a challenge to make them look regulation issue, but I think you'll find that I managed it.'

As Jake checked out the drivers' licences inside, he had to admit that it did indeed look as if the snapshots had been taken in one of those photo-booths you saw in post offices and some big supermarkets.

'The birth certificates are especially good work. It's getting the thinness of the paper just right. They look like the original issue, don't they?' Gordon said smugly.

Indeed they did. Both sets of documents looked authentic.

Jake nodded. 'And you're sure they'll stand up to scrutiny?'

'Oh, guaranteed, old boy. I know this little lad who can hack computers like a dream. The social security numbers are golden, I assure you.'

Jake nodded, well pleased with the results. He held out his hand. 'Well, it's been a pleasure doing business with you, Mr Tate.' Even as he spoke the cliché, he felt slightly absurd.

Gordon Tate took his hand and held on to it a shade longer than Jake felt comfortable with, and then grinned wolfishly and led him back into the hall. 'Of course, we never met, Jake,' Gordon reminded him. As he reached for the front door to open it, something in those wide, hazel eyes made Jake's blood go cold. 'And if it ever comes to it, my word will be believed over yours. You understand that, don't you?'

Jake, who had been guilty of finding the gay crook somehow pitiful, or at least an object of amusement, suddenly found himself feeling very differently about him indeed. He forced himself to meet the man's big, hazel eyes.

'Sorry,' he said flatly. 'Do I know you?'

Gordon Tate laughed softly, and patted one chubby hand on Jake's shoulder. 'That's the ticket, old boy.'

Jake left the house walking far more swiftly than he'd gone in. As he slipped into the E-Type Jag, he was forced to conclude, once again, that he was probably really not cut out for all this. Still, he congratulated himself on the progress he was making. He didn't have to be comfortable with the people he was forced to use or work with, after all. Besides, it was a good thing to be reminded of just how careful he needed to be.

Outside, Jimmy closed his laptop thoughtfully, and reached for his phone. He bent down out of sight as Jake's E-type roared past, and then straightened up again, listening to the dialling tone in his ear being answered.

'Hillary Greene.'

'Guv, it's me. Can you talk?'

'I'm driving to North Aston with Wendy. We're going to attend a meeting of the Forget-me-not Club and talk about Sylvia.'

'Oh right. You'd better just listen then. Young Jake went off early. Nothing in that, his hours are flexible as you know, but I just thought I'd tag along behind. He led me to Aylesbury, to a very nice des res that he wasn't at all familiar with. When I ran it through our database, it turns out that it belongs to one Gordon Tate.'

'OK,' Hillary said neutrally.

'Do you know the name?'

'Can't say as I do.'

'No real reason why you should have come across him, guv. He's not got form,' Jimmy said. 'Well, not officially anyway. But, as the old saying goes, he's known to us. He's a bit of a fixer. Mostly he provides documents to the needy. Financial aid, that sort of thing. He's also been known to act as a go-between. For instance, if your Picasso is stolen, and the kidnappers want to ransom it back – and strictly no police involved – you might use Mr Gordon Tate to be the middle man. If you want to disappear, and need a new name and identity that'll stand up under pressure, again, you might want to talk to our Mr Tate. You want a new face, but don't know which plastic surgeons are discreet and willing.... Get the picture?'

'Oh yeah.'

'So I reckon our Boy Wonder wants something fixed. And whatever it is, he's just arranged for it to happen. Want me to go in and have a word with Mr Tate, see if I can persuade him to let us know what that might be?'

'Hell no.'

Jimmy nodded, with some relief. 'I was hoping you'd say that guv,' he confessed, with a smile. 'From what I've been learning about our friend here, he's well connected. Working both sides of the fence, so to speak, he's got friends in high places – in both the criminal world, and the so-called respectable spectrum. So I doubt that he would have been much impressed by the likes of me. By the way, he does a fair bit of business with Crimmins and Lloyd, that PI firm Jake's been using. You could see why a high-flying outfit like them might find Tate useful. It's my guess that's how our Jake got put on to him.'

'Sounds logical.'

'You want me to get back to HQ and learn all I can about Tate?'

'Right.'

'OK, guv. Talk to you later.'

In the Mini, Wendy watched curiously as Hillary put the phone away. 'Anything breaking on the case, guv?' she asked hopefully.

'Nope. Just admin,' Hillary said. 'So, ever been to an old folk's club meeting?'

Wendy blinked. Today she was wearing a black pants suit that had a complete, life-size skeleton depicted on it. She was wearing full white face paint and had gone heavy on the kohl-lined eyes. She looked like a member of the walking dead. 'Oddly enough, guv, no,' she said.

When they got back to HQ it was just gone four o'clock. Although the members of Sylvia's club had been eager to talk about her and to try to help, they hadn't really been able to add much to the investigation.

There'd been plenty of tales about their victim though – how tough she was, how fair, how funny, how generous. But nobody had any idea who might have killed her or why. And they were all fairly united in their views on the Ruby/Maurice/Sylvia love triangle, the general consensus being that Ruby would have been the first to back down, and that Maurice would have scarpered sooner or later, once he'd realized just what a handful Sylvia would have been. Hints that either one of them might have had something to do with Sylvia's death had been met with either hoots of derision or consternation and disbelief.

'I think we can more or less rule out either Maurice or Ruby from the equation,' Hillary said as she undid her seat belt. 'Look, it's not worth you coming back to the office for just for an hour. Why not take off early.'

'Really, guv? That's great. I've got a hot date tonight with a rower from Brasenose. He's got muscles out to here.' And Wendy used her hands to demonstrate the size of his biceps.

Hillary, who'd been in the act of getting out of the car, turned and looked at her curiously. 'Oh? But I thought you were…. Never mind.'

Wendy, who easily guessed the direction of her thoughts, grinned. 'I'm bi. Well, probably. Mostly.'

Hillary hastily held up a hand and began to scramble out. 'None of my business, and I'll expect you to work off the extra hour some way or other, yeah?'

Wendy rolled her eyes. 'Whatever you say, guv.'

Hillary grinned, but walked a shade wearily towards the entrance. Wendy tooted derisively as she shot off past her, and Hillary gave her a familiar two-fingered salute.

Her smile quickly left her face, however, as she made her way down into the basement. She made sure to shut the door firmly behind her as she went into the office, and Jimmy reached for a sheaf of papers as she slumped into Wendy's now vacant chair.

'OK. So tell me what you've got,' she demanded flatly.

Later that night, over a dinner of pasta and salad, Hillary related to Steven all that Jimmy had learned about Gordon Tate.

'And that's not all,' she went on, taking a sip of orange juice. 'Jimmy managed to find a match on that skinhead Jake met up with at the fireworks display.' She reached for the file and handed it over. 'His name—'

But Steven, who'd just caught sight of the photographs, pulled in a sharp breath, and beat her to it. 'Darren Chivnor.'

Hillary's eyes hardened. 'You know him?'

'Oh yes,' Steven said grimly. And told her exactly how.

For a long while then, they were both silent, their dinner going cold in front of them. Finally Hillary sighed heavily. 'Just what the hell is Jake playing at?'

Steven leaned back and rubbed a hand across his face. 'Whatever it is, it can't be good. Chivnor is seriously bad news, Hillary. I don't think Jake can possibly have any idea what he's getting himself into.'

'No. I agree. But just what does he want with one of Medcalfe's right-hand thugs, and a top-of-the-range Mr Fixit? I just can't see the connection between them,' she said in frustration. 'Gordon Tate is way above Medcalfe's league. He's used to doing deals with Arabian princes and South African diamond dealers, for pity's sake. He works for museums who want to recover "lost" items, and arranges it for Mafia Dons to disappear to Chile or where-the-hell-ever it is that the supergrasses go to die. Medcalfe's just a common or garden scumbag, and he would be way too dodgy for someone like Tate to risk doing any business with him.'

'Hillary, it *is* just a coincidence, isn't it, that Jake Barnes joins the team just as I'm getting this new job?' Steven asked quietly.

Hillary, who'd been just about to take another sip of her drink paused, and straightened up in her chair. Then her frown cleared. 'It has to be. Jake Barnes was already installed at the CRT *before* Donleavy picked you to head up the new task force. He might be many things, but I don't think Jake is clairvoyant. Nor does he have a crystal ball. And in real life, coincidences do happen. So let's not get paranoid and start seeing conspiracy theories everywhere,' she said dampeningly.

Steven saw the sense in that and let out a breath of relief. 'OK, fair enough.' He thought about it some more and then frowned again. 'In which case, perhaps it's the other way around,' he tossed out diffidently. 'Could my getting this new job have triggered whatever it is that Barnes is up to?'

Again Hillary thought about it for a while, then shook her head reluctantly. 'I just can't see how. Unless Jake's got some sort of vigilante complex. You know, you've been set the task of taking out the sexual predators, so he's decided to become some sort of real-life Batman and help you out under the guise of harmless playboy millionaire.' She laughed. 'Somehow, I really don't think the Boy Wonder actually truly believes himself to be, well, the Boy Wonder. I don't think he's crazy, Steven.' She took a swallow of the juice and forced herself back to reality. 'I think we'd have spotted it, if he was actually bonkers. No, he joined the CRT with something specific in mind. We just have to find out what it is, and before the silly sod goes and gets himself killed. We both know that Medcalfe and Gordon Tate have the clout, albeit in very different ways, to arrange to have *that* done.'

'We need to wrap this up sooner rather than later, Hillary,' Steven warned her sharply. 'We can't keep Donleavy in the dark for much longer. You promised that we'd go to him when we had something more solid to go on. Well this' – he tapped the file of photographs and data significantly – 'definitely qualifies as that.'

'I know,' Hillary said flatly. 'And I agree. It's beginning to get out of hand. Just give it another day or two, then we'll tackle Jake together. See if we can't get him to spill it to us first.'

'You're still hoping you'll be able to get him out if it, whatever it is, with his skin intact, aren't you?' Steven said softly, leaning across the table and covering her hand with his. 'Well, who'd have thunk it?' he drawled. 'Hillary Greene is just an old softy at heart.'

She cocked her head to one side and regarded him through narrow, sherry-coloured eyes. 'Actually,' she said coolly, 'I was hoping that he'd spill the beans to us, because if Jake somehow *has* managed to get an inside scope into Medcalfe's empire, it might prove very useful to you in your new job. Just think how much glory you'll get if, during your probationary period no less, you're able to give Donleavy Medcalfe's head on a silver platter.'

And then she smiled sweetly. 'But if you choose to be delusional and go about thinking I've got a soft heart, you go right ahead, sweetheart.'

Steven grinned. 'I knew there had to be a reason why I love you.'

'I knew there must be one, too,' she said smiling softly. 'Now let's go to bed.'

The next day, Wendy went in early. Since she had to make up her hour from yesterday, she thought she might as well make a start. Even so, Hillary was in before her.

'I hope you notice the time,' Wendy said, knocking on the door to her tiny office and sticking her head around.

Hillary pretended that her watch had stopped. 'How about we early birds see if we can't catch Farmer Gibson at home?'

'Back to Caulcott then?' Wendy said, with a groan. 'Well at least, for once, the sun is shining. Think we might have a nice weekend for a change?'

'I wouldn't bank on it,' Hillary laughed. As they drove off in the fitful sunlight, Wendy regaled her with tales of a wild night spent watching a six-foot rower getting into high jinxes with the rest of the rowing team. But when it came to an incident involving eight blotto men, one highly surprised neighbourhood cat, and a can of squirty cream, Hillary stopped listening.

Or pretended to.

Randy Gibson was in the sheep pens, eyeing a lame ewe when they eventually tracked him down. Around Hillary's own height at five feet nine or so, he was in his mid-sixties, with pale-brown hair rapidly turning grey. A thickset man, dressed in dirty blue overalls, as Hillary and Wendy stepped into the odoriferous barn, he looked up, spotted them, and sighed. 'The missus told me you lot were hanging around, asking questions. I wondered when it would be my turn.'

Hillary nodded. 'I hope this isn't a bad time, Mr Gibson,' she began pleasantly, although she wasn't particularly worried if it was. 'We won't keep you long.' As they'd been talking, they'd walked up to the pen and now Wendy drew in her breath sharply as she saw the woolly sheep limping around.

'Oh poor thing. Will she be all right? Have you called the vet?' she asked, leaning over the metal bars and tweaking her fingers together, making little sucking noises through her lips. The ewe, not surprisingly, gave her an alarmed, wall-eyed look and backed away, intent on having nothing whatsoever to do with her.

'I don't know, and yes I have.' The farmer – with a somewhat sour look – answered her questions in order. 'In fact, he's due to arrive soon, so perhaps we can get on with it.'

Hillary nodded, and decided to go straight for the jugular. Sometimes it paid off. 'Do you know that your wife suspects that you killed Sylvia Perkins?' she asked, almost amiably.

Wendy stopped the sucking noises she was making to the sheep and gawped at her. Randy Gibson gawped at her. Even the ewe, after some consideration, seemed to gawp at her.

'What? What are you on about? Of course she doesn't, why would she?' the stupefied farmer finally spluttered.

Hillary shrugged. 'I've been a police officer for more years than I care to think, Mr Gibson, and I've become pretty adept at reading people. So I think you'll find that she does. You might want to talk to her about it, especially if she's worrying about nothing. Is she?'

Randy continued to gawp.

'Did you, in fact, murder Sylvia Perkins, Mr Gibson?' Hillary pressed.

'No. Of course I bloody well didn't.'

'You didn't call on her that day? Tackle her about certain issues?'

'What? No. What issues?' he asked, obviously struggling to keep up with the sucker-punches she was shooting his way, and failing.

'We've heard all about how Sylvia blamed you for her husband's death,' Hillary said flatly. 'And we know she went out of her way to slander you and cause you, shall we say, inconvenience, whenever she could.'

'Oh that. Look, it wasn't my fault what happened to old Joe. The poor old beggar had a heart attack. It could have happened to anyone, although I'd always thought that Joe was the sort who'd go on forever, you know. A stringy, tough little ferret of a man, he was the sort you thought would live to be a hundred and still bike to work. So no one was more surprised than me when he died the way he did. And contrary to what Sylvia said, we weren't overworking him or asking him to do the heavy stuff.'

'When he died he was haymaking, wasn't he?'

'Sitting in a baler, yes,' Randy Gibson snapped. 'We don't use pitchforks and shire horses anymore, you know. And the baler was air-conditioned, and had bloody good suspension. The cost of farm machinery nowadays, he might as well have been sitting in the cockpit of a luxury jet!'

'But Sylvia didn't let it go, did she?'

Randy Gibson turned and glowered at the ewe. The ewe, perhaps not surprisingly, limped over to one corner and turned her back on them all.

The farmer waved a hand vaguely in the air. 'Oh, I took no notice of her. And it wasn't as if anybody else took her seriously, either. And no, I didn't visit her that day. And no, I didn't hit the old lady over the head. All right?'

Hillary sighed. He was probably telling the truth. In fact, she was only going through the motions and she knew it. She now had a good idea who had killed Sylvia Perkins and why: she was just putting off the inevitable. Time, she thought, to get on with it.

'All right, Mr Gibson, thank you for your time,' she said, and nodding to Wendy, turned and headed for the barn door.

Randy Gibson watched them leave, in silence, but couldn't quite manage to keep it up. 'Were you serious? About my Van thinking I killed the old bird?'

'Oh yes,' Hillary called over her shoulder. 'You really should put her mind at rest, Mr Gibson. You can tell her, if you like, that we'll soon be making an arrest in the case, and that we won't be calling on *you* with the handcuffs.'

Beside her, Wendy trod in something black and slippery because she wasn't looking where she was going and said something distinctly unladylike under her breath.

Back in the car, Hillary watched, highly amused, as Wendy very fastidiously tried to rub her boots clean on the grass verge before slipping in behind the Mini's wheel.

'Guv, were you serious? About making an arrest soon?' she squeaked.

'You think I was bluffing?' Hillary asked, punching in buttons on her mobile phone.

'What? No,' Wendy said, then repeated more thoughtfully, 'No, I don't think that. But … who are we going to arrest?'

Hillary held up one finger as the phone was answered. 'Hello. Yes, can you put me through to Dr Partridge please,' Hillary said.

Wendy knew that Dr Steven Partridge was one of the pathologists called in by the police and that he and Hillary had worked together on many of her previous cases, when she'd still been a full DI.

And her heart began to race.

Bloody hell, the case really was breaking! But what had she missed? She'd read every word in the murder book, and so presumably, knew everything that Hillary did. So what had she not seen? She quickly ran the list of suspects and witnesses through her mind, but couldn't begin to guess which one was in the frame.

Her only consolation was that she was pretty sure that the Boy Wonder didn't know either. He was probably back at the office right now, totally out of the loop and not realizing what was going on out here.

'Hello, Doc. Long time no see.' Hillary smiled at something the pathologist said, then laughed. 'Good grief, no. I just wanted to pick your brains on a medical issue. Don't worry, it's nothing I'll ask you to back up in a court of law. I just need some basic information.'

But even after listening to Hillary Greene's end of the conversation, Wendy still had no idea which way the wind was blowing.

'OK. Got it. And would something like that affect a person's personality?' Hillary was asking now. And Wendy's mind raced.

This was sounding more and more as if there was some sort of psychological aspect to the case, but Partridge wasn't a shrink. Then she wondered which one of their suspects had come across as the most crazy. Robbie Grant was surely a budding sociopath in the making, wasn't he?

Or maybe she'd spotted something off in one of Sylvia's daughters?

'OK. Yes, that's pretty much what I thought. Yes, OK. No, don't worry, like I said, I'm not going to put you up as an expert witness. I'm just about to break a case, and I wanted a bit of ammo to work with,' Hillary said now. 'Thanks a lot, Doc. I owe you a drink sometime.'

She listened, laughed, then hung up.

'So, guv, who is it?' Wendy asked eagerly.

'Who do you think?' Hillary asked, reaching for her seat belt.

'*Guv!*' Wendy wailed.

Hillary Greene smiled. 'Drive to Freda's place,' she said quietly. 'We're going to tell her exactly what we've just told Randy Gibson.'

Wendy blinked, but automatically turned the ignition. 'And what's that, guv?'

'That we're about to make an arrest in the Sylvia Perkins case, of course. I dare say Vanessa Gibson will have spread the word before the day is out, but Freda might take the rumour with a pinch of salt. But if she's got it straight from the horse's mouth, so to speak, she won't be able to ignore it.'

Wendy pulled away and drove towards the artist's cottage. 'So she did it? She's the killer?' she asked.

'What do you think?' Hillary could not help but tease.

'*Guv!*'

CHAPTER TWELVE

Freda de la Mare had probably been upstairs painting when they rang her doorbell, for they could distinctly hear her coming down the stairs as they stood in front of the door. When she opened it to them, she had on an outsized dress that was paint smeared and obviously stood in for an artist's smock.

'Oh, hello. Come on in,' she offered.

Hillary surprised the other two women by shaking her head. 'No need, Freda. We've just come to tell you that we'll soon be making an arrest in the Sylvia Perkins case. We've just finished talking to Randy Gibson, and I'm about to phone my superiors to ask them to get an arrest warrant. I just thought, since you were such a close friend of Sylvia's, that you'd like to know. I would appreciate it, though, if you didn't tell anyone just yet. We need some time to apprise the family members, and cross the Ts and dot the Is – that kind of thing.'

Freda de la Mare held on tightly to the doorframe and stared at her. 'Oh. OK,' she said uncertainly.

Hillary smiled and nodded, and then turned and walked back to the car. Beside her, Wendy was nearly doing a hop, skip and a jump in her excitement and bewilderment. But she knew better than to show her confusion when there was a witness or suspect watching; Hillary's training was beginning to show dividends.

Once in the car however, she was about to erupt, when Hillary again forestalled her by holding up a warning finger to be quiet. She got out her mobile.

'Sir, it's me,' Hillary said. Back in HQ, Steven Crayle sat up a shade straighter in his chair. Hillary only called him 'Sir' when she meant business. He glanced up and looked across at Rollo Sale at his temporary desk and beckoned him over.

'Just a moment, Hillary, Superintendent Sale is with me. I'm going to put you on speakerphone. OK, go on.'

'Sir, I hope to be bringing in a suspect in the Sylvia Perkins case very soon. I want you to be ready to interview and arrest Freda de la Mare. Can you obtain a warrant, in the first case for attempting to pervert the course of justice? The CPS might also want to add aiding and abetting, or accessory after the fact as well, I'm not sure yet. It will depend on how things go in interview. But I'm not really expecting too much trouble, to be honest.'

'OK,' Steven said, jotting down notes. 'I know just the judge. With a bit of luck I'll have it within the hour. Do you need me to come out and make the arrest?'

'I don't know yet, sir. I've just lit a fuse which, I think, may very well do most of our job for us. I just need a little time to see how it pans out.'

'You have Jake with you?' Steven asked abruptly. 'You're in Caulcott I take it?'

'Yes, sir, and I have Wendy with me.'

'I'd be happier if I could send out Jimmy to back you up,' Steven said.

'Sir, Freda de la Mare is an old lady,' Hillary said gently. 'I'm pretty sure that Wendy and I are the best ones to see this through.'

Steven didn't need much time to see the sense in that. Not only was she probably not much of a threat, but the police service also had a duty of care to the people in their custody.

Going in mob-handed and causing a frightened old woman to have a heart attack would have the PR department pulling out their hair.

'All right. But I want to be kept apprised of developments.'

'Yes, sir. It may take Ms de la Mare a little time to ponder her options, but either way, we'll be bringing her in some time within the next few hours.'

'OK. I'll speak to you soon.'

He hung up and glanced across at the man who would soon be replacing him, and raised a dark brow. 'Well, she's had the case less than a week.'

'She clearly didn't want to say much over the phone,' Rollo Sale said thoughtfully. 'I can't say as I blame her. What with journalists hacking phones, and so many electronic listening devices out there, it's a wonder we're able to keep anything under our hats for long.'

Steven nodded. 'I'll get going on the warrants.' He picked up the phone. 'Do you want me to sit shotgun with Hillary whilst you and the youngsters watch from the viewing room? Or do you want to take the plunge and oversee the interview yourself?'

Roland Sale thought about it for a moment, then shook his head. 'I've heard a lot about Hillary's interview technique, and I can best see it for myself as an observer. Besides, this is probably your last cold case – you'll want to see it through to the end, right?'

Steven smiled. 'Thanks. Perhaps you can round up Jake Barnes and tell him what's going on – what little we know, that is, and— Yes,' he said into the phone. 'Can I speak to Judge Martin Combs, please....'

'Guv, that's her!' Wendy hissed. They'd been sitting in her Mini for less than half an hour when Freda de la Mare came out of her front door. In her hand she had a large bunch of mixed evergreens, with several plumes of creamy-white flowers. They looked a bit like laurel flowers to Hillary, but she wouldn't have bet money on it. The artist walked down the road just a little way, and then climbed in behind the wheel of a green hatchback and pulled away.

'OK, Wendy. You've always wanted to tail someone just like they do on the telly,' Hillary said with a small smile. 'Here's your chance.'

'Wicked!'

'Let her pull around the bend. This is a single-track road, don't forget, so there's only one way she can go.'

'The pub at the end of the road, I know. But then she can turn either left or right guv,' Wendy said urgently, revving the engine a little too hard.

'Calm down. Put your seat belt on. OK, now, off you go. Speed limit,' Hillary said sharply.

Less than a minute later, they could see Freda's car up ahead, the brake lights coming on. 'She's indicating right, guv.'

'I can see that. Let her pull away before speeding up. OK, off you go.'

Wendy was tense behind the wheel, but Freda de la Mare was going less than a mile or so away, to the next village along. Middleton Stoney was bisected by a busy road, and just before the set of traffic lights that filtered traffic across, Freda indicated right again, turning down a narrow lane.

'Drive on past,' Hillary said urgently. 'Don't try and follow her down there, she'll spot us in an instant. Here, pull over into the car-park of that pub,' she said, pointing out the Jersey Arms on their left.

'Come on,' Hillary said, amused by the way the girl shot out of the car as if rocket propelled. Thankfully, today, she was dressed in a fairly simple outfit consisting of black jeans with a feather decorated black T-shirt and a black and red leather jacket.

'That lane she went down, I think it probably leads to the

church. Just nip down there and see,' Hillary ordered her.

'You're not coming as well?' Wendy asked, a shade nervously now.

Hillary smiled. 'I think Freda might spot two women following her, don't you?'

'Do you want me to find out where she's gone, guv?'

'No!' Hillary said quickly. 'I've got a fair idea already and if you just stopped and thought about it for a moment, so would you,' Hillary informed her.

Wendy danced about, thinking about how much time was passing. 'Guv, she might be getting into her car and driving off! We could lose her.'

'Think, Wendy,' Hillary said, ignoring her impatience. 'You've got to learn to be observant, and think about what you see. What was she carrying when she got in the car?'

'A bunch of greenery and flowers,' Wendy said obligingly.

'And if that lane does lead to the church…?'

The Goth thought about it for a moment, then her face lit up. 'Oh. Right, you think she's gone to visit someone's grave. You want me to sneak around the wall and see which one?'

Hillary again sighed. 'I don't think that'll be necessary.'

'But it might be important, guv.'

'Oh I'm sure it is,' Hillary Greene said softly. 'Wendy, start using your noggin. How many graves in a small rural churchyard do you think will have a bunch of evergreen foliage with pale cream flowers on them?'

'Oh.'

'If we need to, we can wait and then check it out without danger of being seen. Go on, off you go. Make sure she can get to the churchyard from down there, and then come back. Don't let her see you if you can avoid it.'

'Where will you be?' Wendy asked, both pleased and a little in awe to be given such an important task.

Hillary raised one chestnut-coloured eyebrow and indicated

the Jersey Arms. 'In the pub having a drink, of course,' she said, surprised the Goth had to ask. 'Where else?'

In the bar of the pub Hillary sipped her orange and lemonade and eyed the old photographs lining the wall. A football team, dressed in the comical, knee-length shorts of the 1930s showed a fine-looking bunch of men from a nearby village being awarded the Jersey Cup. The caption at the bottom informed them that the well-dressed and elegant woman doing the awarding was none other than Lady Jersey herself.

Hillary had nearly finished her drink when Wendy came in, looking red-cheeked and bright-eyed. 'You were right, it does lead to the churchyard, guv,' Wendy whispered, eyeing the bartender warily. 'But I didn't go inside, like you said, and I couldn't see the suspect.'

'Her name's Freda,' Hillary said, much amused. 'What'll you have? My treat. But bear in mind you're driving.'

'A Coke, ta, guv. But aren't we going to go back to the car and see where she goes from here?'

'Don't you think that she'll eventually notice that she's being followed by a Mini? A car that she'll have seen you driving around in on a number of occasions?' Hillary asked. 'Besides, I have a feeling that the only place Freda's going to go now is back home. So come on, sup up, and I'll treat you to a pub sandwich.'

At HQ, Jake Barnes took the news that the case was apparently going to break with a blink of surprise and a slightly worried glance at his watch. Over by his desk, Jimmy noticed the tell-tale movement and began to look very interested.

'I hope you don't have somewhere else to be, Mr Barnes?' Roland Sale said gently, also having caught the direction of the younger man's glance.

In truth, Jake Barnes *was* worried that the day might run over into the evening, because he had just made plans – very important plans indeed. But he flushed under the implied rebuke of his new superintendent, and smiled diffidently.

'Of course not, sir,' he lied crisply.

Sale nodded. 'Good. I take it you've been doing some research into Freda de la Mare for Hillary?'

'Yes, sir.'

'In that case, perhaps you can come and brief myself and Superintendent Crayle on what you've learned so far?'

'Of course, sir.'

After disposing of a prawn and salad baguette apiece, Hillary and Wendy got back in the car. As Hillary had expected, Freda's green hatchback was no longer parked in the narrow lane, and she experienced just a little pang of worry as she ordered Wendy to drive back to Caulcott. What if she'd got it all wrong?

But when they turned down the old Roman road, they saw almost at once that the little green car was back in its usual place.

'Pull in just behind it,' Hillary ordered.

'But that's right outside her house, guv. She's bound to see us,' Wendy objected.

'Yes,' Hillary said. And looked at her. For a moment, Wendy looked confused, then smiled cautiously.

'Oh I get it. You want her to know we're here, right? You're applying a bit of the old psychological pressure.'

'Something like that,' Hillary agreed, lips twitching. 'Also, it's to let her know that we're available to give her a ride, whenever she's ready. It'll save her having to take her own car to Kidlington.'

Wendy ruminated on that for a moment, but then gave up. Besides, she had something else on her mind. 'Why didn't you ask me to go and find the grave she'd just visited, guv?' she asked instead.

'Because I didn't need to,' Hillary said simply. 'I already

know whose grave it must have been.'

'Oh,' Wendy said. 'But it can't be Sylvia's grave, guv. She was cremated, and her ashes were scattered.'

'I know,' Hillary said drily. 'I have read the reports.'

'Sorry, guv.' Wendy flushed, and sighed mournfully. 'I don't think I'm ever going to get the hang of this, guv. I don't think I'm clever enough.' She sounded so despondent that Hillary had to smile.

'What? You going to just hand the floor over to Jake without a fight?'

Wendy snorted. Then suddenly stiffened. 'Guv.'

'I can see her,' Hillary said softly. For Freda de la Mare had just opened the door of her cottage. For a moment she stared down the path at the two women clearly visible in the front seats of the car, then retreated back into the house. She was only gone for a moment or two however, before she reappeared, wearing a coat and carrying something in a clear, plastic bag: something long and thin.

As Freda walked, stiff-backed and tight-faced down her garden path, Hillary got out and opened the rear passenger door, holding it open for her. As she approached, Hillary nodded at the bag she was holding. Inside she could just make out a glimpse of something gold-coloured.

'That the murder weapon?' Hillary asked casually.

'Yes,' Freda agreed. She seemed to hesitate for a moment, as if unsure of the etiquette of such a moment. 'I imagine you want to take it?'

Hillary smiled and agreed, reaching out gently for it. Then she turned and placed it on the front passenger seat, aware of Wendy staring down at it, wide-eyed and open-mouthed. She then followed Freda into the rear of the car. From the back seat, she leaned forward a little. 'Back to HQ Wendy,' she prompted gently.

Wendy swallowed hard and turned the key in the ignition.

'Right, guv,' she croaked.

'Speed limit,' Hillary reminded her gently. But for once, the Goth needed no prompting, and drove very circumspectly indeed back towards Kidlington.

In the back seat, the other two women sat in a mutually reflective, calm silence.

Wendy followed them towards the interview rooms, then veered off to one side, not at all surprised to find both Jake and the new superintendent already in place in the viewing room.

Jake eyed the pale but keyed-up girl with a rueful smile. 'Trust you to be in at the kill. What's going on?' he whispered.

But Wendy, with a wary eye on the new boss, shrugged. 'To be honest, I'm not quite sure,' she admitted.

'Where's the boss?'

'She's dropping off what we think is the murder weapon with Forensics.'

Jake whistled silently through his teeth, and nodded at the older woman now being shown in by the custody sergeant, and being introduced to Steven Crayle. 'So she did it then?'

'I don't know,' Wendy whispered back. 'The guv asked Sexy Steven to get warrants for practically everything else on her *but* murder. And there was something going on just now about a visit to the local churchyard.'

Jake frowned. 'I don't get it.'

'Me neither. But our Hillary's got it all sussed, I can tell you. Jake, I think she's amazing.'

'Who's got a crush on Miss then?' Jake whispered, nudging the top of her arm with his shoulder.

'Oh shut up!'

'That sounds like a good idea to me,' Superintendent Sale said, still facing the viewing mirror and hiding a smile. He'd heard from Steven that the two wannabes were good kids, with plenty of brains and enthusiasm between then, and that they got on well, which was good to know, but there was a time and a place for everything.

Besides, he was keen to see his prime investigator in action, and he didn't want to be distracted and, he had to admit, he was already impressed. When Steven Crayle had outlined the Perkins case just five days ago, he'd secretly decided that it would probably never be closed, let alone within a week. Just like the two kids behind him, he was keen to see how it all panned out.

It wasn't beyond the bounds of possibility, after all, that the much-vaunted Hillary Greene would fall flat on her face.

At the super's rebuke, Jake and Wendy fell silent, but not before Wendy gave Jake a retaliatory nudge back.

In the interview room, Steven Crayle was just going through the necessary details for the benefit of the tape recording, citing his name and that of Freda, the time, the date, and reading Freda a list of her rights. Just then, Hillary came into the room, and he duly added, 'Hillary Greene, civilian consultant has just entered the room at….' He read off the time, then leaned back slightly as Hillary took a seat beside him.

Freda de la Mare smiled at her wearily.

'Freda, thank you for coming in today,' Hillary began. 'This shouldn't take long. We know most of what happened the day Sylvia Perkins died. We just need you to corroborate it. I take it that you're willing to do that?'

'Of course I am,' Freda said flatly. Her red hair looked dishevelled, as if she'd forgotten to comb it before coming out, and she was still huddled in her coat, as if she found it hard to keep warm. It made Hillary wonder if the artist might not be suffering a little from shock, in which case, she needed to speed things up.

'I don't suppose I can smoke in here,' Freda asked, then quickly waved a hand, answering her own question. 'No, no, I know. Let's get on with it, shall we?'

'The brass poker that you brought in with you. You understand that that's being forensically examined?' Hillary got that in first. She knew that barristers and solicitors liked good solid evidence to be dealt with promptly.

'I imagined it would be,' Freda agreed, with a tight smile. She looked tired, but not defeated, and in the viewing room, Jake couldn't help but smile.

'She's a game old bird, isn't she?' he said admiringly.

'Shush,' Wendy said, fascinated.

'All right,' Hillary began. 'Let's start at the beginning. This all began, really, when Maureen Coles started to show signs of dementia, didn't it?' she said, surprising everyone else listening.

Beside her, Steven, who had the most experience of Hillary's habit of pulling rabbits from a hat, reacted the least by merely shifting slightly in his chair.

'I suppose it did,' Freda agreed slowly. 'She always was a bit flighty, I suppose. A bit of a dreamer. So when she started becoming forgetful or confused, it didn't register at first that it was more than just Maureen being silly old Maureen. Sylvia was the first to realize it was more serious than that.'

'What did you do?' Hillary asked gently.

'Well, between us we managed to persuade her to see her GP. They did some tests – you know, memory stuff, what day of the week was it, who was prime minister, that sort of thing. And ... well ... there it was.'

'Alzhiemer's,' Hillary said flatly. 'Yes, I talked to the police doctor about it. He said, without having access to her notes, that she probably suffered from a thinning of the veins in her brain, restricting blood flow and slowly causing parts of her brain to ... well—'

'Dry up. Ossify. Wither and die,' Freda supplied bitterly. 'Yes. It was awful. Her mind seemed to quite literally get narrower and narrower. The woman we knew, the friend we loved and laughed with, slowly turned into this woman we didn't recognize. Sometimes she thought I was her mother.' Freda shrugged, fiddling with her hands, obviously longing for a cigarette. 'But we took care of her. Sylvie, me, and one or two others. It wasn't hard. We both lived right next door – one of us on either side. We did her shopping, set up direct debits so that all her bills were paid, did her housework, took care of her garden, made sure Sputnik was fed. We were coping.'

Freda paused, then sighed.

'Yes,' Hillary said. 'Sputnik. Poor old Sputnik.' Then realizing that she had to get it all down for the tape, added, 'Sputnik was the latest in a long line of ginger tom cats that Maureen adored, wasn't he? We've been told how she doted on her cats.'

'They were the children she never had. And to be fair, the cats all loved her back. Whenever either Sylvie or me called on her she'd be sitting in her favourite chair with Sputnik curled up on her lap. He used to sleep on the bed with her as well. Kept her company.'

'And then, one day, Sputnik wasn't there,' Hillary said flatly.

'No. She found him dead in the garden. She came round to me, carrying his poor little corpse. She was beside herself. We just couldn't console her. Especially Sylvia....' She paused. 'You do know that she got it into her head that Sylvia was the one who poisoned Sputnik, right?'

'Yes,' Hillary agreed. 'Several of your neighbours and friends remembered that. Apparently Sylvia had complained about the cat taking garden birds and scratching up her vegetable patch.'

'But that was before Maureen got ill. She told Maureen that she should put a bell around his neck. It was something that Maureen latched on to later. It was odd, you know, some of the things she'd remember and the things that she didn't.'

'Yes,' Hillary agreed quietly. 'But Sylvia wouldn't have put poisoned meat down. Not to kill her friend's cat, or any other wildlife for that matter.'

'No. It was that twit over the road,' Freda snorted. 'The one who fancies himself as a smallholder.'

'Paul Quinlan. He admitted to putting out poisoned bait to keep the fox numbers down. But you couldn't persuade Maureen of that, could you?'

'No,' Freda said sadly. 'The trouble was, once she'd got an idea into her head, you just couldn't shift it. You'd tell her, you'd explain, and she'd seem to take it in and accept it. Sylvie used to swear over and over again that it wasn't her fault poor old Sputnik was dead, and Maureen would cry and believe her and they'd make it up. But the next time Sylvie came around, Maureen would have forgotten, and would accuse her all over again. It was so distressing for both of them.'

Freda sighed, and leaned forward on the table, dropping her face into her hands for a moment. 'In the end, we agreed that perhaps Sylvie would have to stop visiting, which was a bit of a blow, since it meant most of the work then fell to me. Looking after Maureen, that is. She didn't have any family left, see.'

Hillary nodded. 'So tell me about that day. When Sylvia died. You were in your home, I take it? Painting upstairs?'

'Yes, that's right. I heard someone downstairs. I shot down, thinking some low-life was after the silver, and found Maureen instead,' Freda said. 'She was just standing in my living room, looking puzzled. At first I didn't realize … I didn't see what she was holding. I just thought she'd come round to borrow something, and then forgotten what it was. Then I saw the poker in her hand. Her dress and arms were splattered in something red. She just …' Freda faltered, took a sharp intake of breath, and blurted, 'she just said to me "I've killed her then. My poor Sputnik has got his revenge." That's what she said. Her exact words; I'll never forget them. Then she looked at me, and smiled, and said, "Oh, hello Freddie. Have you popped round for a cup of tea?" I just … gaped at her. I made her sit down and I dashed down to Sylvia's and went in and … well … you know what I found.'

'Yes. But if you could describe it to us for the tape, Ms de la Mare.'

Freda nodded. 'Oh, right. Yes. Of course. Well, I saw Sylvie lying on the living room carpet. She was bleeding … her head … I could see that she was dead. She wasn't breathing. Her eyes were open and staring. I just … backed out and went back to my place. Maureen was in the kitchen making a cup of tea. She was still holding on to the poker. I took a plastic bag and gently prised it out of her hands. She looked surprised and puzzled, and asked me if I wanted to make up a fire. She recognized the poker, you see, but not what had happened. She never did remember what she'd done and for that I was grateful. Really.'

'Ms de la Mare, why didn't you call the police?' Hillary asked firmly.

For a long moment, Freda de la Mare stared down at her hands. Then she looked up at Hillary and gave a wobbly kind of smile. 'Oh, I thought about it. Long and hard. Believe me, more than once I went to the phone and was about to call them. But then I thought about what would happen if I did. To Maureen.'

'But you must have known she almost certainly wouldn't have stood trial,' Hillary said. 'You're an intelligent woman: we're not living in the dark ages any more.'

'Yes, I know all that. But they *would* have had to take her away and question her, wouldn't they?' Freda said. 'To make sure she wasn't faking it. Maureen hadn't left Caulcott in years. She hardly ever left her house, even. The confusion she'd have felt. The fear. The trauma. And you know what else? What really stopped me from doing it?' Freda said, her voice more urgent now, and begging for understanding. 'I knew that Sylvia would have been furious with me if I had let it happen.' Freda looked from Hillary to Steven, who was looking down at his hands expressionless. 'Don't you get it? Sylvie was the one who was dead, she was the real victim, and I just knew, if she was standing there beside me, if her ghost was there, she'd have been urging me to look after Maureen. To do the best that I could for her. To keep her safe.'

Freda shook her head helplessly. 'Oh I can't really explain it. I just knew I had to do it. But I wasn't completely reckless. I took the murder weapon and kept it safe just in case anyone else was ever accused of the crime. I knew that I had a responsibility to see that no one else was blamed or suffered for it. I also wrote everything down and left it with my solicitors. It's to be opened when I die.... But I suppose I can get them to relinquish it early now.'

'Yes, but Freddie, *what about Sylvie's girls?* All this time, they've been thinking that some heartless man, some faceless stranger, killed their mother and is still walking around scotfree. Didn't they deserve to know the truth?' Hillary asked helplessly.

For a moment, the artist stared at her, her face working. But she managed to hold back the tears. 'I know. Believe me, I do. It's been heavy on my conscience all these years, don't think it hasn't been. But th ... would it really be better for them to know the truth?' she asked desperately. 'I can't say any more. I've thought about it so much. Is it easier for them to think that some nameless man did it, or for them to know that it was her best friend? That it wasn't anything like an evil act that robbed them of their mother, but the desperately sad, confused actions of the friend she'd loved and tried to take care of? Which is worse, do you think?'

Hillary stared at the artist for a moment, then, defeated, simply shook her head. She looked at Steven, who roused himself and began to tell Freda that she was under arrest for attempting to pervert the cause of justice, and for being an accessory after the fact in a case of murder.

Freda merely slumped back in her chair and said nothing.

In the viewing room, Wendy chewed nervously on one of her black-painted fingernails. She knew now whose grave Freddie had visited just before coming here. She'd been taking the flowers to Maureen, of course, as an offering – a way of saying sorry, because she was just about to betray their secret.

'They won't make her go to prison, will they?' she asked, but neither Jake nor Roland Sale could answer that. In the end, it would be down to the CPS whether or not they pursued a case against Freda de la Mare.

CHAPTER THIRTEEN

I N Steven's office, Hillary was making her report to both her bosses. Steven, who knew what to expect from previous such briefings, was calm. Roland Sale, however, looked fascinated.

'Well, right from the start, the real puzzle for me was the question of motive,' Hillary began. 'Sylvia simply wasn't the sort of woman to attract real enemies. And the crime didn't look particularly opportunistic, either. It was unlikely that she had simply been in the wrong place at the wrong time. So until I could understand why someone wanted her dead, I realized that we were really up against it. Well, that, and the lack of any real evidence, of course. DI Jarvis did a great job, but there simply weren't any witnesses to be found, and all the forensics evidence was pretty much inconclusive. It wasn't until we got around to interviewing Freda, that I finally sensed a witness who was holding back. Even then, I didn't really twig to what it was all about for quite some time. But it gradually dawned on me how everyone knew about Maureen Coles blaming her friend for the death of her cat, and when I learned more about her dementia, the more I began to wonder. As I said, I quickly became con-vinced that Freda knew more than she was telling, but she was clearly not going to spill it voluntarily, so I had to think of some-thing that would make her come forward of her own volition.'

'So you told her that you were about to arrest someone,' Rollo

Sale said, nodding approvingly. 'And it worked a treat. Her conscience couldn't let some innocent person go through that, it seems.'

'Sorry your first cold case wasn't more of a triumph, sir,' Hillary Greene said quietly. 'The killer herself is deceased, so there'll be no arrest or prosecution. And I really can't see the CPS going after Freda.'

'I can't say that I'm particularly worried about it. She's hardly a menace to society, is she?' Rollo shrugged. 'And don't apologize. You've closed a case, and brought the truth to a grieving family. Sometimes that's worth more than conviction rates or statistics.'

Hillary nodded, glad to hear him say so. The more she learned about her new boss, the more convinced she became that she was going to be able to work well with him. 'Can I leave the clearing up to you, sir?' Hillary asked, turning back to Steven, who looked slightly surprised. 'Jimmy has something he thinks I need to see to,' she added neutrally, by way of explanation.

Steven caught on at once. Jimmy had only one priority at the moment and that was finding out what Jake Barnes was up to. 'Well, better get on with it then,' he said with a brief, tight smile. 'It'll give me a chance to fill in Superintendent Sale on how things progress from here. Besides, the paperwork is usually our domain anyway.'

Rollo Sale groaned. 'Tell me about it.'

'Sir,' Hillary said briskly, and got up.

When the door had closed behind her, Rollo Sale smiled across at the younger man. 'You're going to miss it around here, aren't you?'

And Steven Crayle, with a small, rather sad smile, agreed that, in spite of the challenges and the excitement of the new job beckoning him, that he probably would.

*

It was dark before five o'clock, and for once Jake Barnes was glad of the long, winter hours of night-time. As he reached for his coat, relieved that they were clocking off on time after all, he was pleased that he wasn't going to be late.

The last thing he wanted to do was keep Darren Chivnor waiting. 'Well, have a good weekend everybody,' he called, and saw Jimmy raise a vague hand his way. Wendy, who was busy applying black lipstick, prior to a night's clubbing somewhere out Reading way, waved cheerily.

The moment he was out of the door however, Jimmy got up, reaching for his mobile, and by the time Jake was pulling out of HQ in his distinctive Jag, Hillary and Jimmy Jessop were already heading for her car and also glad for the long hours of darkness as it meant that Jake wasn't likely to spot that he had a tail.

'He's not heading for his place, guv,' Jimmy said, when they'd been on the road for less than five minutes. It was in the rush hour, but since they were going towards the city and not away from it, they weren't getting caught up in the worst of it. 'His place is near the Banbury Road roundabout. He's going past it, see?'

'Headington,' Hillary agreed, as they watched the sports car take the first exit on the approaching roundabout. 'Perhaps he's visiting someone in hospital,' she said. There were several large hospitals out that way.

'Perhaps,' Jimmy said. 'But hospitals have long visiting hours and I had the feeling, from the way he was antsy to get off on time, that he's on a tight deadline.'

Hillary said nothing. It was possible they were on a wild goose chase, but she trusted the old ex-sergeant's nose. When he'd told her that he suspected something was in the air, she'd been more than willing to ride along with him and see if he was right.

'He's heading for the park,' Jimmy said in surprise, some

twenty minutes later. 'Why would you want to visit the park after dark on a cold November night? Especially if you haven't got a dog that needs walking?'

Hillary shrugged. 'Maybe he's meeting a girl for a romantic rendezvous.'

'In November, guv? They'd have to be desperate. He's got a nice, warm, cosy mansion waiting for him back in north Oxford.'

Hillary smiled in acknowledgement. 'But perhaps they're al fresco freaks,' she said wryly.

When the E-Type pulled in opposite the long line of black iron railings that bordered the park, and tucked itself into a line of cars on one side of the residential street, she was careful to turn off down another side street rather than pass him. Even though the orange-coloured streetlights would probably have made her pale-green Volkswagen look a different colour, she couldn't risk him spotting them now.

She pulled in at the very first available spot and jogged briskly back up the road. Jimmy, puffing slightly, was right beside her, and they were just in time to see Jake pass through one of the sets of gates.

'Do you know what time the park closes?' she asked.

'No idea, guv. Probably not till late, though.'

Hillary nodded, waited for a break in the traffic, then dashed across the road. She was wearing a long black woollen overcoat and flat sensible, heavy boots. Jimmy was dressed in a rainproof parka jacket in sage green and similar footwear.

'Can you see him, guv?' Jimmy asked. His night vision wasn't the best, these days.

'Yes. Over there. It looks as if he's heading for the public loos.' As she spoke, both of them had the same thought at once.

'Surely he's not cottaging?' Jimmy said.

'No,' Hillary said flatly. 'He's not gay. And even if he was, he'd be too smart for that.'

'He's definitely going inside guv,' Jimmy said. As they moved closer to the unlovely, square, brick built convenience, several people passed by them, walking quickly, heads down, intent on getting home and out of the cold November night.

'I don't like this,' Hillary said quietly. 'If he's meeting someone inside, there's no way we can go in without being spotted. If he gets into trouble, we won't know about it until it's too late.'

'We'll just have to wait outside. Pick him up again after the meet,' Jimmy agreed.

'We might be better off waiting to see who else comes out later. Right now, we need to know who he's been seeing, rather than where he goes afterwards – which is probably home anyway.'

'But what if this is just the first stop of the evening, guv? He might be going on somewhere else even more important after this.'

Hillary sighed, then tossed her car keys over to the old sergeant. 'If our boy comes out alone, follow him in my car. I'll hang around and see if I can clock who he was meeting inside.'

'Guv, we should do it the other way round,' Jimmy said. He didn't like the thought of her alone, in the dark park, with who knew what sort of low-life hanging around. 'I'm more likely to recognize anyone he may have met up with than you are.'

Hillary, who knew what the old man was thinking, smiled grimly. 'I've seen the photos, Jimmy. Besides, there are plenty of bushes I can hide behind. Don't worry, I'm not going to do anything stupid.'

Inside the men's lavatories, Jake Barnes was hoping Darren Chivnor wasn't going to do anything stupid.

He'd chosen this place for their meeting simply because he had reasoned that the thug would probably feel safe here. After all, a men's public toilet, in the middle of a public park on a cold, dark November night, was hardly the place where either of them might run into anyone they knew and, by now, Jake was aware that Chivnor must be getting very wary, if not paranoid, about being seen with him. His connection with the police was in the public domain after all, and Chivnor's boss wouldn't be any too happy to hear about them getting chummy.

Inside, standing over a chipped sink, Chivnor was looking in the mirror and checking out his spots. He'd arrived a good hour early, and had clocked who was about. The fact that there were definitely no cops about was a good sign. He'd also checked on the stalls. The two which were occupied had quickly emptied, and his own shaven-headed, tattooed presence had sent the few others who'd come in to take a leak, quickly scurrying through their business and leaving.

Now all was silent.

'How'd you get my mobile number?' Chivnor asked, the moment Jake Barnes stepped through the door. 'It's supposed to be fireproof.'

'When you have money, you can buy anything,' Jake said easily. In fact, his PIs had tracked it down. 'Like what's in this envelope for instance,' Jake added, wanting to get down to business as fast as possible.

The scent of urine and the cold chilly air reminded him just how alone and isolated he was here. He knew this man's reputation, Chivenor had to have a knife on him somewhere, and if he'd decided that whatever it was Jake was peddling wasn't worth the risk…. Well, what better place could he ask for than this to do something about it? If Jake's body were to be found here, Hillary Greene and the other cops at HQ would surely assume the worst, that he'd either been cottaging or mistaken for someone going down that route, and had fallen foul of a gay-basher. Or maybe that he was simply the victim of a straightforward mugging gone wrong.

Either way, he wanted to get Darren Chivnor's attention focused on something else. Now he had it.

'What's that then?'

'Well, money, for a start. But something much more impressive,' Jake said.

Darren snorted. 'Nothing's more impressive than money, my friend.'

'Take a look and see,' Jake said, stepping forward and very carefully placing the fat brown envelope in the sink beside the skinhead. He was careful not to get too close.

Darren eyed him with something of a knowing smirk, then shrugged, and reached for the envelope. First he took out the wads of cash.

'Nice. Twenty grand?'

'Good guess.'

'I never guess. Here, what's this?' Now Chivnor was looking at a driving licence, but although it was Lisa's face that was looking back at him, the name on it was that of Chelsea Cordwainer. If Barnes knew about Lisa, what else might he know?

He rooted inside and came out with another licence. This time, it was his photograph, but it bore the name of Michael Rawlings. He tipped the envelope up, and quickly sorted through the documents, becoming more and more excited: birth certificates. Social Security numbers, tax information. Passports.

'Shit,' he said, inspecting them carefully. 'This is top quality gear.'

'It'll pass any inspection, by anyone, anywhere. You can set yourself up in a new life with that. You and your girlfriend both.'

'Not on twenty grand, mate. Get real,' Darren Chivnor sneered.

Jake shrugged magnificently. 'Oh that's just spending money. The real money on offer has a lot more zeros after it than that.'

'How many more?'

Jake smiled. 'Enough to buy the dream,' he promised. 'What is it, Darren? A beach bar in Mauritius? A boat-hire business in

Benidorm? Luxury holiday lets in Australia?'

Darren carefully stuffed all the impressive paperwork back into the envelope and shoved it inside his leather jacket. 'OK, so just what is it that you're after? It has to be about Dale, right? If you think I'm gonna shop him to the cops you're out of your mind. I wouldn't live a day.'

'Don't let the fact that I'm a civilian consultant at Thames Valley fool you,' Jake said flatly. 'I couldn't give a shit about whether or not they take down your boss,' he said – more or less truthfully. 'I have my own agenda.'

Darren smiled wolfishly. 'I thought you might. Go on then. Surprise me.'

But just then, before Jake could do just that, the door opened and a man came in. His name was, of all things, John Smith, and he was a janitor at one of the hospitals on the other side of the park. He was walking home via his regular route through the park since he'd lost his driving licence in the previous month after failing a breathalyser. He was in his mid-fifties, and there was nothing out of the ordinary about him at all – save for the fact that he had a lot of curly ginger hair.

Darren Chivnor knew a man called Curly Monroe who worked for Dale in one of his clubs. For a split second, seeing all that curly ginger hair in the poor lighting of the men's loo, all his paranoia and fear burst out like a leopard from ambush.

When he'd got the text message from Barnes requesting this meeting, he'd been amused by the choice of location, but also relieved. If on the wild off-chance any of the other lads who worked for Dale spotted him here, he could tell them that he'd been bored and had gone out for a bit of gay-bashing. It was widely known that Dale couldn't stand poofs, so it would have given him the perfect cover and alibi.

Now, seeing whom he thought was Curly Monroe coming through the door, Dale reached instantly for his knife. It was a switch-blade, and sprang open instantly, glinting wickedly in the dim lighting.

Three things happened at once.

Going into his act, Darren snarled viciously, 'Get out of it, you bloody wanker! Poofs like you make me sick.' So saying he suddenly lunged for Jake. He made sure to feint a little as he did so, missing him completely.

The second thing that happened was that John Smith, realizing that he'd just innocently stepped into a very nasty situation indeed, took a step back, putting him directly under the full light, thus showing him to be much older than Curly Monroe, and a fair bit shorter.

And thirdly, Jake Barnes, after one wild look at the knife, turned and legged it at a very creditable rate of knots indeed through the door and out into the night.

Darren Chivnor swore viciously. John Smith very quickly followed Jake's example and also legged it.

Outside, Hillary Greene had positioned herself slightly to the left and rear of the toilets, and heard a door bang open explosively. She was thus the first to see Jake Barnes flying out and running away down the path. She'd taken one step forward when she saw the ginger-haired man who'd just entered also come back out, looking over his shoulder fearfully, and running off down the path.

She shot a quick look over to the right where Jimmy was standing concealed in a laurel bush. She took another step out, then froze, as the skinhead from Jimmy's photos shot through the door.

In his hand was a viciously sharp-looking knife.

Chivnor hesitated in the doorway, wondering if he should go after Barnes to explain, but quickly realizing that that would be a mistake. The millionaire would be bound to think that he was trying to race him down and finish the job with the knife.

He also doubted that Barnes would be in any mood or condition to listen to reason.

He swore again, viciously, when he realized that he might have just blown his best chance to earn a big enough stake to strike out on his own.

Still, he consoled himself, it wasn't a complete waste of time. He had twenty thou to add to his bank account, plus a set of grade-A documents for his and Lisa's get-away, when the time was right.

Besides, he knew how to contact Barnes. He'd just give it a few days, and then telephone him and explain what had really happened. Once he'd had a chance to get over the fright, Barnes would have to understand why he, Darren, had to be careful. And if that *had* been Curly Monroe back there, they'd both have been toast if Dale Medcalfe had found out what it was they were up to.

Not that Darren knew, even now, just what it was that Barnes really wanted. But to go as far as he already had, the man must want it bad. Badly enough to take another chance on him, surely?

As Darren Chivnor stood there in the dark, watching the richest man he knew running hell for leather down the path, he wanted so badly to believe that Barnes had been telling him the truth. That he really wasn't working for the coppers, and didn't care about bringing down Medcalfe, because then, maybe, just maybe, he could grab the real cash prize, start a new life with Lisa, and not even have to double-cross Medcalfe for it.

And that was the equivalent of Darren's Holy Grail.

For her part, Hillary Greene remained frozen. She kept her eye on the skinhead who, much to her relief, didn't give chase, but slowly closed the knife and slipped it into his back pocket. Then he turned and began to walk off in the opposite direction from Jake.

Seeing that the Boy Wonder was safe, she turned her head to look for Jimmy. She spotted him at once. She raised two fingers to her eyes, pointed at Jimmy, then stabbed them in Jakes's direction, indicating that she wanted Jimmy to follow him.

She then pointed in the direction Chivenor had taken, indicating that she was going to follow him. Jimmy didn't look too happy about it, but dutifully took off after Jake. Hillary, giving the skinhead plenty of time to get ahead of her, set off after him.

Her heartbeat was slowly returning to normal by the time she'd followed him to one of the park's other exits. As she'd half expected, he got into a car and drove off. She sighed, then reached for her mobile.

She dialled Jimmy's number, knowing that the canny old man would have set it to vibrate, and not to ring.

'Guv? You all right?' His voice was lowered and gruff, but he didn't sound breathless. She'd been a bit worried, at the rate Jake had been burning shoe leather, that the old man might not have been able to keep up with him.

'I'm fine. Our tattooed friend left by another exit and got in a car. Where are you?'

'Not far from where you left us, guv. When Jake realized that he wasn't being chased he slowed down.'

'What's he doing now?' she asked curiously.

'Being sick in a privet hedge,' Jimmy said succinctly.

'Good,' Hillary said vindictively. 'It's time that boy learned a hard lesson or two. He's had things too easy, and all his own way for far too long.'

'Shall I let him know we're here, guv?'

'No. Go back to the car. I'll be right behind you.'

'OK. Guv …' Jimmy began carefully, 'I really thought Chivnor was going to stick him back there.'

'So did I for a moment or two,' Hillary agreed. 'Don't worry, I'll be speaking to Steven. It's time we got to the bottom of this. When young Jake's had a chance to get his nerve back, we're going to tackle this thing head on. Whatever it is.'

'Guv,' Jimmy's relief was palpable as he hung up.

But when Hillary dropped the old man off at HQ before

motoring back to Thrupp, she found that Steven, waiting for her on the boat, had other things to talk about.

And this time, he wasn't going to be put off.

'Hey, you look beat,' he said, standing up as she walked down the narrow corridor towards the small living area in the prow. 'So I won't keep you. I just wanted to talk. About us,' he said. He had that determined look in his eye, and she felt her heart sink.

'I know you keep avoiding it whenever I try to bring it up, but it's been nearly two weeks,' he carried on. 'Whilst I don't want to crowd you, or hurry you, I just don't know how much longer my nerves are going to be able to stand the waiting.' He managed a brief, if rather tight, laugh.

Hillary, who'd just been about to tell him about Jake, slowly took off her coat instead and looked at him warily.

Barnes could keep until Monday: clearly, this couldn't.

She'd always known that she would have to come to a decision soon, of course, but she still had no idea what she was going to say. She'd allowed the Sylvia Perkins case to push the dilemma to one side, but suddenly, here she was, facing it like a deer in the headlights, and feeling just as paralysed.

'Steven,' she said tentatively. Why couldn't they just stay as they were? It was what she wanted to wail, like a spoilt little kid not getting her own way. Suddenly she felt ashamed of her cowardice.

She'd been mucking him about, and he didn't deserve that. Again she opened her mouth, this time to apologize, but Steven was already holding up a hand, forestalling her.

His suit was slightly rumpled and he looked a little tired, but still his devastatingly good-looking, elegant, and sexy self. She'd become so used to having him in her life, in such a short space of time, that the idea of losing him left her feeling oddly panic-stricken.

'I just want to try and make things clearer for you,' he said.

'Please, just hear me out. It's simple, really.' He took a slow, long, breath. 'Hillary, I love you and I want us to be married. I really think we'll be good together, and good for each other. I want to live with you full time, like proper grown-ups, either at my place, or we can buy another place together, I don't care which. I'm not asking you to sell the *Mollern* – it'll make an ideal holiday home, and we can spend weekends on her whenever you like. I know you love her. And I'm not asking you to give up your job, or do mine for me, or run your world around me, or mother me, or do any damned thing that you don't want to do.'

He paused, then smiled a shade helplessly. Something about his sudden air of vulnerability tugged at her heartstrings. She swallowed a hard, tight lump in her throat, and wished that she could sit down.

'I'm not Ronnie Greene. I don't feel the need to tom cat around, and I wouldn't be unfaithful to you,' he swept on. 'I'm ambitious, yes, but I'm straight as a die and you know that. I won't hurt you. But … and this is really what it all comes down to, Hillary,' he said, taking a step closer and looking down into her wary, troubled eyes, 'if you can't trust me when I say all this, then we might as well call it quits.'

Hillary winced.

'Yes. I know. It hurts, doesn't it?' Steven said. 'That's the only thing that's given me hope.' He put a gentle finger under her chin and lifted her face to his. 'I think you love me too.'

Hillary opened her mouth, then closed it again.

He smiled a little sadly. But he didn't really need to hear her say it. He knew how hard it was for her to open up.

'But I need an answer, sweetheart,' Steven Crayle said gently.

Then he kissed her.

Then he left.

And for a long while Hillary Greene simply stood where she was. And thought.

She thought about women's lib. She thought about growing

old alone, and whether she was letting that niggling little worry influence her. She thought about her own fears. She thought about Steven Crayle and admitted to herself that she loved him. And believed him when he said that he loved her, but then she wondered if love was enough.

But mostly she thought about Ronnie Greene, and the scars that the bastard had left. Just how much she'd let them affect her life, for so many years.

And when she'd thought about all that, it all came down to one, simple question: was she going to let Ronnie Greene ruin what might be her last chance at real, personal, happiness?

When she put it like that, Hillary finally realized that the answer was equally just as simple.

Was she hell.